A Chain of Devils

Also by Thomas Corcoran

Novels

Waiting for V-J Day
Decoration Day

(In Commodore Hilty, Afloat and Ashore):
The Flag List
Commodore Hilty's Second Act
Hilty Defeats Entropy

Stories

The Hobbledehoy

Non-Fiction

Afraid of Less: What To Do About the Future

A Chain of Devils

a novel by
Thomas Corcoran

Bernice Feigenbaum & Company

Philadelphia ~ 2025

ISBN (HC): 979-8-218-84357-1
ISBN (PB): 979-8-218-84358-8

First printing

This is a work of fiction, set in the imagined past, occasionally depicting historical figures and places.

Cover image a composite of details from:

"Chinese junk, Victoria Harbor, Hong Kong, China," Bob Henry / Alamy

"Bow view of USS Gray off the coast of California," U.S. Navy photo, National Archives.

Sources for the epigraphs:

Richard Henry Dana, Jr., *Two Years Before the Mast* (New York: Signet Classics, 1967), p. 350.

George Eliot, *Romola* (London: Penguin Books, 1980), p. 287.

Thanks to literary agents Damaris Rowland and David McCormick for their help with earlier versions of this novel.

To Linda

The past was real. The present, all about me, was unreal, unnatural, repellent.

—Richard Henry Dana, Jr.

Tito was experiencing the inexorable law of human souls, that we prepare ourselves for sudden deeds by the reiterated choice of good or evil which gradually determines character.

—George Eliot

Contents

Part One
Dropped into History

The Lottery Drum

My father, who taught me to sail, showed me in his mild way that you cannot push a rope. A lifetime regarded as successful—successful beyond my merits—has shown me that you cannot really pull it either. All right, you can take a little strain on it and trim a sail here and there. But ordinary people are powerless before history, and even the extraordinary few that make history seldom know what they are doing or what will become of their actions.

Now that we have had a pandemic, I will say that the war in Vietnam was the pandemic that ended my childhood. Offended to my very being, I devoted every spare moment to opposing the power that waged the war: my own government. Not infrequently did I break the law; four times was I arrested, and once I was sure I was going to die. The passion I felt, in the grip of which I went to bed each night planning what to do the next day, lasted from the murder of Diem in 1963, arranged by our CIA, until the first of December 1969, when I all but won the national draft lottery.

At a stroke now I too was powerless before history. Becoming a foot-soldier was out of the question—clumsy as I was, I would surely fall into a punji pit. Yet otherwise I was healthy and strong. I had no religious beliefs to justify my going to divinity school. I couldn't say that I *conscientiously* objected to war, only to this war. And either prison or running away to Canada or Sweden would have broken my parents' hearts. On the other hand, I loved boats and ships, and after a gentle upbringing I thought I deserved to be treated as an officer. So I accepted the advice, specious as it was, of reforming the system from within. Feeling mostly superior to the men around and in front of me, I raised my hand and spoke these words:

> I, Christopher Higginson Clarke, do solemnly swear (or affirm) that I will support and defend the Constitution of the United States against all enemies, foreign and domestic; that I will bear true faith and allegiance to the same; and that I will obey the orders of the president of the United States and the orders of the officers appointed over me, according to regulations and the Uniform Code of Military Justice. So help me God.

In this way I found myself, in July of 1972, during a violent spasm of the war just over the horizon from me, standing in the doorway of a helicopter that seemed to be struggling to stay airborne while I waited to be dropped by something like a hangman's noose to a tiny bullseye on the after deck of a ship that looked too ugly to keep out the sea.

Another new officer had gone first, someone I had just met in the helo, with that exchange of glances by which cats declare enemies. Though he seemed to know what he was doing. Springing from the jump-seat, he slipped into the noose and was lowered out of sight. Time passed while the cabin trembled and the helo wandered about the sky and I was given too much time to think.

Finally the noose was retrieved and held out, level with my waist. How to put it on: dive into it or surface through it? That other officer had known. There was no clue in the the crewman's sun visor, where the only image was of someone tall and raw and trying not to look afraid. I dived. As if expecting this, he stopped me and threaded the collar over my arms and head and pushed me to the edge of the door. Eternity beckoned, one way or another. Hands crossed over my chest, I swung into space.

They were waiting for me below, a crowd of them in their cranial helmets and color-coded vests. A man in yellow held two wands out from his sides, as though the helo were a circus lion he could keep in place by hand gestures. The deck came up—how easy! It was going to be fine! I was halfway there, halfway between two lives, when I felt a small tug and the lowering stopped.

Overhead the rotors woofed: the downdraft beat upon me in warm waves acrid with jet exhaust. The crewman in his harness was leaning from the doorway, one hand testing the cable. He signaled—two fists and then someone's throat to be cut. The cable was fouled. Mine was the throat. Reasonable enough: I gave him a thumb's-up.

From bridge wings men watched...what? The emergency? The entertainment? Perhaps the impediment to victory, for I was holding up the war.

More engine power and the deck heaved as suddenly as a vomit. The pilot was trying to set me down by almost landing on top of me (the *almost* being a secondary consideration to the safety of the aircraft: they would scrape up my paper-thin body with a tire mark on it). Just my bad luck. On the other hand, as a new and clumsy soldier I could only have looked forward to those punji stakes. The water was there in cobbled blue wavelets. During my training some switch had been thrown to make me ambitious and reckless, then and afterwards. I shucked off the noose and jumped.

Keep your knees bent, I thought. Roll when you touch, I thought. Paratroopers do it all the time. No church steeples to catch your chute and break your neck. No Germans shooting machine pistols at you. Easy.

My self-conceit was superior to rolling when I fell. I kept my feet under me as I hit the nonskid, and I stayed

upright for the moment, but I couldn't prevent three running steps as the helo hauled away with a roar. On the
third step I fell forward, and the safety nets came up. Of
course: how logical to have safety nets. My hands seized
the frame as if I were a gymnast performing on the high
bar, and arms extended I turned a flip, a clean, slow-
building pirouette until I was hanging from the frame
against the side of the ship with the water tickling my
feet.

Captain Marchand

Several hands pulled me from the water's edge and set
me on my feet again. A man took my inflated vest and my
cranial helmet and led me through the ship, saying that
the captain had called for me. No doubt he had, after that
arrival! It was an equal probability that I would be the
ship's clown or the ship's lucky charm; neither of them
the proper role for an officer. My mother used to say you
get only one chance to make a first impression. With the
captain I should keep my cool and not say too much.

My escort was a chief petty officer, a senior enlisted
man, a sonarman by rating. His name was Beatty. When
I hesitated over the propriety of asking his first name, he
added, "You should just call me *Chief,* sir." We shook
hands while walking, and he gave me a friendly look along
with the shake. In the same way that I knew the other
ensign and I were certain to hate each other, I felt that
Chief Beatty and I were going to be friends, if such a thing
might be permitted between an officer and enlisted man.

The ship was bigger on the inside than she had looked from the helo. I had no idea where we were going—only a vague idea that we were going forward and up—until we had walked a couple of hundred feet through a passageway divided by watertight doors and had climbed a couple of ladders to the bridge. The chief opened an ordinary door, called, as I was to learn, a joiner door, which sounded more encouraging than it was; and suddenly we were in a different world, with the sea open before me.

Apparently we were in a hurry. The ship, ever thrusting ahead as powerfully as navy standard fuel oil could be turned into steam, was trying to surmount her element. She was driving into the otherwise moderate sea, rising, falling, twisting, sometimes all at once. Every so often she would bury her head, shoving us forward as white spray arose from her bow and blew back over her gun mount to fall upon the windows like some primal rain. Something unpleasant awaited me from this.

The captain was sitting in his chair, a monarch on his throne, with his court around him. In the moment I forgot his name. He was about forty, short-legged, wide, and powerful—his khaki shirt was stretched to the seams. Bareheaded, with red crewcut hair and a sunburned face, the kind of pig-eyed officer who had given us Vietnam. Yet a hero at the Naval Academy—I did remember this—where he had anchored the line for Roger Staubach, the famous quarterback. Hating the military though I did, I loved the Navy Hymn, and I had rooted for Navy on TV, anonymous in their blue and gold uniforms, faces bulging from their helmets.

Certainly he was powerful: I identified my misgivings as reasonable, only I must overcome them.

In our service it is incorrect to give or return a salute while uncovered, as both of us were then. Coming to attention and saluting him, I reported for duty.

Instead of a salute he returned a superior smile. As I was to learn, everything amused him as beneath him, or already known, and a waste of his time. This, if nothing else, would have put us on a collision course, for two people can feel superior to everyone else but one of them must be superior to the other.

"And you are?" he asked.

"Ensign Clarke, Captain. Chris." As if this were purely a social occasion, I leaned forward and offered my hand. He swiveled his chair a few degrees away as if something—anything—must interest him more than I did.

With my hand out, I pivoted to the other new officer, who of course, had already reported and introduced himself.

"Chris Clarke," I said coldly.

"Billings."

"Pleased to meet you. How do you do?"

My politesse was out of place. Billings, the captain, the officer courtiers, and even the enlisted watch exchanged grins. This was an American ship, we were west coast sailors, this was not the Royal Navy.

I remembered: the captain's name was Marchand. He swiveled back.

"You two young men have never met before."

"First time," I said brightly. Billings was silent.

"Yet you rode out here on the helo together."

"We did."

"From *Yorktown,* where you've been living for the past two days."

"Along with four thousand other men," I reminded him.

"And at Subic Bay before then. Future shipmates."

The universal grinning couldn't last much longer with-out guffaws. Hearing them I was silent; perhaps I low-ered my head a fraction.

"XO, what lucky departments are getting these para-gons of sociability?"

The executive officer, a man in his thirties with soft lines and kind eyes, though they too enjoyed the amusing moment, was standing beside the chair as major-domo.

"One to Louie and the other to Tyler, Captain. Damage Control Assistant and First Lieutenant."

"Which is which?"

"Mr. Billings to—let me see, I have it here."

Not quick enough off the ball. The captain looked me with his superior and now accusatory smile. "Where are you from, Mr. Clarke?"

"Boston, sir. Well, Cambridge."

"You went to Harvard?" He drew out the long *A;* there was more grinning.

"No sir. My parents teach at Harvard. Or my father does, now. I went to M.I.T."

"Ah, an engineering degree. XO, here's your DCA."

"No sir," I corrected him. "English." If I were making a full disclosure, I would have added *civil disobedience.*

"Actually, Captain," the XO offered, "I was going to recommend Mr. Clarke for First Lieutenant." I didn't like this, and I would bet the captain saw it. The first lieuten-ant was in charge of the deck hands, the sailors whose low test scores didn't qualify them for a specialty. On the other hand, he was also in charge of the boats, knotting and splicing, steering and looking out upon the sea: my passion for so many years. On the other other hand, when not standing watch or doing the fun things, his people sanded and scraped, primed and painted.

"Then you must be the flight drop," the captain said.

Billings nodded.

"Before that you went to—I don't need to refer to the XO's notes—your state school."

"University of Missoura," Billings agreed.

"Majored in agriculture. A technical subject. Not many people know that, how technical it is."

"Yes sir."

"And you went through four years of ROTC instead of a few weeks at OCS, like Mr. Clarke."

Mr. Clarke, who had been commissioned, he seemed to imply, only by act of Congress, without whose foolish intervention he would be carrying an M-16.

"So you'll be DCA. Actually, gentlemen, I don't care about your commissioning source. Or why you joined the Navy," he added, looking closely at me. "Time will tell whether you have what it takes. My need is a little more immediate. I need an officer of the deck. This ship is short-handed. I assume your training has taught you something about standing watch on the bridge, and your enlisted men will keep you straight—will you not, bosunmate?"

"Yes sir, Captain," cried one of the enlisted dutifully.

"And I'll give you Chief Beatty as your junior. Your first watch is the mid tonight. It should be quiet enough, an independent transit to our station. All you have to do is get us there. Which one of you is it going to be?"

In my swollen guise, so unlike my personality and values and mood, and which was to last about forty years, I glimpsed the usefulness of a drop of humility: "Neither of us is qualified," I declared.

"You don't say." He looked at Billings for a more zealous response, and I cursed my stupidity.

"I guess so, sir."

"How hard can it be, eh, after flying a T-28?"

"I'll do it," I said. "I got an A in shiphandling at OCS."

"You've actually handled a destroyer, Mr. Clarke?"

"Simulated. But realistic. The school's simulator."

Which gave rise to my nickname for a number of weeks. Not the Clown. Not Our Good Luck Charm. The Simulator."

"I see. Very impressive. Though you do know that out here they don't reset the computer if you make a mistake?"

"Of course, sir."

He reflected, or pretended to. He studied the sea. "There's a bit of weather kicking up. North in the gulf you'll find the fishing fleet, each of them looking to cut off his devils. But the navigation is a straight shot. You won't get into trouble as long as you follow two simple rules. Do you know what they are?"

"Don't hit anything and always throw up to leeward."

Among the courtiers, general disapproval at my cheek, not unmixed with enjoyment of my sense of humor.

"One," Marchand said, ignoring both, "keep me informed. Day or night, I don't care. If you have a question, call me and let me help you with it. If you need to ask whether you should call me, that means you should. Don't try to command the ship yourself."

"Aye-aye, sir," said Buster, who apparently felt in the running still.

"And the other rule?" I asked.

"Don't ever make me look bad. Tell me something, Mr. Clarke. When you went ass-over-teakettle back there—"

"I wasn't thinking about either rule, sir."

"I was going to say, when you went ass-over-teakettle back there, at what point did you pull the cord on your life vest? Before or after you grabbed the safety net?"

"Before," I said, the first lie. "While I was in the air."

"That's what I thought." He turned to the court for con-firmation. No one contradicted him. "Forehanded of you, a good quality. Now, gentlemen, who is it to be? Don't worry, the loser will get his chance in time."

Neither one of us would say, but my own heart sank. Surely the question was rhetorical. There couldn't be any doubt who should be promoted to the responsible posi-tion, which they had told us in training should be the aim of every officer going to his first ship. Ensign Billings was as impressive in his military bearing as Commander Marchand was in his. He was well muscled, and his uni-form fit like a glove. He stood on the uneasy deck as if he'd been planted there. His shoes were spit-shined. His chin was tucked into his chest. He had a presence. If you wanted something done, if you wanted someone to keep this four-thousand-ton destroyer escort and her two hun-dred and fifty men safe from harm, you would give the responsibility to him. Having spent so much time in flight school, he must be senior to me. He was no smart-ass, dripping water onto the captain's deck.

An order was given. The ship changed course, heeled a few degrees, and fell off a wave. I lurched against the chair, and the captain grabbed my arm to steady me. On the new course the sun shone upon us with a garish light. We seemed arrested in the moment, and perhaps each of us felt that we would be more to each other than senior and subordinate, mentor and protégé, monarch and cour-tier. Or perhaps he just felt that I was a bug, swollen with the blood from some other, hapless host before he flat-tened me.

"Very well," he said. "You take the watch, Mr. Clarke."

Billings snorted. I was thrilled and then ashamed, as if I had been unable to take my eyes away from pornog-raphy.

Buster Billings

I don't remember the next few hours. No doubt the XO, Lieutenant Commander Schmid, introduced us to our department heads, assigned us to our quarters, and sent us below to the ship's office with our service records. It was a Sunday, and the crew was at holiday routine—conveniently at leisure to witness my lubberly arrival. The only energy in the ship was driving our single propeller shaft.

We were not a real destroyer. We were a "destroyer escort," USS *John Shafer.* We had just the one propeller, and therefore no redundancy in case of a breakdown; and just the one gun, a weakness if ever we were called upon to fight, as ship's company wanted with such bloodlust. Instead of firepower, we had an advanced sonar, and we carried a helicopter. In theory we could sweep the seas clear of submarines so the rest of the fleet, especially the six aircraft carriers at Yankee Station, pounding away at the enemy, wouldn't be troubled by them. But the Gulf of Tonkin was shallow, North Vietnam had no subs, and any belonging to China—for China shared the eastern half of the gulf—well, back at OCS, when one of the pundits at the Naval War College, in a symposium to give our class a taste of the intellectual basis of our profession, had been asked about the Chinese navy, he replied that they rowed like hell.

No, we weren't worried about submarines. We were a misfit thrown into the maelstrom of an American offensive that Richard Nixon and Henry Kissinger had devised to gain an advantage at the Paris Peace Talks...just as the North Vietnamese were putting their all into attacking us to improve their own bargaining position.

I knew these things, but on that first day what I most disliked about the ship—my place of work, my new home, after all—was its ugliness. From the helo *John Shafer* might have been a needle afloat on the sea, perhaps with one end magnetized to point north, as we were heading now. From the vantage of standing on her weather decks, the blocky lines of her hull and superstructure looked like tract housing. Behind the bridge was a pagoda-shaped tower combining the functions of a mast and an exhaust stack (with the same lack of feeling the designers had named this *the mack*). The mack failed its criteria of form and function both, and as I tasted the tang of sulfur it emitted I pictured how the ship would look without it— say, if a North Vietnamese bomb blew it away. The thing it proved most useful for, as I would find out, was a hiding place for dopers.

Nor did I like my quarters. Ensign Billings and I were assigned to the junior officer bunkroom, just below the bridge. The space had originally been intended for a com‐ modore, but the ship had proved too limited to be a flag‐ ship, and at the first refit the VIP furnishings had been replaced by four utilitarian bunk beds with four lockers and pull-down desks, all standing on a green—and why green?—presumably fire-retardant carpet.

We were on the port side, though without a porthole. The captain's cabin, to starboard, was separated from us by a single joiner bulkhead. This might be too close for comfort—through the vent ducts he could probably hear whatever we said. (Then again, whispered that swollen spirit in me, proximity was power.)

Not that, enemies as we were, Billings and I would be sharing secrets. Because we were short of officers the room was empty. Each of us took the bottom bunk of a tier, about eight feet apart, which felt like privacy in‐ vaded until I saw my division's berthing compartment.

After we had unpacked our sea bags, each of us waited to see what the other would do. I had the greater pa-tience. When Billings saw that I was settling in for a nap, being the one with the night watch, he strode from the room. The joiner door, perceiving the tension between us, hissed and clicked behind him.

His feet rang on the ladder, a distinctive rhythm, and the alcove was silent. Presently I got up. I would like to say that professional curiosity moved me, but it didn't. There couldn't be much on this ship to interest me. I would learn the few places I would absolutely need to know and black-box the others, like all of engineering. I got up to find the wardroom, the officers' mess, for I was hungry, and perhaps also at some level I hoped that the Nelsonian ideal of a band of brothers might be true.

The destroyer escort had two continuous decks, one above the other, and the wardroom was on the upper, the so-called main deck. Trying to fly down the ladder as Billings had done, I failed to duck under the hatch comb-ing. I saw lights and stars, I fell three rungs, and it sounded as if the whole ship must have heard me. I lay on the green tile—again green!—rubbing my head, where a lump was rising and blood was sticky in my hair. I may have groaned a little. Then I picked myself up as any hero would. The next ladder was right there, awaiting me, and I descended warily and wandered fore and aft among amused sailors until I found myself not in the wardroom but on the enlisted mess decks.

Evening chow was being served. One of the cooks ges-tured me to the mess line, and with my head ringing and submissive as a sleepwalker, I picked up a tray and let him fill it. Dessert was a container of peaches in syrup and a sheet pan of squares of coarse-crumbed vanilla cake. Following the example of the man in front of me, I pinched a piece of the cake, dropped it in its convenient hollow in the tray, and laved a spoonful of peaches over it. At once he turned on me.

"You can't touch the cake, sir. Now they're going to have to throw out that whole sheet pan."

"But you—."

Just then I saw the cook smiling and shaking his head. He handed me a chit—apparently I was supposed to evaluate the meal—and I carried my tray to the tables. I was tempted to sit next to the lying sailor and read him out; perhaps put him on report. However, I turned away and sat with three petty officers who seemed less likely to play tricks on the tadpole.

What now? How was I to talk to them? I had never really talked to enlisted men before. To put off the moment, I completed the evaluation and gave it to the cook. When I returned to the table one of the men asked if I were sampling the meal or just simulating sampling.

"Eating it," I replied, cutting into a ham steak that seemed to have been stamped out by a machine. "You'd be amazed what an appetite you have when you fall from an airplane."

Here were some smiles. Humor. I could win them.

"So where are you guys from?"

This was less successful. One of them was from Neptune, Nevada. The second was from Trident City, Texas. The third was from Popeyeville, Pennsylvania. The best I could manage in return was that their recruiters must have had an easy time with them. I forced myself to make eye contact, which revealed to me that each of them badly needed a haircut. Later I learned that except for the senior enlisted and the Naval Academy graduates—the "lifers"—no one wanted to be here any more than I did.

The three sailors picked up their trays and left with no *by-your-leave;* maybe that was the protocol. Although the food was deplorable—six months of this would ruin my health—I looked as if I were enjoying it. I was so out of sorts that it felt like kindness when the man in the steam-filled scullery, as he took my tray, hardly gave me a glance. A sweep with his sprayer and he shoved it into the hot box and pulled down the cover. If only all un-sightly leftovers could be boiled away like that.

Consistent with my awkward timing, I entered the wardroom too early for dinner. (Dinner for the crew was at four-thirty; the officers ate more fashionably an hour later.) Besides the Filipino stewards, unfolding the white tablecloth, only two people were there. Billings sat on the couch with another officer at right angles to him who had his back to me. They were playing acey-deucy and puffing up cigars, in whose stinking cloud they were already bond-ing: trash-talking like brothers indeed. Billings gave me a glance devoid of interest, at which the other looked over his shoulder. It was Captain Marchand.

"Don't interrupt your game, sir," I said. "Just passing through. I've been sampling the crew's mess."

On the excuse of having the midwatch, still more than six hours away, I skipped the wardroom dinner and went to bed. The room was cold, and the speeding ship was working heavily: the intakes of her forced-draft blowers, just aft of me, were roaring and banging. My head hurt. The nausea that I had never felt when sailing with my father seemed to rise from the noxious green carpet to drown out every other thought and allow only self-pity. I was eight thousand miles from home in a steel prison too ugly to hold back the sea. I had made a fool of myself join-ing the ship and in my first two encounters with my cap-tain. My shipmates were insubordinate and cruel and would never give me the benefit of the doubt. When first impressions meant so much, my absence from tonight's dinner would be ridiculed by my brother officers. If they learned of my past I'd be condemned as a hippy. The whole world was unkind. Just over the horizon a bloody war was going on, a moral obscenity that I had opposed for seven years but that I was now sworn to support even if, as was likely, it killed me. Although I had graduated near the top of my class at OCS, I knew nothing of my new profession or leadership or life itself. Before God I was a danger to everyone. Surely it would be better if I walked out to the fantail and climbed the lifeline and threw myself into the wake. Lost to sight, unrecoverable, and quickly forgotten: the thing that should have happened when, knowing so much better than the pilot, I had jumped from the helo hoist this afternoon. I had no chance of making a life here. If I managed to survive, somehow I would betray myself.

The door opened, letting in the light from the alcove. Ensign Billings, the captain's new best friend, had returned from dinner and the bosom of good fellowship.

As he crossed the room, his body carried a nimbus of cigar stink. Without taking off his mirror-black shoes, he lay down across from me and laced his hands under his head.

In a moment a penlight played up and down my face.

"If you want to pretend that you're asleep, Clock, you'll have to do better than that."

"But I *am* asleep. My unconscious maintains a residual level of vigilance against obnoxious intrusions."

"Rally? Let's test it, shall we?" With a scissors kick out of the bunk, he materialized at my side. Yelling "Clear!" he pounded his fist on my chest. If my heart didn't stop then it should have. Two days later I still had the bruise.

"What the hell?"

"Piggy's off her swill, is she? I can fix that." A hand grabbed my shirt front, another my web belt, and the next thing I knew he had heaved me onto the deck and was pulling my ears. I could have resisted, but I was caught in the weirdness of the moment and I doubted that he meant to hurt me.

A moment later we were both sitting on the carpet with something like a demilitarized zone between us. The penlight played on my face again.

"All right, I'm awake. What now?"

"Why weren't you at dinner?"

"I told you. I ate on the mess decks."

"I'm senior to you."

"Yes, I would think so, after flight training."

"If I'd had flight *training* I wouldn't be here."

"What happened? What's your name, anyway?"

"My friends call me Buster. You may call me Ensign Billings."

"Mine is Chris. Clarke, not Clock."

"But Clock in *Bos*-ton." He drew it out.

"What happened in flight training?"

"We'll get to that. What was your draft number?"

"Three. What was yours?"

"Three hundred and forty-four."

"So you were safe. Why join up?"

He rose, as a dancer does without using his hands, went to the door, and turned on the lights. The bare utility of the room was revealed and the reality of my life confirmed. Thanks to him my khaki shirttail was pulled from my pants. He himself looked ready for personnel inspection. Taking a desk chair in each hand, he flipped them around to put their backs together and straddled one. I did the same thing with the other.

"I want to fight for my country," he said quietly. "I feel a patriotic obligation."

"You've got me there."

"We Billings have always fought since the Civil War. Plus it was either this or farming. Plus I'm married—or I was, last time I heard from what's-her-name—with two children. Though by now she may have run off with Joe Sorensen, who owns a bunch of grain silos. Her folks always did favor him."

"How old are you?"

"Twenty-six. Are you for the war or against it?"

"Against it. Not that that matters now. What about flight training?"

"Are we going to be friends? Clock and Buster?"

I looked at him. "That's up to you."

"You've got *lifer* written all over you."

"You volunteered!"

"Not for this."

"So what happened?"

He smiled. When he wasn't acting out he had an appealing smile, without art. "My record says I was dropped for an inner ear problem. That's a lie. I don't understand relative motion. I flunked formation flying."

"But you could fly something else. Cargo planes don't fly in formation."

"They do in air shows. The point is, flight training is a series of gates, and you have to pass through each one. Any fool could do it. *You* could do it. Not me. I flunked the very last one. I can lead a bird all right with a shotgun or hit a teammate making a break for the basket. Or if *I'm* the only one moving I'm just fine. But I freeze up when I'm moving and others are moving around me. I don't have the knack. And when they're moving slowly, like ships, I overthink. I should have gone straight home from Pensacola. They offered me that. I told Marie, 'I don't need to be here, doing this.'"

"I could teach you," I offered, although that might have unintended side-effects. "It's just practice." True enough. After hundreds of maneuvering board plots at OCS, often well into the night, something had clicked.

"Give it up, Clock. I wasn't looking for help. Save your leadership for your men tomorrow."

"I'm sure you'll do better than me anyway."

"I might. Why are you acting so strange?"

After a breath, I blurted, "My mother died." Instantly he looked troubled, so I told him the story.

"That's terrible," he said. "Dear God."

"I feel as if I weigh three hundred pounds."

"I hope to shout." After a moment his face brightened. "So friends, yes?"

"Okay." We shook hands across our chairbacks. Yet I couldn't help a feeling of satisfaction, that I was the better officer and would leave him behind and our being friends would give me an advantage in that.

My Mother

Almost all the protestors I had known were slackers. Sex, drugs, rock-and-roll: essentially, that's all they had, the pastimes of a drawn-out kinderhood as they postponed their future in corporate America. And that was me. At M.I.T. the English major was at its lowest ebb of rigor. My calculus exam was an essay test. My science requirement was met by a course on flying saucers. I took the subjects I wanted without any design. Only one English professor required me to memorize poetry. I skimmed the prose readings with my mind somewhere else—I don't know where.

When I got to OCS, someone threw a switch in me. I had always known I was capable; it was a surprise now to discover that I needed to excel. The academic program was easy; oddly enough I also won top marks in military bearing, most of which were based on fitness and athletics. At the end of seventeen weeks I graduated third in a class of two hundred. Third in the draft, third among recruits: three was my number.

At home in Cambridge my parents gave a party. Their guests, all university people, were kind to a young man just starting out but condescending to his uniform. That wouldn't do. My mother's feelings were sometimes hard to read within her general amiability. One radical colleague, going too far, drank to me and Ho Chi Minh: she pinned him against the bookshelves and let him have it. After that only their closest friends stayed to wish me well.

The next morning I got up early to run, which seemed worthwhile as good for me though it was good for Nixon too. My mother was sitting on the porch in her favorite chair holding *The Times.* I went to say that if she would wait for me we could have breakfast together. Something was odd in the way she was sitting; some compaction of herself within her pink quilted bathrobe. She didn't turn her head in gentle delight when I came around the corner of her chair. Her face was grey. Her dull half-closed eyes looked upward, sightlessly. Her mouth was open, as if she had wanted to call out until she thought better of it. In a few seconds the pain must have grown from a curiosity to a revelation. It wouldn't be reasonable to call, she must have concluded; too late for that.

I sat on the ottoman below her feet, wondering how still and small and real she was. Then I sought my father.

He was just coming out of their bedroom, to begin a day like any other, a day that she would complete. He smiled a greeting; here was the gentle delight, which saw further than hers did, into my future. I made a sound like a sob, choking on the words, and all I could do was point. He knew at once what I was saying, but he couldn't believe it. He held his chin with his thumb and forefinger while he looked at me. During twenty-five years of marriage he had never thought of this. No one was more alive than she. He himself was related to life only through her. How could this be?

The day after her funeral I got on an airplane to join the war that all three of us abhorred.

Watch and Work

Nothing memorable happened on the midwatch. We arrived at our station and slowed to three knots, a brisk walking pace known in ships as *bare steerageway*. For the next two weeks we seldom went faster. We were a backup in case any of our aviators, returning from strikes on Hanoi or Haiphong, bailed out in the Gulf and needed to be rescued. Until nearly the end of our patrol this didn't happen. Hundreds of planes went up and came back every day. Tons of bombs were dropped. Countless enemy were killed. Le Duc Tho, the North Vietnamese representative in Paris, must have been greatly sobered. Besides the carrier strikes, B-52s from Guam pounded the country day and night. Our losses were the greatest of the war, but when anyone bailed out the rescue call always went to a Big Mother helo stationed on a nearby cruiser. Except for the work in our Combat Information Center, CIC, keeping track of the strikes, we might have been sailing alone. Actually, it was an ideal environment for learning. Hour after hour the quartermaster took the weather data: light and variable winds, sea state zero or one, barometer high and steady. The water looked like its name: *Pacific.* I never did see a shark fin. The only danger, about which I was warned by the conscientious sailors and tempted by the jokers—"Good eating, Mr. Clarke: jump right in and grab that one"—were the short, sinuating sea-snakes, full of their deadly poison.

I should explain some roles on the bridge, which meant so much to me from the beginning. I was the officer of the deck, or *OOD:* in the captain's absence from the bridge I was in charge of the ship, subject only to his orders or to those of the XO. I had *the deck,* as it is called; when relieving I told the bridge watch, "This is Mr. Clarke, I have the deck." I might also have *the conn*—"This is Mr. Clarke, I have the deck and the conn"—which meant giving commands to the helmsman, who actually steered the ship, and to the lee helmsman, who rang up the ahead and astern bells on the engine order telegraph. Anyone might take the conn. In battle or other emergency that person would be the captain, with his ultimate responsibility for the safety of the ship, the most experienced and presumably the best shiphandler onboard.

The officer of the deck might have an assistant, the junior officer of the deck, or *JOOD,* who on a small ship like ours might be a senior enlisted. My JOOD was Chief Beatty, a better watchstander than many in the wardroom, who in the quiet moments of those quiet watches gave me a lot of good advice and more than I deserved of interest and sympathy. Early on I told him about my scholarly parents and my mother's death. "Oh, that's sad," he said, and this was just right. He looked something like an academic himself, in his thick glasses with heavy black frames. Most of his offerings were couched as "What if this happened?" or "What if we did such and such now?" but his experience was far from hypothetical: after brushing him off once or twice to my cost, I listened. If all my relationships with the men had been this easy, I would have learned the craft of leadership much earlier and been happier as well.

For with my men and around the enlisted crew generally I was the typical dumb new officer, or worse: a laughingstock who might get them killed. That first day at quarters, standing in front of twenty sailors who hadn't qualified to do something better, I thought it incumbent on me to make a speech. Half a minute in I could see that I had lost them. In another half-minute they'd be drifting away. Whatever enthusiasm I had, for my task, for the ship, for the service, bled out. I looked at them. Homer Williams, my leading petty officer, issued that day's orders to fill the silence. When I tried to speak to them in less official circumstances (believing that these included, for example, the times when they were chipping paint), all I got was short answers, with or without the *sir.* The truth was they frightened me. I didn't know how to be with them. I didn't know what they liked and didn't like. I didn't know their slang. Whatever their background, in today's parlance they were *other* to me. I was sure that soon I would have to write to my father about the mutiny in First Division. Instead of growing up in the academy, I should have worked on the Boston docks or pumped gas or tried burglary. Alternatively, I should have had the self-confidence not to care what they thought of me.

On the other hand I was great on the bridge, greater than I deserved. Part of this was my experience in sailboats, learning that devotion to the elements and the forces acting upon a vessel in a fluid medium. Part was an ability to see the picture at a glance, sort quickly through priorities, and make snap decisions. Part was that I loved it.

Then too, I must say, every time the captain came to the bridge I pretended to be all-knowing and infallible. Chief Beatty, loyal as he was, never gainsaid me, not even by a glance, but every time I lied to Captain Marchand I got the hollow feeling that he knew it. Strangely enough, not only did he go along with my lies, they seemed to please him. Of course it was possible to read his sarcasm differently, but the things he wrote in my watchstander's log and a supercilious comment or two decipherable as praise made me think I was off to a good start. At the end of this patrol period I received a letter qualifying me as Officer of the Deck (Independent Steaming)—news I could share with my father—and after one particular episode I became generally regarded, at least in the chiefs' mess and the wardroom, as something of a natural (winning respect among the first group and alienating my brothers in the second).

It would be nice to report that Buster too progressed, that he was mistaken in his weaknesses; but having declared himself incompetent to evaluate moving objects he seemed to allow, even to welcome, evidence that proved it. He was standing watch with the communications officer, a reservist, who saw this quiet patrol as an opportunity to study for graduate school (after the deployment he would leave the Navy to become a hospital administrator). The reports that flowed to the bridge from CIC or the lookouts were always received by him in the same way: "Very well, thank you," with no further action taken. Whenever advised to change course, he let Buster do the conning.

This led to a misfortune. Because no one had taught Buster to stand in the direction of the turn, to ensure the course was clear, one day he nearly ran over a fishing boat just as the captain came up to the bridge. I doubt that Marchand would have cared if we had cut the boat in two, drowning the family onboard, but he had found a weakness in Buster, as he looked for in everyone, and from then on he wiggled his knife in it.

Of course it was the short-timer he should have dealt with, the officer of the deck, his immediate subordinate. Instead he lost no chance to find Buster wanting. For days afterwards he would question him until Buster silently shook his head. With some captains, taking a more positive approach, this might have been a form of training, an act of generosity. With Marchand, who led as he'd been coached, it was a crude attempt to break him down so he might be rebuilt as a winner. Since Buster shared his opinion of his faults but without any faith in the rebuilding, both of them colluded in the breaking down, and the captain's judgment of the incapable ensign spread throughout the ship.

The incapacity was a lie, just as my success was a lie. In every other way Buster was a born leader of men, fearless and inspirational. *He* knew how to talk to them, without simulating interest. Knew how to kid them and be kidded by them without taking offense. He asked their advice. If he decided not to take it he always explained why. Even a barnyard word from him pleased them. Whatever his problems on watch, he was welcomed as a shipmate.

Windward and Leeward

Those first two weeks felt like two months. After Chief Beatty praised my shiphandling to the captain he let me take us alongside the oiler, something I managed well and which gave me unalloyed pleasure. While I was doing this, my division were making a hash of bringing the rigs across, despite the presence of Lieutenant Tyler Brock, my department head. Once again Marchand showed little respect for the chain of command. Tyler, USNA Class of '67 and the most competent officer in the ship, was untouchable anyway, so instead he chewed out Homer Williams, my leading petty officer, directly and in public. I paid a price for this, but not from the captain, who signed my final qualification as OOD (Independent Steaming) that night.

"We are climbing Jacob's ladder," Buster sang in our stateroom when the yeoman brought me the letter with the grin of a footman bringing a love note to the master. "We are climbing Jacobs ladder | Soldiers of the boss."

The next afternoon, when Buster had the conn, the cruiser in charge of our station advised us that her Big Mother helo was out of commission to change out a gearbox. The communications officer, who was OOD, replied with his usual "Very well. Thank you" and did nothing. As if to punish him, an aircraft then appeared off our bow trailing smoke, and quicker than the mind could distinguish them there were two double splashes, one small and feathery, the second a walking splash that gave the glimpse of a silver wingtip as it disappeared in the sea.

Our own helo was chocked down in the hangar. We had a boat at the rail, but the captain decided on a shipboard recovery since we were so close. It was a vital moment with the pilot's life and also the ship's reputation at stake; as captain I would have taken the conn myself. Marchand let Buster make the approach.

He began well. Knowing by now to conn from the engaged side, Buster eased the ship alongside the pilot. For once my division was on the fo'c'sle in good season with the rescue davit swung out and the cargo nets dropped over the bow. The head of the pilot, in his cheerfully decorated helmet, was *right there* below us. He raised one hand to signal that he was alive and ready to be hauled to safety. But Buster, not knowing that the wind and seas would push the ship faster than the pilot, had put him on the windward bow, and after he stopped the ship, before we could lower the rescue collar, we were already drifting out of position.

The pilot asked conversationally where we were going.

In my frustration at the opening margin of water, I shouted at the bridge wing. Buster's face and Marchand's too were passive, as if the situation were beyond their control. Backing and filling would be awkward, even supposing they came to their senses. My people weren't helping either. By the time Williams thought to fetch a heaving line, we were too far away and the wind blew his toss back in his face. With a curse meant to be heard I jumped overboard.

My first sensation was how delightful the water was, warm and clear. I floated easily without a life jacket, buoyed by the salt. The pilot's vest had already inflated. He and I would tread water until the command figured out what to do.

Close to him rust-colored blobs rode to and fro, as if from a giant eyedropper.

"You're bleeding?" I asked.

"Seems like it. The ground fire that took out my engine nicked me with a piece of shrapnel."

"Where?"

"Left arm."

"Better let me have a look."

"Sure."

His heroic taciturnity was infectious. All under control, despite those flames in his cockpit. Instantly I wanted to be an aviator. I wouldn't have flunked formation flying.

The arm was raw and pulsing blood. His face was pale and his breathing rapid. How often death comes disguised as trivial. I wrapped my hand over the wound, squeezing hard until the blood stopped rising through my fingers. The pilot winced but said nothing. The ship had stopped to lower her boat. I beckoned, two quick arm-waves. She surged ahead, turning to give us her lee bow. Tyler Brock had taken the conn.

"Look out for the sea-snakes, Mr. Clarke," Williams called, but that might be his sense of humor. He liked to send new sailors to fetch a bucket of vacuum or a hundred feet of waterline. Still, I looked. Two of the snakes were tracing sinuous lines on the surface about ten feet away, moving towards us ever so innocently. Were they, like sharks, attracted by blood?

"No point in lingering here," I remarked to the hero.

But now the situation had flipped: competence on the bridge, stupidity on the fo'c'sle: my people hadn't thought to swing out the rescue davit on this side. A couple of men clambered down the cargo nets as I steered the pilot underneath. "Grab your arm," I said as casually as I could and lifted him out of the water enough that the men could take him. I don't know how I managed his weight except that the water was so buoyant. "Severed artery," I called.

"Get the medic." But Doc Daltry, the hospital corpsman (only the Army called them medics), was already there with a tourniquet. We got the pilot onto a stretcher, still conscious and still nonchalant, and down to sick bay, where some unlicensed surgery—every corpsman's dearest wish—and several units of blood saved his life.

In the little pulse of glory I was brought to him to be thanked. The manly thing was to chide him for misplacing his aircraft. When he was stable our helo medevacked him to *Yorktown,* one of the carriers at Yankee Station, and perhaps in recognition of our performance we were ordered to the gunline, our own dearest wish.

(I cannot dismiss the possibility, of course, that the real reason for this good fortune was a lobbying campaign by James Marchand, celebrated by Naval Academy alumni as the anchor of that famous 1963 football team.)

After the rescue I asked Buster if the captain had said anything to him.

"Looking for dirt are you, Clock?"

"That's unfair. I thought you might be feeling bad."

He started to shadow-box. "Wake up old Charley," he said. "He's never seen a fight like this."

"I have the reach of you by half a foot, shorty."

He stopped. "No, he didn't say anything, but he was kind of the way people are when they knew all along that someone was going to disappoint them."

"Now you know windward from leeward, anyway."

"As if I cared," he said.

The Gunline

Halfway down the coast of the reunited nation of Vietnam is Quang Ngai province. During the war its story was told by the sun, as so often in fairytales. During the day U.S. troops and the Army of the Republic of [South] Vietnam (ARVN) generally managed to maintain control. At sunset the spell came alive: the peasants of Quang Ngai put down their tools and picked up their weapons. First as the Viet Minh then as the Ba To and finally as the Viet Cong, they had been fighting for their freedom since 1941. What was different when *John Shafer* arrived off their coast was that the regular troops of the North Vietnamese Army (NVA) had joined them; men, tanks, and artillery.

My parents and I and millions of Americans had been right that the Vietnam War, apart from the dishonor of it, was unwinnable. Whatever Nixon hoped from the Paris Peace Talks, the reality on the ground in 1972 was the impending withdrawal of the United States, completing a strategy he had campaigned on and put into effect three years earlier (his term for it, *Vietnamization,* sounded about as convincing as the reports I was feeding Marchand). In a few months only the irresolute ARVN would stand between the NVA/Viet Cong and their great goal of national liberation. For the remaining U.S. forces, then, the mission looked like a deadly marketing campaign, fighting as hard as we could to sustain the appearance of resolve, defending the rump half of a country that didn't want to be defended, at least by us.

Sailors are fatalists. To ship's company, all this was like the weather, except perhaps to Tyler, to whom war was life, as it was for Sherman and Patton. Most of my shipmates just wanted to do their jobs and not be the last man killed in the war, which wasn't likely anyway, and return home with some medals on their chest and a sea story or two to tell. At least they knew what they wanted. Between my old obsession and my new ambition, I was like the sad, much maligned friend of my parents who had left his wife and family but wasn't sure about his lover.

On August 1, then, having steamed overnight, we arrived at our station off the village of Mo Duc, in Quang Ngai province. The crew came topside for the arrival. There was fabled Vietnam, five thousand yards away. Most of us, though we had been pulled in by its gravity, had never seen it before.

The spot looked deceptively peaceful. All around us was an industrious fishing fleet. A narrow beach fronted a forest rising into a backdrop of old green hills which seemed to overlap each other. According to our gunnery charts the village lay in a clearing tucked behind a foothill. We couldn't see it from the ship. We hoped we weren't going to be disappointed.

(Like fools in a fairytale, we forgot it was daytime.)

The line of fire was of particular concern to Buster, who, having made his near-fatal mistake on the bridge, was demoted to standing watches in the gun director, rotating with Chief Letourneau, the leading gunner's mate. The director was mounted on top of the bridge and artificially stabilized against the motion of the deck. When synched to the gun it looked wherever the gun pointed. On the other hand, if the director officer saw a target through his rangefinder, the gun could be synched to him. In theory Buster might aim the gun from there—might defend us against North Vietnamese tanks and artillery, hero as I thought him. But that seemed unlikely, especially in such a peaceful setting.

He gave me a demonstration. The interior was like an aircraft cockpit with its instrument panel, its outstanding visibility through the rangefinder, and the sense of being master of his own confined world. If the motions of the gun mount threw him into an odd attitude, his pilot training had accustomed him to that.

I was encouraging. A good fit for him, I said. I must admit his demotion pleased me.

"When the XO and Brock called me in," he said, "they reminded me of how much I like pheasant hunting."

"What did you say to that?"

"I said I was getting tired of all you surface pukes anyway. It's nice to be downwardly mobile, don't you think?"

"You'll come back," I said. "You'll be an OOD before the deployment is over. People have short memories at sea." This bit of wisdom came not from me but from Chief Beatty, who, speaking of Buster, said that the half-life of seawater was about one week.

"I'm not a brownnoser like you, Clock"—grabbing my arm with both hands and giving it an Indian burn until I pulled away. "I just want out of here."

"Says the man with draft number 344."

"I didn't sign up to shoot people with a cannon. Inside my armored keep. Seems unfair, don't you think?"

Unless we considered the coming darkness.

On one of the hills—*330,* named for its height in meters—a Marine detachment had set up an observation post, or *O.P.* Its leader was a captain whose call sign was *Charlie Brown.* The detachment spotted for their battalion, who were blocking the highway between Mo Duc and Quang Nai City; our mission was to support them. From his O.P. Charlie Brown could look down on the village clearing, innocent in the light, murderous in the dark, and beyond it the scratches of roofline broken by occa-sional smokestacks that suggested, as Rembrandt's etch-ings do, the city in the distance.

I had the first dog watch that day—from 4:00 to 6:00 P.M.—after which I ate dinner and returned to the bridge, sensing that we were going to begin. The hills were sil-houetted in the red and orange glow, and a few lights were just showing through the trees, like the first of the evening stars when you wait with your sextant. On the starboard bridge wing a crowd of officers stood holding binoculars. They had given the captain his privileged place by the compass repeater and the sound-powered phone. All the binoculars were in use. Louie DiGiovanni, the chief engineer, kindly shared his with me.

Since it was too dark for us to see any targets, Charlie Brown would call in the fire mission and spot our fall of shot. Over the speaker came his voice, slow, clear, and confident: grid coordinates and height, number and type of rounds—all the data we needed to aim our gun. We were actually going to shoot, then. Tyler in CIC directed the mission; he had come to us from a ten-gun World War II destroyer, and the captain had so much confidence in him that he stayed up here as another spectator.

Our radio talker repeated the data and after a moment reported "Ready."

"Ready break fire," ordered Charlie Brown.

Nothing happened at first. Well, what?

Servos humming, both the gun mount and the director slewed out to the beam, and the gun barrel rose and fell as regularly as breathing to adjust for the roll of the ship.

Still nothing. Marchand spoke into the phone: "What's the delay?" I brought the binoculars down from my eyes to give them to Louie.

"No thanks," he said. "Not my first prize fight."

Just as I took another look, seeing nothing really in the dark, there was a tremendous bang, smoke and flames shot from the gun, my world tilted like a TV camera upset by the unexpected, and the binoculars hit me in the face. The muzzle of the gun was scant feet away with nothing to shield me from the blast.

Louie smiled.

"Right one hundred, drop one hundred," said the voice.

This time I had a moment's warning as the first round's empty powder casing was ejected from the mount, to clatter on the deck and tumble against the lifelines. Then another blast, against which I steeled myself.

"Repeat. Five rounds. Fire for effect."

Marchand nodded, and a mutter of satisfaction spread through the observers. In the lexicon of spotters this meant that we were on target.

A series of blasts, then another series, then an adjustment to a new target and another series. Then I lost count. Although I was warned by the ejected casings, each shot seemed to come before I was ready. The gun blasted me, blasted all of us as if we were shooting ourselves. My ears roared, rang. My mouth tasted bitter, and cordite prickled my skin. That slender tube couldn't possibly contain such force. No wonder guns burst.

But I was only feeling the explosion of the propellant, not the payload. We were shooting into the dark, and unless we got a secondary explosion—say of an ammunition cache—we would never know the result. Most of the time Charlie Brown, keeping his transmissions to a minimum, didn't tell us.

At the target the detonation of the payload must have been unimaginably horrifying. Nothing could survive a hit. You'd be dead no matter which side of the war you supported. To preserve your will to fight against such a weapon must be remarkably brave. And how many of the dead and the maimed were noncombatants—women and children?

None of the old hands seemed bothered by this. That night and in the days that followed, their tone was cheerfully destructive, like hunters who assume that everyone, even the quarry, shares in their love of the kill. Being on the gunline was indeed a plum, with so many multi-gun destroyers in the fleet and *John Shafer* having just the one. As Louie boasted in the wardroom, we would show them we could punch above our weight.

It wasn't only the officers. The gun became the ship's obsession. Seaman Wolford, in the laundry, kept as good a tally of the rounds fired as Tyler Brock. Fireman Jurgelevicius, the welder, who repaired a tricky piece of hydraulic line in the recoil system, never paid for a drink—or a girl—on the deployment. No one minded the lack of sleep or other inconveniences from the constant firing and the frequent rearming. Led by Chief Letourneau, the gunner's mates were mess decks celebrities.

We were there three weeks. We fired night and day—the stately, unrelenting *shot...shot...shot* which was like someone with a sledgehammer beating the bulkheads. We fired while others of the crew ate and slept and watched the movie. We fired while the fishing fleet fished around us. We fired rounds that became shrapnel, rounds that pierced armor, rounds that exploded above people's heads, and—a red-letter occasion—the much admired *Willy Peter* or white phosphorous rounds, which burned the flesh like napalm, never stopping while the fuel lasted. Many days we fired our entire magazine, five

hundred and ninety-nine rounds, and then hauled away
from the shore at best speed to find the duty ammunition
ship. Sometimes we fired all day and replenished all
night, officers passing shells side-by-side with enlisted
men.

When he could see the target Charlie Brown spotted
our fire. At night, or when he and his Marines needed to
rest, we generally fired "harassment and interdiction"
missions into a circle drawn on the chart and presumably
containing our foe; but these had no more reality than
pencil marks, since we never heard the results.

In an emergency, for example if the O.P. were under
attack, Charlie Brown might call for illumination rounds,
but this hadn't happened yet even though it seemed odd
that the enemy would leave undisturbed a voice so dangerous. They knew him, voice and call sign, which occasionally they would spoof, since they were listening to our
spotter circuit. They were clever as hell. By the evening
they had figured out our daily changing authentication
codes. One of the continuing lessons of the Vietnam War
was that the enemy, though not American, were smarter
than we gave them credit for and that they often used our
superior technology against us. Haven't we learned and
relearned that lesson since then!

Public Relations

There were respites. One quiet morning, after we had re-
armed during the night and most of the crew were sleeping in, Chief Beatty and I had the watch on the bridge.
Captain Marchand appeared, big, squat, powerful, light

on his feet. Sitting in his chair, he picked up his binoculars with their macraméd strap (courtesy of my boatswain's mates) and raised them to his eyes. Being ever aware of him, I looked in the same direction, as did the chief.

"That northbound bulk carrier, Mr. Clarke?"

Yes, I knew it was there, headed our way, and knew vaguely too that it didn't appear threatening. In general I paid little attention to real ships, assuming they would stand clear of a destroyer looking to shoot someone. The fishing fleet, on the other hand, was all around us all the time, annoying as gnats; every so often a boat would dart across our bow close enough to make me wince. If the enemy had been given to terror attacks at sea as they were on land, we would have been unprepared to stop them. It was by no means out of the question that *John Shafer* might have joined the doleful list of military units caught by surprise. The memory of our laxity frightens me today.

Marchand swiveled his chair around. "Are you comfortable with her bearing drift?"

"Yes sir, certainly."

"What *is* her bearing drift?"

"Left"—although I hadn't taken it, that geometrically, legally-binding prediction of whether two ships will collide, maintaining the same aspect to each other as they approach.

"Are you sure?"

Salty sailor as I thought myself but inexperienced as I was, I assumed that he couldn't know such a thing at a glance. "I've taken it twice, Captain. Always left."

His roughcut cauliflower lips formed a superior smile. "Take it again."

I did, theatrically lingering at the compass repeater. No amount of wishing would make the reading change.

"Oh yes," I said, straightening up. "She must have changed course."

"Changed course, did she. Coming up the coast."

"Yes, she must have. Chief, let's give her some room."

Chief Beatty opened us to seaward, while the enlisted watch, mostly my men from the division, looked like dopers who, on the approach of Authority, had thrown their roaches overboard. The captain's pleasure seemed to grow at the charade.

Having commanded ships myself, I don't know why he didn't punish me for lying—a court-martial offense. In those weeks I was two men depending on whether the captain was present. If he asked me a question I couldn't answer, even the most trivial thing—even if it had nothing to do with the Navy—I lied. I lied when there was no point to it, just to fill the silence. I lied to appease and sometimes to disagree, to show him that I had a mind of my own. I lied to him when alone and also with others. The lies multiplied, requiring feats of memory. My behavior surprised and confounded me, it often sent me to bed to pull the blanket over my shame, but I couldn't help it. I became not the Simulator but the Dissimulator.

He nodded as if everything were under control and jumped down from his chair. At the door he turned and said across the bridge, without needing to raise his voice, "Oh, and Mr. Clarke, may I see you for a moment?"

"Aye-aye, sir. Now?"

"If you would."

"I'll just call my relief."

"Oh, I think Chief Beatty is more than capable of taking the deck, don't you? Since we've crossed that bulk carrier's bow."

He left before I could go with him, which might have made us more like shipmates. After Chief Beatty relieved me, I went into my stateroom and checked my appearance then knocked on the cabin door as my heart beat painfully.

"Come in, Chris. Sit down." He spoke in a tone of voice I hadn't heard before, gentle and unaffected. A voice for reporting bad news from home, perhaps; I hadn't heard yet from my grieving father. "Coffee?" On the small conference table was a silver service—a gift from the ship's sponsor. Before I poured a cup for myself, I replenished his, which pleased him. He shifted his big body in the chair. Over a sip he looked at me. His eyes were ice blue behind the wild tufts of red eyebrow. They gave a curious feeling of disjunction, as if a second, alien intelligence were using them to look at me.

"What did you think of yesterday's shooting?" he asked.

"Outstanding, sir." The truth was that after two weeks I still hadn't seen a single target.

"Did you read this from *Newport News?*" He held up a radio message.

"Yes sir." I would read it afterwards.

"You know, we ought to sell ourselves like that. Sure, she's the flagship, with a big staff. But this message was undoubtedly written by some ensign like you with a flair for catching the reader's attention."

"Maybe a future Pulitzer Prize winner."

He didn't see a joke. "My point is, it reads like *Newport News* is winning the war all by herself. I want you to write a message *about us* every day."

Are we winning? I thought. "A message?" I asked.

"A daily operations summary—give it a format, make people think it's a regular report. We have a terrific story to tell. Yesterday we silenced an enemy mortar emplacement." This was a stretch: probably the enemy troops had shouldered their mortar tube and moved on. But who was

I to criticize his exaggerations? As I thought this, I began
to understand why he had chosen me. "We are firing at a
greater rate," he went on, "than any other ship, including
the heavy cruiser. We are firing so much we may have to
re-gun in Subic—wouldn't that say something! But Commodore Lewis, who writes my fitness report, hasn't noticed. That's what I want you to address: tell our story.
Can you do it? You *can* do it."

Gone was all gentleness of manner. He was ready for
the snap of the ball, speaking now only because speech
was customary. I didn't really need to be persuaded: there
was no escaping the strength of will that swelled his chest
and squeezed out the space between us. He was a man
who despised what he could dominate, and I was a boy
who wanted to be loved.

"What do you say, Chris? All right?"

"Aye-aye, sir."

"All right?"

"Yes *sir!*" I exclaimed, *Hooyah!* not being sailor talk.

"All right, then."

The mechanics of data collection I knew from college.
I made up a form that the gunnery team must complete
after every mission. In the evenings I collected the forms
and went over each target on the chart. Then I drafted
the report on the typewriter in the weapons department
office, double-spacing the lines so the captain could make
his changes.

There were many of these. I was slow to learn the style
of naval reports—that understated bragging, as if about
your gifted children. More important, despite—or maybe
because of—my own struggle with the truth, I resisted the
practice, widespread in the war, of inflating the numbers
at every turn. Under Marchand's quick red pen *damaged*
became *destroyed, engaged* became *silenced.* A targeted

structure always concealed an enemy arms cache. The fall of our shells always triggered secondary explosions. Body counts were higher than enemy troop strength.

No doubt, with all my lying, he had assumed a certain corruptibility in my character. But these were official records, whose falsification might send me to prison; and once, forgetting who he was—or wishing that he was someone else—I challenged him: "Everyone I've talked to didn't see a secondary."

"Well, now you've talked to me," he replied, underscoring his correction. He set down his pen. The branched veins stood out in his forehead. His hands gripped the edge of the desk. How he would like to press his short broad thumbs against my throat.

After that I simply stood behind him and watched, absolving myself from responsibility. When he changed a fact, often he would look up at me, daring a fight, but he understood that I wouldn't get up from the playing field again. "I *saw* a tank," he might say. "I was there." More and more he was pleased with me not for what I wrote, not for how adroitly I wrote it in the accustomed style, but just because he had cowed me. I was his creature: typical of Marchand, he was pleased and contemptuous at the same time. It was humiliating to carry the messages to Radio Central and have the radioman say, "Someone bled all over this one." But it was worse to sit at the breakfast table while my brother officers read what we were supposed to have done the day before. The department heads, who had actually fired the missions they were reading about, made pointed comments at first; comments which XO Schmid countered by exclaiming, "Good message, Mr. Clarke!" Buster acted as if anything the captain did must be disgusting.

Charlie Brown

The other part of my public relations duties was to maintain a rapport with Charlie Brown, without whose spotting I would have no news to hype. I kept him and his Marines supplied with candy, cigarettes, and magazines from our ship's store, paid for from the XO's slush fund and flown to the O.P. by our helo. Once a day, in between fire missions, I read the news to him over the spotter circuit. Though I didn't hear them in the background, I guessed that his Marines listened in.

As did our enemy, vocal in his enthusiasm.

I hammed up the news a bit, trying to sound like Walter Cronkite, but I censored nothing. When eleven Israeli athletes were taken hostage by Palestinian terrorists at the Olympic Games in Munich, I reported it. When they died in a rescue attempt, I reported that. From five time zones away, neither event seemed as bad as it was.

"Eleven, huh," he said, who was responsible for more lives than that at the O.P. "Well, in a hand-to-hand fight it would be hard to save them."

"Fuck you, Charlie Brown."

"Fuck you too, Victor Charlie, my little yellow friend. Don't you know it's rude to eavesdrop? Go on, Chris."

"Fuck you, Chris."

"Ferguson Jenkins is on a pace to win his twentieth game for the Cubs." I said. "That's six years in a row."

"Fergie."

"And Milt Pappas of the White Sox no-hit the Padres."
Charlie Brown was from Chicago. His real name was A.C.
Jackson, and at the Naval Academy he had been a classmate of Tyler's. "In national news, domestic counselor
Daniel Patrick Moynihan has advised President Nixon
that race relations in America might benefit from a period of benign neglect."

"That so?"

"And in international news"—bringing out my best
item—"the White House announced today that all combat troops have left Vietnam."

"Too bad for you, Charlie Brown. Stinking Marines no
combat troops. You the last fucking man to die here."

"Thank you, Victor Charlie. You can tell your gook
friends that we'll be packing up any day now. Sorry we
can't drop a couple of Willy Petes on you before we go.
And thank you, Snappy"—our call sign. "A pleasure, as
always."

"And that's the way it is," I signed off.

The way it was was that Captain Jackson had become
our hero, the present source of our self-esteem. Even
Marchand, once a celebrity himself, who had basked in
the glory of heroic teammates, spoke of him with respect.
Toward the end of our line period, as the area remained
generally calm, he invited him to the ship. Hero worship
aside, he wanted a kudo from him—or from his battalion
commander, whatever he could get—and even more important he wanted to be asked to return to Mo Duc.

Louie DiGiovanni instructed me on the politics at
work. There were eight destroyers in our deployed squadron, under Commodore Lewis. At the end of the deployment he would rank the eight commanding officers in
their fitness reports, and only the top one or two—to be
safe, only one—would survive the winnowing to become

a commodore himself. James Marchand must be the one. But Lewis was vicious: he loved to throw chum in the water. Mad Joe Montgomery of *Bausell,* a six-gun World War II destroyer, was Marchand's chief competition, and Lewis liked Montgomery and held up *Bausell* as the squadron exemplar. She was remarkably clean and smart for her age, she answered every bell, and she'd been on the gunline longer than we had and had been widely praised for her shooting.

The rivalry was personal—Buster and I grown up. Once, back in San Diego, when *John Shafer* had moored outboard of *Bausell,* Montgomery had put rat-guards on the mooring lines between them. A new ship with rats: ha-ha, a great joke, enjoyed by the commodore himself. According to their style Marchand must grin and bear it. At the start of the deployment he had taken Montgomery ashore as his drinking buddy. Montgomery now wore a tattoo he would have trouble explaining back home. Such was the way old salts competed. Louie grinned.

Charlie Brown got permission from his battalion commander, and the next afternoon our helo brought him to the ship. The main door opened and a tall Marine officer in jungle fatigues stepped down. He chatted with the two pilots for a moment than gave orders to the lance corporal uploading our tribute of geedunk. Then he walked forward, taking long strides. I met him on the flight deck, brought him into the helo hangar, and took his safety vest and cranial helmet. His head was nearly shaved—the first black person I had seen without an Afro since our cleaning man at home. His eyes were wary and tired, but his manner was composed: alert, attentive, confident. He was as tall as I and powerful with the power of leverage. The sleeves of his blouse were rolled up to his long biceps. He set down an oddly shaped canvas bag. We shook hands.

"Chris Clarke." *The voice of Snappy,* I wanted to add.

"Captain Jackson." No first name: *Call me Captain.* But I was merely an ensign, and formality concerning rank, even among junior officers, was the Marine way. A first lieutenant might have to order a second lieutenant to charge up a hill, sacrificing himself and all his men.

"How are you?" he asked. "What now?"

"First the wardroom. The captain has the officers and chiefs there so you can give us an idea of what's happening on the ground. And then the gunnery team would like some time. *They say* it's for any pointers you might have, but really it's because they're so pleased with themselves—rightly so."

He nodded. If he understood that hero worship was implied, it didn't move him. The thrill of being admired, as Marines were, even in those antiwar days, had nothing to do with Hill 330.

"There's Charlie Brown!" the captain said in the wardroom, where the khakis were two-deep at the table and everyone was standing. "Jim Marchand. Always good to know the play-caller."

"Captain Jackson, sir. How are you?"

Marchand introduced the XO and the department heads, and the officers sat by seniority. I stood by the pantry door among the chiefs. Jackson used the same formula to greet the other department heads, but when he came to Tyler Brock, his classmate at the academy, he grinned. Sixty-seven broke the mold, they agreed: there were no plebe years since theirs.

"Colonel Jones asked me to give this to you, sir," said Charlie Brown, in character again, picking up the canvas bag and taking from it a short-barreled rifle with a pistol grip and a curved magazine. "A Soviet-made AK. We found this near the NVA major you killed in the fire mission last week. Be careful of the stock," he warned as Marchand, with an insipid smile meant to show pleasure, reached for it. "The glue on the brass label is still wet— Battalion just had time to put it on the helo."

Marchand read aloud:

CDR J.M. Marchand, U.S. Navy
CO, USS *John Shafer*
Our Great Friend "Snappy"
Mo Duc, Quang Ngai, RVN, 8/72

He held it up for all of us to see. After checking the chamber and magazine and feigning disappointment that they were empty, which raised a few chuckles, he passed it to Tyler, who passed it to Chief Letourneau to be kept in the ship's armory. "Very kind," Marchand added. "I'll tell my superiors how helpful Colonel Jones has been." (As he did, with an inspired use of the passive voice, in my summary report that night.)

The welcome concluded, both men sat, Jackson on the captain's right, across from the XO. Rogelio Gozum, the leading steward, brought a glass of iced tea on a little round napkin scalloped at the edges and embossed with the *John Shafer* seal. Jackson lifted the glass to look at the napkin, mimed a face, and whistled softly. I laughed. He heard me and looked across, catching my eye. *I have a lot of black friends at home,* I thought-messaged him.

Louie, next to the XO, fancied himself a strategist (though Tyler was always correcting his facts). "So, has the Battle of Mo Duc begun?"

"That's a new one. The Battle to Pry Future General Jackson Off Hill 330, I call it. Battalion has entered the city, but there's chatter the NVA are moving south."

"Then they'll have to get through you, won't they. What are your static defenses?"

"You mean the terrain?"

"Exactly."

"Well, it's a lot harder to attack uphill, of course. We've got a perimeter out, mines and wire, and a decent field of fire in case they do come."

"That can't be enough." Showing two teeth beneath his black moustache, Louie wheedled for the tabloid truth.

Jackson said softly, "If the enemy wants to take my position, and he's willing to commit enough force, he'll take it."

"Not if we're around," declared Marchand.

"Thank you, sir. He's very patient."

"Yes, and we're coming to the end of our line period. But we'll be relieved, certainly. I hear back-channel it may be *Providence*—light cruiser, twelve six-inch guns and twelve five-inch. Your next great friend."

"That *would be* Providence," Charlie Brown said, drawing a laugh, but there was no change in his eyes. I was wrong: it wasn't wariness, it was distance. Or maybe acceptance.

"And we'll certainly come back here if we're invited. That's a hint, sir."

When Charlie Brown had no answer for this, the XO, to degrease the conversation, returned to the professional problem, asking how the O.P. would know if an attack was coming.

"We'll see them getting ready. A general movement of people and equipment during the day. Waiting for dark."

"Movement in the open?"

"In the open. Pretty obvious. They're confident."

"Why not hit them then?" asked Louie. "Christ, Captain"—he was speaking to Marchand, not Jackson—"drop some frag on their heads. Attack them in daylight, before they get in position." There was a murmur of agreement around the room, and Louie nodded his own agreement.

"It's a rules-of-engagement thing," said our spotter. "Quang Ngai province is where Binh Hoa and My Lai happened."—the infamous massacres, which had helped fuel my antiwar protests. He emptied his glass in a long drink with his head back, his Adam's apple throbbing.

"How do you know you're not shooting at civilians?" Buster asked.

Marchand frowned.

"You have to make a judgment about that."

"Who does?"

"I do," Jackson said.

The briefing ended on this note. For a few minutes the senior officers continued with him around the table as the rest of the wardroom emptied. "Old Clock has a new love," Buster said as he walked past me, waggling his nose with his fingers.

Jackson laughed. "You're the duty tour guide, right?"

"Yes sir, happy to. What would you like to see?"

"Your radio room."

"Aye-aye, sir. And, maybe then, the gunnery team...?"

"Radio first," said the XO, giving me a wink.

I led my hero up the ladder and down the passageway to the locked joiner door, where I pressed the buzzer. We were quickly admitted. The spotter circuit was monitored continuously here: Charlie Brown was their hero too. The watch supervisor showed him the banks of transmitters and receivers and test equipment, the switchboard, the teletypes. Jackson took it all in like a visitor on a factory tour, waiting for the free sample at the end.

"What else can we show you, sir?"

He smiled. "Any chance of a MARS hookup back to the States?"

"Not allowed during daylight, sir. Sorry."

But the communications officer, the blasé short-timer who wanted to run hospitals, had overheard us. He came forward from the crypto vault. It might be possible, he said, to raise a ham operator in the States who could make a phone patch. His eyes gleamed in the pleasure of subverting regulations while he flipped switches on the patch panel as fast as human hands could move. He warned, however, that propagation might not be so hot.

Propagation turned out to be amazingly hot. The signal seemed to be coming through a long submerged pipe, and in the background was a constant undulating tone, like a police siren in an old movie about the Nazis, but the words were clear enough. A woman in Modesto, who sounded like a grandmother, answered the call. Next was the voice of the Camp Pendleton operator, who sounded like a great-grandmother. Then Jackson's wife was on the line, a young eager voice.

The short-timer snapped off the speaker, and he and I retreated from the patch panel. In the brotherhood of petty criminals, we told happy stories about our other victories over The Man while on a green oscilloscope in front of us, two traces rose and fell, and in the soundproofed booth my Marine captain, cradling the handset against his ear, rubbed the top of his head and hugged himself.

Part Two
Comfort Women

Olongapo's Origins

All line periods end. Eventually the war would end too, and the ships would go home, and the sailors would be reunited with their families to take their chances in the sunlit world, whatever that might bring.

As expected, a day or two after Charlie Brown's visit and with no further sign of the enemy, *Providence* came over the horizon with her overwhelming firepower which no sane enemy would challenge, and we were detached to proceed to Subic Bay.

Subic Bay, in the Republic of the Philippines, is now a commercial port attached to the City of Olongapo, which is modern and thriving. Fifty years ago it was an American naval base, and Olongapo was its excrescence, subject to its authority and taxed as such. It comprised two different realms, representing humanity at its best and worst.

The first was the port itself, called the naval *station,* the piers and shipyard, clean, efficient, and safe, where fifteen thousand Filipino workers earned a decent wage using—in some cases learning—the skills that industrial economies require. Working to a high standard, they serviced and repaired more than two hundred U.S. ships each month. For off-duty sailors the attractions of the naval station were wholesome: a chapel, a movie theater, a bowling alley, a library, a putt-putt green, a sailing center, a USO, and a Navy Exchange, where otherwise unaffordable luxuries could be purchased at cost. In the service clubs drinks were a bargain too, food was served to soak up the alcohol, local bands played songs from home, and the quitting time was respectable. Occasionally the shore patrol might be called to some place like the Chuck Wagon, an annex of the officers' club, but any rule-breaking there was usually harmless, resolved by the appearance of the uniform and guard belt, and never reported. No one might be murdered at the naval station.

At the main gate a sign on the archway said

JOB SAFETY STARTS HERE

It greeted the arriving workers each morning, but it ought to have faced in both directions. For beyond the gate, across a bridge over what everyone called Shit River, the other realm began. This was Olongapo. Until the U.S. became entangled in Vietnam, Olongapo was farmland, poor but decent. As the ships began arriving at the naval base in their numbers and the rich American sailors came ashore and the payroll soared, a shantytown sprang up offering the most degraded pleasures an exploited population could devise. When I was there in 1972 it was a hellhole.

Everything was for sale, every appetite could be sated. Family elders might take your arm on the boardwalks or casually offer their relatives while they drove you in their jitneys. Of course the offerings were mostly of women—a shocking range from pre-pubescent to wrinkled and toothless. But men and boys too sold themselves, openly; the Filipinos seemed to think that a disproportion of American sailors were what they called "benny boys." The idea of personal sovereignty was unknown then, not only to the sailors but also to the hookers—the accepted term, not *prostitutes* or *whores,* certainly not today's euphemistic *sex-workers.* From the naval station, pursuing your innocent amusements but always mindful that forbidden pleasures were just beyond the gate, you could almost hear the background hum, as if from a giant power plant, a continuous working of lust excited, sold and bought and more or less slaked, usually in the shortest time possible. The fiction was that you "went over" to have a few drinks and maybe enjoy a pig roast. In reality Olongapo was where the fleet went to get laid.

This realm was not only the opposite of innocence, it was dangerous. Venereal disease was endemic, both drug-resistant strains of the clap and more than a few cases of syphilis. With the hookers had come violent men: sailors were shaken down, robbed, beaten, and occasionally knifed in the clubs or upon the unpaved streets. While I was there a sailor from the cruiser *England* refused to pay his jitney driver a jacked-up fare; as he walked away another man jumped from the back of the car and shot him dead. When you went over, you could get anything, it was true; but anything could happen.

Outside the squalor of shanties, in a rural area loosely defined as Subic City, another kind of bargain took place. Quite often sailors and their hookers shacked up for the duration of the ship's time in port. This offered to the sailor convenient comfort and at least the promise of monogamy and to the hooker a higher and more stable income for fewer tricks. In the ideal there might even be the hope of marriage, that redeeming outcome followed by emigration to a new life in the United States and for the lucky few the chance to bring over an older parent or younger sibling.

Liberty Hounds and Straight-Arrows

So we entered port, that slow, thrilling revelation of the
shore, and I was on the fo'c'sle for my first time to moor
the ship. After so long underway, my men remembered
what to do. The mooring lines were faked out on deck and
the anchor made ready for letting go in case the ship lost
power or steering. The mood of the men was a variety of
feral, not unlike their desire to kill.

"Home sweet home," my leading petty officer, Homer
Williams, emoted from the capstan, where he sat. "Smell
the pussy, sir."

By then I was pretty well disgusted by Williams.

Striking a pose for his fastidious officer, he mended his
tone: "Grande Island to port, Mr. Clarke. To starboard,
sir, if I may invite your attention, is Bataan Peninsula,
where, in 1942, if memory serves, thousands of coura-
geous American and Filipino troops resisted the advance
of the Rising Sun."

"Stand by your lines," the phone-talker relayed. Jumping from the capstan, Williams shouted orders in a voice
meant to be heard on the bridge. Across the flat, gray surface of the harbor, we came up to our berth, slipping in
neatly astern of *Bausell,* our squadron mate. The heaving
lines were tossed, the mooring lines followed them to the
bollards on the wharf, the forced draft blowers wound
down, and all the accumulated energy of the last forty
days ebbed from the ship.

"Well done, First Division!" said the XO, making a loop
through the weather decks to ensure that the ship looked

presentable, a worthy companion to *Bausell*. We had the same desire. My men were frapping the doubled mooring lines and tying on the rat guards. Frapping lines—marrying the three parts into one by wrapping clean white cord around them—was unfashionable among West Coast sailors, but Joe Montgomery had done it to impress the commodore, and so must we. In the same way teams of sailors with garden hoses were washing down the salt from the superstructure to make the grey paint shine. (But we would leave the hundreds of divots cut in the nonskid around the gun mount by the ejected powder casings, the proud scars of battle.)

"And that, if I do say so, sir, is how a ship ought to present herself," declared Williams. "Oh, Mr. Clarke— sir!—I wonder if I might have a word?"

Standing in the bullnose with my back to the titivation, I was feeling an epiphany of sorts. Ships were all around us, decks teeming with sailors and workers. Sometimes the effort of a multitude can bring me to tears. I had never cared before about the different classes of ships, but now I made a resolution to learn them, present and past, capabilities, histories, and silhouettes. I would be *John Shafer's* expert in recognition and identification, the wardroom authority—not Louie or Tyler. If this profusion represented only that small part of the fleet that wasn't at sea, how mighty was my country, making such an effort to win the long foreign war.

Joining me, Williams went on: "I was hoping, sir, you'd look favorably on a request for open gangway."

"For whom?"

"For me, sir."

"You want to take leave, is that it?" We were to have two weeks in port; beyond necessary maintenance and possibly the replacement of our gun barrel, little would be asked of ship's company. Still *open gangway* was something else again: no requirement to be onboard at all except for duty days.

"Not exactly, sir." With an uneasy laugh Williams pulled off his white hat. In the stubble of his crewcut were beads of sweat. His cunning blue eyes were deep-set under a heavy brow. Already they were bloodshot. He was thirty-seven but looked fifty in the morning light. What he needed was leave, a long leave from the life he was living. "I have attachments here," he said.

It was probable that he had already hired someone to stand his duty.

"Attachments?"

"I might be getting married, like."

"Oh, I see. But don't you already have a wife?"

"All that's still to be worked out, Mr. Clarke. Which is why I need the time."

Sailors in civilian clothes were beginning to gather at the quarterdeck. Liberty would be going down soon.

"Nice try," I said. "See you at quarters tomorrow."

"You refuse?" Gone was all pretense of subordination.

"If I let you go then all the men will want to."

"They *are* going. It's the custom."

"Only the duty section onboard?"

"That's right. Depending how much *peso*-nality these swinging dicks can show." He chuckled.

Both the banality of the pun and the low meaning of the chuckle decided me. For six weeks Williams had undercut my authority with the division. It was my own fault, of course: I had devoted my attention to the bridge, to winning the captain's approval, at the expense of my duties as division officer. Still, it was time he learned his place. An ensign with his single gold bar is forever senior to an enlisted man with his crow. By Act of Congress and rightly so. I might have to order him and his men into a burning compartment.

"You can put in a chit if you like," I replied in a tone of voice that told him it would be useless.

"Aye-aye, sir, if that's the way you feel about it." He turned on his heel and walked away. Over his shoulder he muttered, "Doesn't seem quite fair, though."

How unfair it was became apparent that afternoon, when his request chit for open gangway was returned to me by the duty personnelman. Tyler Brock, our department head, had endorsed it, and the XO had approved. Williams went down the brow before eight bells were struck. That evening Buster, on shore patrol, saw him strutting through town with a hooker on each arm.

Chit in hand, I went to my enlisted sensei, Chief Beatty, to ask if it was normal for a department head to overrule his division officer in a minor administrative matter. No, he replied, not normal, and especially not normal for our department head. Then why? He gave me a long rambling answer from which, allowing for his kindness, I was able to extract that each of us has his nature, for better or worse; that Williams's nature was bent and his body diseased; that, understanding this, Mr. Brock yet valued his performance in leading a division of misfits all but forced by Fate to fight an unpopular war; and that perhaps too a hint was intended that my fast start in *John Shafer* had induced in me a certain attitude that might be, well, self-important.

His placid glance hoped he hadn't given offense.

"All right, I can work on my persona. Should I—"

"That's not a sailor's word, Mr. Clarke. Persona."

"How I present myself, then. Should I say something to Mr. Brock about this chit?"

"Remember what's written on the naval academy belt buckle, sir: *Fidelity* and *Obedience.* Mr. Brock knows you'll be upset that he overruled you. If you're silent it will impress him, more than complaining."

"All right, thank you, Chief. Are you going over?"

"Not me, sir. I married my high school sweetheart."

In other words Chief Beatty was a straight-arrow. Ship's company, I found, was divided into straight-arrows and liberty hounds, and in Subic Bay you were one or the other. The first group stood the duty days, did the maintenance, and enjoyed themselves at the welfare and recreation sites that the American people had provided for them. Whatever they may have suffered in manly pride compared to the second group was more than offset by moral complacency, money in the pocket, and a wist-ful, near-pleasurable loneliness that expressed itself in calls and letters home often containing cries from the heart.

The second group rewrote the ship's liberty policy: they went over, stayed over, and didn't return. If a nation makes a claim and no other nation challenges it, with time that claim acquires the force of law. So many of our crew stayed over that the ship's office stopped sending daily muster reports to the XO (who didn't ask for them either). Toward the liberty hounds the straight-arrows felt morally superior, certainly, but also resentful and perhaps envious.

Whatever joys the liberty hounds experienced, they paid for in more than money. Each day men would line up at sick call, pretending camaraderie, to receive their shots of penicillin from Doc Daltry. The first-timers among them might also be sore at heart, for beyond the shock of venereal disease was the banality. Something just for them had been promised. "You butterfly?" the women asked when they shacked up; yet they themselves were butterflies by necessity.

As I learned about Williams, the division between the two groups didn't always follow marital status. Among the married straight-arrows was the XO, the son and grandson of admirals, who loved and understood sailors but lived by his own moral code. Among the liberty hounds were Captain Marchand, Tyler Brock, and Louie DiGiovanni, whose wives all knew each other and spent time together as they waited for the ship to return. I couldn't quite tell with Tyler and Louie whether they meant to break their marriage vows. I hoped not in Tyler's case; in Louie's it would just confirm what I expected of him.

Most important to me, Buster was a straight-arrow; a straight-arrow by character, by devotion to his wife—his childhood sweetheart—and in any case by circumstance. His challenge to Charlie Brown over the rules of engagement had greatly displeased Marchand, who ordered that he be put in hack—restricted to the ship. The XO interpreted the order to mean that Buster should serve on shore patrol. He disappeared. He had a room at the Q— the bachelor officers' quarters—and when off-duty was thought to be spending time with the naval aviators at Cubi Point, his preferred cohort.

With Williams gone, the responsibility for directing the men in my division, those still onboard, fell to me. Like Doc Daltry I had my daily lineup of sufferers. It seemed that many of my sailors had emergencies at home but that Williams had refused to consider them; which was a shame when the solution was so close—Clark Air Force Base, with its daily flights to the U.S.—and so easy—my signature on a request chit.

Perhaps they thought I was an easy mark. The anti-war protests, shared with people from every background (including the literally unwashed), had taught me that other lives weren't as fortunate and decorous as mine in Cambridge. Still, I was shocked by the variety, the desperation, the stupidity, and the ugliness of the problems my men described. Without any modesty they showed me the situational equivalent of their poxes and pustules, and for every ill revealed they demanded just the one remedy: the flight home from Clark. When I wouldn't sign their chits I became their enemy. By now the idea of *fragging* had made its way into the lexicon of the war and become normalized. Two nights running the same low voice called me in my stateroom, promising to dump my body in Shit River. I consulted my sensei: within an hour Chief Letourneau had me sign for a .45 from the armory. I put it in my safe and locked my door.

At the Texas Bar

I went sailing. When the director of the center, a retired warrant officer named Ruthven, signed my qualification card, he mentioned that they were short of instructors. I made a face and shoved off. Mine was a twenty-five foot sloop, their biggest boat. Contrary to the rules, I sailed her out of the harbor and around Grande Island. The wind was fresh, and on the long legs out and back I sailed a beam reach, heeled way over with the water sluicing down the lee gunwale. Here was happiness. For the first time in two months I thought neither of the ship nor of home. When I returned to the basin, Mr. Ruthven, with a smile, reminded me of the rule against leaving the harbor and asked again if I would like to teach. We agreed on a schedule.

More happiness might come from that, inconvenient as it was. I returned to the ship in a better mood, resolved to work on my persona.

Someone knocked and tried to enter: the XO.

"Why the locked door, Chris?"

Did he know? Had Beatty or Letourneau told him? Did he know that I was such a poor leader that my men had threatened to frag me?

"I think it locks when it closes, XO. Always has."

"Ah. Come on, now. We're going over to celebrate."

"Celebrate?"

"We've been praised. Everyone's going. Get dressed and meet us on the quarterdeck."

"Is this what the Navy calls a *command performance?*"

The XO counted on his fingers. "First, young sir, it's not *the Navy*: it's us. Second, you don't care whether it's a command performance: *I'm* telling you. Third, unlikely as this might seem, it will do you good."

Whether it would do me good to experience a wretched side of life or do me good to give my ambition a rest or do me good to show my shipmates that I was, after all, just a regular guy—he wasn't clear. Perhaps he thought it didn't matter. I changed my clothes and left, locking the door, and went below to the quarterdeck.

Except for the command duty officer and Buster on shore patrol, the entire wardroom was going over, to some place that Tyler and Louie had found. The kudo had come in from Charlie Brown's battalion, and the gunline wanted us back. We gathered on the quarterdeck in our "appropriate civilian attire": for me, a polo shirt; for the XO and the other veterans, embroidered guayabera shirts, which in the Philippines were appropriate for all occasions. The junior enlisted mostly wore T-shirts with snarky messages or tie-dyed like an LSD trip.

The captain came down in a summer sports coat, which concealed the bulk underneath. Four bells in two groups of two were rung, and the word was passed *"John Shafer,* departing." After glancing aloft to see if the halyards were taut and the radar centerlined and over the side at the neatly frapped mooring lines, for we must be as smart as *Bausell,* he went down the brow and along the wharf without waiting to be followed. The officers scrambled after him roughly in order of seniority; that is, I was about to step onto the brow when the blasé short-timer cut in front of me with the explanation "George goes last."

Resolved to work on my persona, I told myself to act like George, the junior ensign in the wardroom, ignorant, interested, and inconspicuous.

At the gate the Marines checked ID cards. A typewritten notice posted under plastic reminded us of the curfew: failure to return by midnight or to find places in town would cause a report to be sent to our commands. And we were reminded that the Philippines Constabulary, the PC, had stated that curfew violators of any nationality were subject to arrest and confinement.

On the bridge over Shit River, some of my fellow Americans were tossing coins, and children in boats or along the riverbank were diving to retrieve them. Both sides had the same look of avarice. The children took turns according to some hierarchy that an anthropologist would find interesting. The Americans tossed as the spirit moved them, sometimes two or three at a time to confuse the children...but every coin was retrieved.

With a cry one of the children held up a slug washer and shouted a pidgin stream of filthy terms at the tosser, who laughed.

The others had gone ahead, and I had to hurry to catch them, pushing my way through the crowd of vendors. The main street was a dirt road with a desultory boardwalk. The vendors were selling jewelry, watches, clothing— *Property of Olongapo Yacht Club* T-shirts—monkey meat on a stick, airline samples of liquor with authentic labels, and, just as openly, the various sexual services I've described. I was soon tired of being solicited. As the crowd pressed around me—collusively for all I knew—I shifted my wallet to my front pocket and kept a hand on it. The street smelled smoky and fetid. Late tropical sunlight filtered between the buildings, which were two or three stories high and thrown together like a boom town in the gold rush days. It would be dark before I came out.

From every doorway music blared. Some of the clubs were *The Flamingo, The Desert Inn, The Professional Club, Charlie's Angels,* and *Casablanca.* We entered through the narrow doorway of *The Texas Bar,* which advertised

ABSOLUTELY NO COVER | WELCOME FRIENDS

but where a bouncer about the size and shape of the captain demanded twenty pesos from each of us and stamped the back of our hands.

Inside we were met by a middle-aged Filipina in a cowboy hat and a fringed bikini. The place had a stage, a dance floor under a faceted silver ball, which threw colored gleams of light in every direction, and about twenty tables mostly filled by Americans sitting with women; more women than men. Tyler and Louie were holding a long table on which pitchers of San Miguel beer were sweating, and the rest of us took seats. There was no protocol in such a place: I sat between Tyler and a tall, square-shouldered man with prematurely white hair who introduced himself as Joe Montgomery, CO of *Bausell.*

The music was so loud the air throbbed, and on the stage a young woman was dancing naked, a sight that was hard to watch or to look away from. She turned every

which way to show as much of her as there was. The most
explicit views were received by the tables as common-
place, and once or twice men got up to put money on the
stage, which she raked in with her foot as she danced.
She might have been about twenty, lissome, unravaged.
Perhaps she was only there to dance and be tipped. She
had a very good sense of rhythm. Her breasts made me
think of antiwar protestors who took off their tops before
the bayonetted lines of national guard troops. Her loins
were troubling.

Captain Montgomery was speaking to me.

"So you're Jim Marchand's star ensign."

"So you're Commodore Lewis's star captain."

He beamed. His skin smelled of Mennen aftershave. I
wondered where his incriminating tattoo was.

"How'd you like to come to a real destroyer?"

The XO stood over us. "Don't be poaching my officer,
Captain," he said with a grin.

"How'd *you* like to come to a real destroyer, XO? Get
in the war instead of pinging the empty ocean."

"Last time I checked, sir, we needed to regun."

"One gun, big deal. I have six."

Now Marchand stood over us; at his chesty voice I
swiveled my head.

"Look down your nose all you want, Joe. Our *one gun
big deal* is superior in every respect—payload, range,
rate of fire, accuracy—to any of your old museum pieces."

"Until it breaks. Then where are you?"

Now the battle was joined. The air was filled with technical terms, including classified information about the
gun and shore bombardment tactics, which any of these
women might pass on to the enemy. (And why shouldn't
Ho Chi Minh have agents in Subic? Even as we lost the
war, we continued to underestimate him.)

I was eager to show what I knew, but before I had the chance, I was sent as George to get more beer. The bartender filled four pitchers and nodded in lieu of payment. Tyler and Louie would settle the bill and then collect from us on the ship. That was how we officers, we gentlemen of the colonial world, paid our debts. By chit, by honor.

Off the main floor was a small room viewed through a picture window. Inside, provocatively dressed women wearing paper numbers sat on benches. One woman, seeing me pass the window, came out to our table and sat on my lap. Almost at once a Filipino in a white guayabera came by to ask if I would like to buy Angel a drink. I hesitated. She left, and another woman, who might have been forty, took her place and began to rub her muscular rump against my groin. Actually, she was older than she looked and reeking with perfume, but she knew what she was doing, and I had to shift positions under her. The man came by again and asked if I would like to buy Melody a drink. I would prefer not to—no hesitation about it—and Melody jumped off, pinching my thickened groin and tickling my ear with a wet tongue: "You benny boy," she whispered.

No one else came to tempt me for about five minutes, during which my blood went cold and I looked around for what I might judge. Women were taking men upstairs and disappearing through a doorway. To a song with suggestive lyrics a fat woman did a striptease around a pole. There was nothing attractive about her, she danced like sin. Stone sober, I was thinking about leaving, hoping no one had ordered food, when what must have been the most beautiful woman in the bar sat on my lap and lighted a cigarette.

She was tall and striking, with skin like satin; her face was so beautiful in repose it needed no animation. She knew what she was, how far above the rest of the women, the *prima* of the bar. When the man came around, of course I bought Tiffany a drink, which cost ten pesos, about seventy cents. Her glass appeared with a cocktail umbrella; something fruity, non-alcoholic. Apparently indifferent to the lap she was sitting on, she disdained to talk to me. Perhaps I had a reputation in the bar already. Perhaps she was waiting to perform, and I was a kind of green room.

Tyler said to me, "You've just validated a principle of market economics." A nice-looking woman was sitting on *his* lap, enjoying her drink, and he had his arms around her waist.

"Make them throw strikes," I agreed. "What bell did you use coming into our berth?"

"Back two-thirds."

"Why so much?"

"You get more authority from a short powerful backing bell than a drawn-out weaker one. And you can wait longer to decide when to use it."

"And why were you so steep?"

"A single screw ship backs to port. I had to get the stern swinging to counteract the side force when I backed down."

"I don't understand."

"Give me your number," he said to the woman. She took it off, and he unfolded it and began to draw on the back of it with a stub of pencil. He drew a line for the wharf and successive hull shapes, like bullets, with arrows to show all the forces at work. As I leaned toward him to look, Tiffany left my lap as unpetted cats will and crossed over to Montgomery. Feeling superior, I pushed my chair closer to Tyler's. The fat woman, while her song was still playing, got down from the stage and dressed. The lissome dancer took her place.

"So how did you know when to back down?" I asked.

He shrugged.

"All right. What were you looking at to decide?"

"The water, the aspect of the wharf, a flag flying over one of the buildings, I don't know."

"You don't get it, do you," I said.

"Get what?"

"I've just watched Ted Williams, and I want to be able to hit a baseball that way."

Tyler took the flattery in stride. He woke up every day with pleasure in his choice of careers. Like Tiffany, a star in his own realm.

"You will," he said. "You've got natural ability."

After a pause he added, "Now that you care about it."

Something Montgomery did or said displeased Tiffany; perhaps, like Custer, he was too importunate. She stood up, turned about, and dropped into the lap of Marchand. A moment later she was leading him upstairs. Several officers exchanged glances, but no one said anything. Nor did he look at us, but something in the way he claimed her, with his hand in the small of her back, was meant for Montgomery and his six-gun ship.

Muttering that at least he knew where to draw the line, Montgomery left the bar.

A tawdry strip song was playing, and the lissome dancer was naked, but she was graceful and expressive beyond lewdness. Her dancing spoke of where she had come from, what her hopes had once been, and how her path had narrowed since then. For her and thousands of her countrywomen, ten years compassed life's chances. As young as she was now, presently she would be doing this work in garish scent and with hardened contours.

Another woman sat on my lap, and because time was wasting, the pimp stated at once the price for having sex with her. Fifty pesos to buy her out of the bar. Fifty pesos for the management fee. One hundred pesos for the room. Fifty pesos for a short time. Two hundred pesos for all night. Put off as I was, I could add it in my head: for about thirty dollars I could own another human being until the sun rose. And she—some Angel or Melody or Tiffany, whose name and, indeed, whose face I wouldn't remember tomorrow—insisted that I take it; I was morally obliged to take it or I never should have walked in here. If I didn't take it, the Navy had no business being in Subic Bay. If I didn't take it, the United States should never have occupied the Philippines in 1898.

An American from the next table threw a coin onto the stage, and the lissome dancer did the splits above it without losing her rhythm. When she rose the coin was gone. Another American threw another coin, which disappeared the same way. The music shifted into a lower key. She gave her back to her admirers, and in her graceful carriage were pride and condescension.

Louie DiGiovanni jumped up. One of the men at that other table was heating a coin over a Zippo lighter. Louie knocked both objects from his hands, and the two tables emptied. Fights are incoherent. I found myself standing next to Louie and confronting a black man with a knife. The point of the knife didn't care where it went; didn't care that I was the star ensign of my ship. His eyes didn't care where the knife went either, as long as it went into a white man. An officer would be best of all. Fragments of light from the mirrored ball ran up the man's sleeve. I stood stark still. Any movement—even raising my hands to appease him—would release the spring. Any movement by anyone.

I sensed people behind me as a moral weight. The man glanced off, and a nightstick hit him on the arms and poked him in the kidneys when he crumpled. The knife clattered. Just as I recognized that I myself was safe, I was dragged backwards by my belt. All the women had disappeared as children did during duck-and-cover drills. The melee consisted of the two warring tables, some Filipino muscle led by the pimp, and our shore patrol in their white uniforms with blue arm bands and ready sticks. Their officer was Buster: it was he who had pulled me out and Louie too, both together. He was powerful in the elemental way of manliness that could deal with knives. "Bar is closed," he announced. "Curfew, gentlemen."

At the Chuck Wagon

We returned to the base, excited or depressed according to our natures: all but the captain returned. Buster came with us to make sure. The Marines at the gate saluted him, and he left us to chat with them about—what?— farm prices for all I knew. The others went on. I waited and so did Louie. Buster returned, taking us by our belts again to remind us of his power, and led us down a diagonal sidewalk. We passed the putt-putt course. On the other side of the windmill was a double Quonset hut with a sign over the entrance:

THE CHUCK WAGON | OFFICER'S CLUB ANNEX

The left hut was a dining area, darkened now. We went through the connecting hallway to the other hut, where a country-and-western band was playing and officers were sitting, drinking San Miguel beer from bottles. The room was lighted and cheerful. If you were to wash the Texas Bar with an astringent bath of American wholesomeness, you would have the Chuck Wagon.

We clinked our own bottles and drank.

"Isn't this more like it?" Buster said.

"Except for the apostrophe in the wrong place," I said.

"What's that?"

"It's not just one officer's club."

"And doesn't that just describe us, Clock. I save your life, and you proofread a sign."

"Christ, Buster, that was awful. What are we doing to these people?"

Louie grinned. "Still worked up, yes? First time you've faced the business end of a knife?"

Still worked up, no. I was tired of his self-satisfaction. Louie was a good guy, but at thirty-one he thought he had learned everything that life could teach and now he was called upon to share his wisdom with the rest of us.

"Not quite," I said. "In Chicago four years ago, while I was exercising my right to free speech, a national guardsman wanted to stick his bayonet in me."

"Come on."

"Someone pulled him off at the last second."

"No, I mean you *protested* the war?"

I took a long pull during which I glanced at each of them. I wanted to tell them about my past, even though it might damage my reputation. Anyway I owed them something more after that facile line about the bayonet, so I told them part of the truth: that I had been arrested at the convention for shouting, among other things, "The whole world is watching" when the real charges were throwing rocks at the array of shielded enforcers and dropping coffee cans of shit on them from our hotel room. I described peacefully occupying the president's office at M.I.T. after hours but not the other campuses in Boston that I helped shut down whose frightened employees were still at their desks; nor the fire I started in an ROTC building and then, intimidated by the enormity of the act, extinguished. I told them that I telephoned the White House fifty times one day with the code phrase "I wish to register my opinion" in order to invalidate a phony poll that Nixon was about to release that the "Silent Majority" of Americans still supported the war. I gestured to show how long my hair had been, which made them laugh uneasily. I didn't mention the drugs or the initiation into easy sex.

"So why in hell are you here?" Louie asked. Under his moustache his crooked grin anticipated the gossip he could tell about me on the ship.

"Draft number," Buster answered. "Look at me in the window: aren't I handsome!"

"So you don't believe in the war at all?"

"The war's a tragedy," I said. "We're caught in it just like everyone else. I'm amazed that we're still trying."

"Here comes Clock's love song to Charlie Brown."

"*John Shafer* too," I protested. "Your people and mine."

"And old watash here," Buster said. "Though I do like shore patrol. I should thank Marchand for trying to put me in hack. Where was he tonight by the way? Oh—I see: getting his beans snapped. He'll catch the pox worse than your leading bosun mate, Clock—whose skin I've saved twice in this hellhole by the way—and go back to his pretty wife with his face all eaten up. Not that anyone would notice."

"Does the captain have a pretty wife?"

"Beautiful," Louie said.

"Well, he's with a knockout tonight."

"Oh, I'd take *her* in a heartbeat," Louie said.

A young woman came to the microphone, smiled at us, and sang a song. If I wasn't mistaken she knew Buster.

No, I wasn't mistaken, for he waved at her. The decal on the bass drum said

BERT AND THE BONANZA BOYS

and taped to it was a paper sign, hand-lettered:

Featuring Lény

"A friend?" I asked.

"You bet," he replied. "Lény's a sweetheart."

By which, I understood, he meant someone to admire. In Louie's parlance I myself would take her in a heartbeat. She was extremely pretty with long black hair and a hopeful smile. Her contralto voice was soft and round: if your favorite sister could sing, this would be her voice. Most surprisingly, it sounded like pure Appalachia.

"Yes, he did me a favor," Buster said, returning to the subject of Marchand.

"Why were you so rude to Charlie Brown?"

Louie nodded at this, he and Charlie Brown and Tyler Brock and Carl von Clausewitz being brothers-in-arms.

"I wasn't rude to him." Buster's eyes were free of their usual mania. "I respect him. It was those other phonies I couldn't stand."

"Are you talking about me, Ensign?" Louie asked.

"If the shoe fits. I don't mean you personally. But yes, you! All you surface officers are phonies. You just stand around and look important. You don't do anything. In Missoura we call you *gentlemen farmers.*"

"Conning the ship is doing something," I said.

"Can you *steer* the ship, Clock? Louie, if you needed to change the burners on a boiler, could you do it?"

"I *have* done it, you asshole. I've punched tubes on a boiler. I used to be a boiler tech as you know very well." Taking up his beer he drained it with theatrical haste, put two dollars on the table, and left us. Lény, seeing this, smoothed a lock of hair behind her ear while she sang.

"Good thing fitness reports don't come out yet," I said.

Buster slouched in his chair. For the first time his immaculate shirtfront had a wrinkle across the chest. He said, "I spent some time at Cubi this week. The air station. Do you know, for a jet jock the window of decision to catch an arresting wire on your carrier—any of the four wires—is about half a second. You catch a wire or you bolter back into the sky on full power or you keep rolling overboard and die: it's that simple. It's more stressful to land on a carrier at night than to dodge antiair missiles over Hanoi: they've done studies. No wonder those guys drink. And what do *we* worry about? A slow approach on the oiler, where *close* is good enough. Submarines that don't exist. Does my captain like me? It's fine for you, Clock, but it won't do for me. I knew it that first day."

That first day, when Marchand chose me over him. Sympathetic for Buster as I might be, and frustrated that he wasn't making a greater effort to succeed, I was gratified that he had settled for second place. I didn't want to compete with my friend, but I wanted to be first. In the Texas Bar I had felt something other than revulsion. It meant a lot that Captain Montgomery thought I was Jim Marchand's star ensign.

"Forget it," Buster said. "I'm happy for you, Clock. Truly. You'll make an outstanding lifer."

"Not a lifer. I'm just trying to do my best."

"When you're Chairman of the Joint Chiefs of Staff I'll say I knew you when you couldn't help falling down ladders."

"So what will you do," I asked, "if not the Navy?"

"Sell farm machinery and chase Marie around the house. Isn't that girl a sweetheart?"

He meant the singer. Dressed in a jersey and a skirt that covered her knees, she looked sweet and wholesome, and she moved to the music, shifting her weight from one foot to the other, as a child would move when especially pleased. She was singing John Denver, and her voice had that rusty overtone.

"How does she do that?" I asked.

"Old Lény," he said affectionately, as if her family's farm had been next to his. "Filipinos beat all for imitation. They spend hours listening to our records. After this she'll come over and I'll introduce you."

"In a pig's eye."

"You'll see." He took a reflective pull from his beer. "I expect she would see you as a catch—poor misguided thing, but that's her lookout. Since you're so shy around women, we'll ask her out together."

"I'm not shy around women."

"Grab your beer now," he said.

"Why?"

"Why do we do anything in the Navy?"

"To win the last war."

"Tradition! Tradition, of course."

Bert and the Bonanza Boys were playing "Knock Three Times," and we, a chorus of lonely men far from Appalachia, some of whom might be candidates for the office of Last One Killed in Vietnam, slammed our bottles down three times on the beat. "Oh, my darling," she sang. She might have been singing to me.

A Song Across Cultures

Buster had turned his seat toward the music, from which position he and Lény seemed to communicate. When the band took a break she walked right up to our table and sat down. Buster introduced us. Like many women she shook hands without unfolding her palm, so that when I felt her small hand in mine all I could do was give it a squeeze. Her eyes were respectful, as if she were being introduced to a business friend of her father. But distant. I didn't know what Buster might have told her.

"Pleased to meet you," she said.

Her speaking voice was foreign, thick in the vowels, soft in the consonants. If after singing in this purely American voice she had spoken with a Cockney accent I couldn't have been more surprised.

Seeing the confusion in my face, she laughed. All the formality was gone, and she looked like a girl, free to laugh at what pleased her. But the laugh had an edge.

"You sing beautifully" was all I could manage.

"Like a round-eye."

"No. I meant.... Well, you *do* sing beautifully."

"It's all right. I was classically trained in Cebu City."

But she laughed again. "I'm just filling in. Bert's regular girl got married suddenly. He's giving me a trial. Maybe the customers will vote to keep me."

"I'll vote early and often."

"That's nice, thank you. You should work for Marcos."

"No politics," Buster said. "That guy over there looks like PC."

"PC?" I asked, though I knew from the sign at the gate.

"Philippine Constabulary," Lény replied. "Our SS."

"I just saved Clock's life," Buster said. "One of the sailors wanted to knife him."

She was startled out of her joking mood.

"At the Texas Bar," Buster added.

"Was anyone hurt?"

"No, no, just the usual thing. We broke it up."

"Are you all right?"

"Fine," I said. "Under the circumstances. Well."

"Well?"

"I don't know how to say it. My own life has been sheltered. I don't want to give offense."

"What do you mean?"

"The bar was awful. Women on display behind a window. Wearing numbers."

"So you could...."

"So you could just order one up."

"Conveniently. But you, you'd rather meet them on the street. Come up to your car. Have some privacy."

"I'd rather not meet them at all. The business of it. Buying human beings who have to pretend to be willing."

"How do you know they aren't?" she asked.

"Well done, Clock. You offended her."

For she was on her feet and moving away from us. But the players were reassembling for the next set, so perhaps that was the reason, to go back to work, to earn her place in the band.

"What'd I say but the truth?" I asked.

"Her sister Rose works at the Texas Bar."

"Good lord."

"Not as a hooker. She manages the place from an office upstairs. She has more responsibility than you and she's only eighteen."

"No way."

"She's a born leader, Rose."

I was ready to go back to the ship. This place, these people, weren't for me. No doubt the war was responsible, no doubt we had corrupted their society, but I couldn't be part of it.

Only Lény, as she sang in front of us, wasn't corrupted. She was fresh, wholesome, innocent, hopeful, loving. And beautiful—my chest went hollow to watch her. Perhaps her sister really was a born leader, who needn't sell herself: Lény would be even further removed from it.

The next set was long, to a dwindling audience. It was getting late. Bert was contracted to play until two, and he gave good service. Despite the empty chairs, the band performed as spiritedly as the Beatles in Shea Stadium. The music was irresistible. "Knock Three Times" almost made me cry.

At the break the players went to the bar. I stood up to go back. But as soon as she had gotten her drink, which the bartender filled from a soda gun, she returned to our table, and her glance as she approached recognized me as someone familiar to her, if not necessarily dear.

I sat when she did and said: "I'm sorry, Lény. It didn't come out right. I didn't mean to imply a judgment on the women who work at the bar. If it isn't an ideal situation for them, it's not their fault, it's ours. I drank there too tonight. I bought drinks for women who sat on my lap—I thought I should. But that was all. One of the dancers was very talented and another, a tall young woman, had an aura like a movie star."

"That must have been Tiffany."

Buster was right, then, about Rose.

"I've just never been in an environment like that. I'm sorry I didn't put it better."

She studied me for a moment—a sincerity check?

"People need to live," she said in a gentle voice. "Life here is hard. My country is poor. Things Americans take for granted—food and clothes and housing and medicine, a salary, a pension—we don't have those. Each day is hand to pocket."

"Pocket to mouth," Buster suggested with a wink.

"No, something else."

"Hand to mouth," I said.

"Yes! Hand to mouth. We eat what we make. We don't have your life. How would it be if my ship was visiting you? Where are your people anyway?"

"Oh, God," Buster said, "don't get him started."

"Cambridge, Massachusetts. On the East Coast."

She laughed. She had a musical laugh, lovely to hear. "That sounds like a rich people's place."

"No," Buster said. "A place for eggheads."

"Eggheads!" She laughed again. "Is there a harbor?"

"Yes."

"Very well. So my ship, the Philippines Navy destroyer *Juan Schafer,* is visiting Cambridge. What might I expect to find?"

She was continuing to make her point, however elaborately; but if I wasn't mistaken her line of questioning also had an element of personal curiosity.

"I'd welcome you and show you the sights," I said. "Cambridge—Boston—is important in our history."

"Oh, Boston. John Adams. You like history."

"Yes. When the Navy is over I hope to teach history."

Buster snorted. "He's a lifer."

She reached over. Her hand rested on mine. "We have a history too. It's partly yours as well. Since *your* ship is visiting *my* country, I will welcome you and show you the sights. I'm free during the day. When can we meet?"

"Whenever you like," I said happily.

At the USO

I held my version of sick call, disapproving all requests to go home while looking closely at the requestor to see if he was the one who had threatened me, then I walked down to consult Doc Daltry about my poxed leading petty officer. In the military, patient confidentiality comes after readiness: Daltry told me that Williams, if he wasn't unfit for duty already, would soon be so and must be put out of the Navy unless he stopped contracting the clap. Condoms weren't enough; it must be total abstinence.

The two of us went to Schmid, who agreed to put him on medical restriction for at least the rest of this visit, and Chief Letourneau, double-hatted as our master-at-arms, went over to bring him back. This done, Williams, looking like a terminally ill man wearing a dress uniform, appeared at XO's screening.

Onboard ship and in the absence of a court-martial, only the captain may administer actual punishment (of a limited severity). Before then the accused appears before the XO, who may dismiss the charge. Schmid was too nice a man to be severe; this so-called disciplinary hearing was more like an intervention.

Even so Williams did everything to avoid restriction—he flattered, he wept, he promised to reform. Then he made the mistake of alluding to the captain's absentee pennant, which, however the XO was inclined before, doomed his case. On medical grounds he was restricted to the ship, not only for this visit but for the duration of the deployment—four more months—and the quarterdeck watch was given a standing order to prevent his crossing the brow.

The look he gave me as he went below suggested that he was the one who had phoned the threats.

I wasn't afraid of him—or I wasn't afraid in that moment. On the other hand, I didn't want him to think I *was* afraid, so I went ashore and held my sailing class as I had agreed to do, then I walked next door in a sudden access of homesickness.

Among the wholesome amenities of the naval station was the USO, where servicemembers could phone home for free. I didn't have to wait for an empty booth, and my call went right through. It was 11 P.M. in Boston. Even before his wife had died, my father had kept late hours.

His voice sounded different, without its usual tone of Socratic investigation. I could imagine the empty room in which he sat: the single cone of light, the book face-down on the chair beside him. All the sounds of the house, even his thoughts, would echo now. He was sixty-two and had never felt old before.

"You must have a great deal to tell me," he said.

"Calls are supposed to be ten minutes. I don't know what happens if we run over."

"Probably condign punishment."

"Let's go Dutch treat. You first."

"My turn won't take a minute, and I want your news."

"Are you teaching?" My father taught international relations at Harvard's School of Public Administration. His usual fall class, about the relationship between war and politics, should have started by now.

"It seemed better to keep to the schedule so soon before convocation. We're a little short-handed, you know, with Henry enjoying his apotheosis. I have a lively group of students, including one submarine skipper."

No shiphandling there, I thought. Nothing to bump into in the deep, just don't lose any neutrons. "What's going on at the Paris talks?"

"Hard to tell if anything's going on. Henry's back in Washington. Uncle Ho seems to have been surprised by the resistance you and your fellows have been putting up. *Operation Linebacker,* you call it. How does it look from your end?"

"I qualified for officer of the deck."

"So soon!"

"They seem to think I'm a better officer than I am."

"All that sailing."

"Occasionally I pretend to be better than I am."

"Don't we all."

"Actually, Dad, there are a lot of inflated claims coming out of here, and I have to say I've been a part of it. Both in the reports I've drafted about our shooting and me personally—I've actually lied to my captain."

He took some time answering, during which I could hear faint voices on the wire. Two women were discussing a recipe for poaching a chicken breast.

"This war was begotten from a lie, Chris," he said, "and the taint of that has clung to the entire project. Johnson and Westmoreland took it beyond even indiscriminate propaganda. It's sanctioned lying to our own people. You did your part to expose the lies when you opposed it."

"But now I've become them."

Leave half the chicken uncovered, one woman said.

My father's musings, thoughtful and convoluted, re-quired an active mind to follow them. "If you can help end this war—finally—you will have done a service to every-one. There's nothing but honor in that."

"But the hypocrisy. Since I used to scream bloody mur-der for the truth, I should have the moral courage to tell it now."

"You're doing so well!" my father exclaimed, and the USO operator broke in to advise us that the ten minutes were up. I didn't have a chance to go beyond confession: to tell him about Buster, Marchand, and Tyler Brock; about Charlie Brown; about Lény.

Lény Rosales

I felt foolish standing outside the main gate, where even in the morning, as the sun shone bright and hopeful upon them, Filipino children waited for my countrymen to throw coins to them. But right on time Lény appeared on the bridge, unsullied by the squalor behind her, wearing a summer frock and carrying her handbag and an expen-sive camera. She smiled at me as if there were no doubt that everything we had said at two o'clock in the morning on first acquaintance we would certainly do.

We boarded a bus to Manila, riding over a one-lane mountain road where overhanging branches scraped the roof and the pavement in the turns was crumbled. Inside, we bounced like eggs in a carton. At the worst moments I believed that I was no different than my sailors: the search for sex was about to plunge me hundreds of feet into the jungle. When we arrived, therefore, whole and not even bruised, it seemed that everything would happen now; that one of us would suggest that we were in love and the other would agree with delight in her eyes.

There was a boat to the island of Corregidor. We explored tunnels and had lunch among the ruins of pillboxes. Homer Williams had known his history. From this place thirty years before, thousands of men my age, Americans and Filipinos as close as brothers, had held out for a month after the fall of Bataan and had then been marched off to slavery, torture, and death, never to see their families again. As close as brothers. Every Filipino schoolchild knew this story, but Lény let me tell it anyway. Then in the rush to the inevitable we opened our hearts. I didn't have to try my words before I spoke them. Sitting beside the tall healing grass, we kissed and held hands and made promises.

Everything I was keeping inside me, all the way back to the draft lottery, I gave up to being in love. Because of the curfew I couldn't leave the base when the band went home. So we turned the day upside-down. If I didn't have the duty I heard her sing. Then we parted until morning. While hundreds of sailors and yard workers were coming in the gate, I alone would go out, over the bridge, a mile or so down a dusty road toward Subic City, and finally to her room at the back of a weathered farmhouse facing a barnyard. The sun was intense; by the time I arrived my hair was hot. We had mornings and afternoons together.

She was small and slim with long sparkling black hair and skin the color of milk. Her eyes were black too and like the surface of a pond over which clouds pass: sometimes I could see my reflection in them, and other times I could see only depth. In the morning after half a night's sleep they had hollows underneath that would disappear when I kissed them. Her pale freckled wrists would reach up for me at funny angles because she was too tired to hold them straight. How I loved to kiss her, to compress her soft wide lips, to feel her teeth against mine, to have her breathe into me, to watch her close her eyes again.

Her room—our world for much of the day—had only a bed, a wardrobe, and a wicker dressing table with an in-verted basket for a chair. Before we went out in the after-noon I would sit on the edge of the bed and watch her get ready. The sight of her, the arch in her back, the way the white slip hung from her little shoulders and breasts, made me desperate. My hands would shake as I reached for her, a background figure coming to life in her mirror, and a minute later we would be making love again—no, the truth was that I had to have her and she was sweetly, humorously compliant: the love-making, when her own desire was so evident, came at other times.

I had never had such wild feelings. Not in anything. Nothing mattered but being with her. Exotic as she was, it seemed that our affair was a great romantic flight that must end in arias and fire. I didn't care. I would be one of those sailors demanding an early out. When refused, I would desert the ship and live with her in her parents' home in Cebu, reprising Eden. The real world might find us eventually and punish me for putting love before coun-try. It would be worth it.

"What are you thinking about?" she asked early on.

"The future."

She smiled that of course the future was unknowable and any hopes she might have for it, with me, it was too soon to mention...but still she might hope.

"My mother died three months ago," I explained.

"And you wonder if she would like me."

"No, not that. Well, yes." Lény was sitting in front of her mirror. I knelt and took her in my arms, mistaking

as resistance the twist in her spine, and kissed her devot-
edly, forehead, eyes, and mouth. The basket protested
against the strain. "She would have loved you, Lény, just
as my father will love you. Both of them were—are—very
good judges of people."

"And you, Chris? What kind of judge?"

"Even better. Infallible."

"It doesn't matter that I'm not a round-eye?"

"God, no. How I hate that term!"

She turned back and acknowledged her pretty self in
the mirror and started brushing her hair with long, careful strokes. I moved from her line of sight, sitting against
the bed, and as I sometimes did, I looked at the photo-
graph on the wall beside the dressing table: an American
naval officer in uniform with aviators' wings.

After awhile the brushing stopped. She set the brush
on the table and covered her eyes with her hands.

"I don't know what to think," she said. She meant that
she didn't know whether or not to believe in her hopes.
What those were were revealed to me over time, like an
exotic bird glimpsed through the tropical forest.

"Do you think I'm pretty?" she asked one day.

"Of course. Don't you see how I look at you?"

"That's just sex. Do you think I'm pretty enough to be
an American tampon girl?"

"In the commercials? You have that same fresh look."

"No, the football. The Dallas Cowboys cheerleaders."

"Ah: *pom-pom* girl."

"Are any of them Asian? I am much older than you.
Old enough to be your mother."

"I doubt it."

"How old are you, Chris?"

"Twenty-three."

"And I'm a hundred and twenty-three. When you go to Hong Kong, will you sleep with other women?"

"I didn't know we were going to Hong Kong."

"You are. After the gunline. The girls always know."

"If I do, I certainly won't sleep with anyone, and they certainly won't sleep with me."

"The Chinese women are beautiful. Glamorous. Those slinky silk dresses. You won't be able to help yourself."

"I think I have more self-control than that, Lény."

"Not that I've seen." She smiled down at me; this might be a compliment to my love-making. "I'd like to live in the United States," she said.

"Yes, and you'd be very welcome in Cambridge."

She turned away from the dressing table, and I leaned against her knees, which she spread a little so my head could lie in her lap. More protests from the basket. With both hands she caressed my face, drawing her fingers along my jaw, circling my lips so lightly I could hardly stand it, gently pressing a path upwards across my cheeks and around each temple, pressing out the pain, making a promise of pleasure. But she overlooked my throat, where it felt as though someone's fingers were taking a grip.

"You are worried," she said, "that this has come too easily for you. That I don't really love you, more than the thing."

"What thing?"

"What I said. But this is a big risk for me, bigger than for you, leaving my home. Do you love me, Chris?"

"Yes. I love you, Lény. What thing?"

She took a breath—her chest rose against the back of my head. "I want to be married and live in the United States and have a family. I want this with you."

I turned to see her face. Above her smile were tears.

"It's a beautiful idea," I said. "It's what I want as well. Do we have to decide now?"

"Why not decide? What could change for you in Hong Kong?—unless some long-legged Chinese beauty is better in bed than me."

"Nothing will change, not in my loyalty, not in my feelings. Do you want me to marry you before I go? Is that it?" I asked this for vanity's sake, seeing myself as someone who could brave enemy fire. From the look on her face I had a moment's certainty that I would go home married.

"No: I want your promise. You won't break it as other men would."

"Other men. Since we're being honest with each other, Lény, are you talking about that other man?" I pointed to the portrait on the wall.

As if I had consulted a curator, she took a moment to analyze its contents: "I had unrealistic hopes, so—yes—he broke my heart. Now he's a friend; I keep him up there because he's an admiral."

"Just a friend?"

"Just a friend. He's been very kind to me. He helped me with a problem, or tried to. Admiral Locke. You see: I don't keep secrets, I name names. I am honest with you. He is married. Are you married, Chris?"

"To the Navy."

"Don't make jokes, please. It's too important for me."

"I wouldn't be here if I were married, Lény."

"Yes you would. I know what I'm talking about. You want what every man wants, and I have already given it to you. Do you think that if the women of America were fighting the war in Vietnam, Olongapo would be filled with male prostitutes?"

But you're not a prostitute!

"No, I don't guess so."

"Men are different than women, and it's a foolish girl who doesn't understand this. Do you have another love back in the States? Someone you write to, who has hopes for you as I do?"

"No, there's no one else."

"Tell me honestly. You have experience as a lover."

"I *am* being honest. There's no one."

"Then I want your promise, Chris. I want it now. If you won't agree to marry me, I must break up with you before another day."

But she didn't mean it, or at least not to the point of breaking up. I wasn't sure how much she meant, how much was playfulness—as in her acquired persona of a country-and-western star—and how much an exquisitely drawn-out negotiation for a purpose written in invisible ink and just now beginning to appear.

"I'll go to Hong Kong," she said the next day.

"Terrific." In fact I had confirmed our schedule.

"No, you don't mean it. You want to shack up with an exotic Chinese beauty."

"You say such things."

"You aren't sincere. I won't go. I won't ask Bert for the time off. Anyway, he would fire me and get another singer, someone he has his eyes on. There's a dress I need," she added.

"A dress. Do you want it as a gift?"

"No, I want you to buy it for me."

"I don't see the difference."

"A gift is ugly, or it is foolish. The ugly man gives a gift as payment and calls it a gift, but it smells bad anyway. The foolish man gives and gives, not believing his good fortune that the girl has shared her body. But if I tell you

I need something and you buy it for me, then you are saying you are serious about our relationship, you are taking
an interest in *my* life, you know how to be practical for
me: there is a future for us under one roof."

I banished the thought that she too had received value
for sex. When I walked back to the ship that day, I con-
soled myself that people make love and they also give
gifts. That was the world. Yet I was never happy to see
her camera.

"I would love to buy you a dress," I replied. "Shall I go
with you?"

"No, that too would be ugly: a sugar daddy and his
girl—or in your case, a sugar boy and his ancient mama.
I know how to shop, Chris. All I want is the money."

The Rosales Sisters

Over time Lény told me more about herself and her sister,
as far as our circumstances describe us. In Cebu City, in
the southern islands, the girls had grown up in comfort.
Their father was a politician. They lived on Colon Street—
"the oldest street in the entire Philippines," she said
proudly—and had servants. Then her father took a job in
Manila with Marcos, and after that they saw him less and
less and their standard of living declined. They moved into
a smaller house, and their mother went to work. The real
parental authority was an uncle, a Catholic priest.

He was a good man, an example to the daughters; not
unkind but strict in enforcing rules. Lény did her best to
please him and with her obliging nature succeeded. But
Rose fought him from the beginning. She was her father's

child, born to command. She would be in charge of her life in every detail, and Lény, though seven years older, had to choose between authorities.

Two years before I knew them, Rose, at sixteen, left home to work for her father in Manila. Lény abandoned her college studies, a year before her degree, to follow her. Something happened there which I never learned. Rose broke with her father and moved to Olongapo. Whatever it was, she broke with Lény as well, and although Lény followed her north their reconciliation was fraught. Rose accepted her back in her life only with the understanding that they live apart. It was then that Lény took up lodgings at the farm, a ten-minute walk from her sister.

"So she lives in Olongapo?" I asked, disingenuously. "In one of those ramshackle places?"

"Ramshackle." Lény smiled.

"Decrepit. Falling-down. Like places in a gold rush."

"But that's what it is for us, don't you see?"

"And what does she do there?"

"She runs a bar—I will tell you this. She runs it as a business person, not as a...."

"Not as a call girl."

"A hooker. No." After a moment she added, as both a judgment and a prediction, "You don't understand us."

What My Shipmates Thought

We didn't leave on time. We were extended another week because one of our boilers was found to have a ruptured tube, which turned out to be five tubes.

Another week of going over wasn't healthy for the liberty hounds or good for morale generally. Whoever wasn't sick or recovering or broke or disillusioned was bored by now. Besides the engineers, whom Louie kept busy, most of the ship's work was done by the eager Filipino craftsmen in their hard hats and with their shop plans, cutting and welding everywhere.

Lény and I too felt the malaise. The delights of discovery, powerful as they had been, were mostly behind us, and our affair had settled into a routine without the joy of making plans. In fact, each of us had planned to be doing something else now. We were like weekend visitors to a country house snowed in before we could get away, and now we must revisit the same old talk and replay the same old indoor games until the roads were passable.

Onboard ship, it seemed typical of my life that I was both proud of my manly exploit and also embarrassed to have fallen for a girl in a port; two sailor's clichés. The XO prefaced his orders to me with *If it wouldn't be terribly inconvenient* and *I hate to intrude on your busy social schedule.* Tyler reminded me that permission to get married had to be approved by the command. Louie, passing through the wardroom in sooty coveralls, said that wasn't true, any more than a ship's captain can perform marriages. He *can* perform them, Tyler riposted. They're good for the duration of the voyage.

The reaction from my men was mixed. No doubt my leading petty officer saw me as a hypocrite; it was obvious in his formal mode of address. But others saw me as simply human, and a few even wished for my happiness. Their personal problems—all requiring repatriation and early discharge—kept pouring in. I kept disapproving their chits even as I fantasized about deserting to Cebu with my—what? What was she? And what was she to me?

When a reference to Lény was made in front of the captain, he tugged on his earlobe and called me *Mr. Clarke.* "She's very pretty," he said, making me wonder how he knew that.

Of course the one responsible for the affair, and whose opinion meant the most to me, was Buster.

"Why shouldn't you marry her?" he asked.

At his request I had taken him sailing, which Mr. Ruthven, the director of the center, counted as a class. We didn't leave the harbor, in part because I had him tacking and jibing nonstop. In between force-feeding him weeks of instruction, we talked about my love.

"Why shouldn't you marry her?" he repeated.

"Sail the boat," I said. "Whatever else happens. Your perceptions follow a routine just like driving a car. The luff of the sails, the sound of the wind in the rigging, the tension of the sheets, the pressure on the tiller, a point of land you head for or a compass course to keep. You're in command, just like a pilot: fly the plane."

"She's a better person than you are."

"I agree. On the other hand, I'd hate to think in my old age that it was you who introduced us."

"Yes, you can't stand to owe me anything. *And* I saved you from catching the clap from those working girls."

"Not to mention being impaled by a knife."

"And the knife. So why not? How is she in bed?"

"Spectacular. Eat your heart out. That's not the problem. Call your maneuver now: ready about. Round up to the wind, closer than that. Very good. Helm's alee. Duck your head, shift your feet, step around the tiller, come up on the high side. *Very* good! See how smoothly she crosses, with no loss of speed. Now fall off and put her head on that buoy."

"So we can run into it."

"Not with the leeway we're making. See? We're drifting to port. What you airedales call side-slip. Easy for
you: only two dimension to worry about here. Always picture how you yourself, your body, is physically moving
across the water. Develop your understanding why it
moves that way."

"I can do this," he said softly. Then, louder, "So what's
the problem?"

"She's not a round-eye."

"What difference does that make? Nobody cares anymore. Louie's wife is Japanese."

"And we've seen how faithful Louie is."

"Piffle."

"Piffle?"

"Bullshit. He's no cheater. He's probably one of those
guys who like to brag, but you catch them at home and
they're completely pussy-whipped. Like me," he added a
moment later, grinning.

"Where's the wind from?" I asked.

"Port beam."

"How do you know?"

"Those telltales on the shrouds."

"How else?"

"The pattern of the waves."

"And?"

"The feel on my cheek."

"Good. Is that the true wind or the apparent wind?"

"Apparent wind. The true wind plus our own motion."

"Could you draw that out on a maneuvering board?"

"Yes." A firm yes.

"Prepare to jibe," I said.

He did this capably, so that the boom swung over our heads as soft and easy as Lény's caress. Our wake drew an angle. The warm breeze with its hint of salt pushed us along.

"Why shouldn't I marry her?" I said.

"Why shouldn't you?"

"You can know someone this fast. Really know them."

"Piffle." With a slight press of the tiller, unprompted by me, he adjusted the course to conform to the channel. "You can spend a lifetime and still not know them. I met Marie in the third grade. We started having children at eighteen. We lost a child. She was with me in Pensacola when I bilged out of flight school. I could tell you I know everything about her, all the good and all the bad, every-thing she's capable of. But there are days when she's a mystery to me—not just her moods but what she really thinks—for all I know she thinks I'm a clown. Before I came out here she told me Nixon ought to nuke Hanoi. She was serious: *Kill them all: they're only gooks.* As much as I think I know her, I can't be *absolutely* certain she'll be waiting for me when I get back."

In my feelings of superiority—not unlike the young soldier's certainty that if half his unit is going to be killed, too bad for the poor bastard next to him—I reminded my-self that Buster and Marie had never been *in love.* Lény and I would always have that to build a marriage on, or to come back to.

"I think you're safe," I said, "if she's coming all the way to Hong Kong to see you."

"You never know. Her father always wanted her to marry Joe Sorensen."

"With his grain silos. Does Marie know everything about you?"

Buster leaned against the tiller, so that I made a grab for it to correct the course. Irritated, he seized it back. "Don't you take the controls from me, Clock. I had it. I can do this."

After his irritation passed, under the blue sky and the soft clouds with the breeze light on our cheeks, he said, "I had a close call once, but I couldn't go through with it. It was too ugly to think about."

"Ugly."

"The dishonesty of it. Pretending to be someone I wasn't, just to get this thing that the good Lord gave us too much of anyway. That's the draw of this place, isn't it, that no one has to lie. Unless you're lying to Lény."

"I'm not."

"Then who are you trying to be? Someone out for a good time? Or someone ready to commit himself for the rest of his life to a woman he's known for three weeks?"

"You do admit that the latter is possible."

"Christ on a crutch! Only people in books say *latter* and *former,* Clock. Sure it's possible, but what are the odds that it's happening here, to you, to her? You're having an adventure, your first one ever—I don't care who you slept with when you thought you were stopping the war. Things are going to look very different when you get back to civilization. Have you asked her to marry you?"

"It's on the table, certainly."

"I do pity her, having to listen to Cambridge-speak. Ready about: I'm taking us in."

With a little, very little, advice from me, mostly a reminder to see how the wind was blowing along the berth, he rounded up and let the sheets fly, judging the drift perfectly, and just touched the dock, so that the fenders hardly squeaked. I handled the lines for him.

Mr. Ruthven was pleased, as missionaries are. Learning to sail would save the world's soul. Buster's face spoke
of quiet confidence. If mine was as candid, it spoke of the
disappointment of returning to the shore, with its un-
charted courses, its uncertain breezes, its lack of control.

"I think you don't know what you want," he said as we
walked toward the ship.

"I don't. I'm confused. Happy, sated, and confused."

The Farewell Party

There was a pig roast. The ship, boiler tubes replaced,
would sail the next day. Lény and her friends—she had
respectable friends among the families of the workers—
were giving the wardroom a sendoff. The way she spoke
of it, the event seemed more personal than that, involving
some kind of public claim not unlike an engagement. I
had been to homes in Cambridge at which such happy
news was revealed. We might be getting married; it only
needed a word. And why not now?

She wore her new dress. Bert and the Bonanza Boys,
in their performance duds, were among the guests. A juke
box played American songs with the volume turned up,
which was almost as compelling as live music. Couples
danced beside the pig, on a tile floor among the folding
tables. We were in a room behind the bowling alley, safely
on base, where the curfew didn't apply. The party could
go on until we got the ship underway. It wouldn't be the
first time, Louie told me, that sailors had left port while
half in the bag from the night before.

The captain, the XO, and Tyler Brock—my chain of command—were received by Lény as royalty. I stood back and watched. If Marchand had designs on my pretty girl-friend, he hid them well. He was cordial and reserved—perhaps he knew her from the Chuck Wagon in the inno-cence of fandom. I didn't want to think that he might have met her "going over."

All her friends wanted to dance with him, a powerful officer with that brute masculinity that had won Tiffany at the Texas Bar. I have since known other men with this quality, unfathomable to the rest of us. Tyler was their second choice. The XO danced once to be polite and then watched with fun in his eyes. I was happy to see my su-periors enjoying themselves, and as I understood my feel-ings I began to think that there might be worse careers than this one. Why shouldn't I be engaged? My father had married much too late in life, accepting that the best part of marriage would be a compatibility of the mind. Why shouldn't I take this step now, when desire and desire consummated were so good; when Lény and I could com-plete a wonderfully romantic story to tell our children?

She may have divined these things—women in love, I've observed, are telepathic: she seemed to fill out and became again the happy, hopeful Lény who fronted for Bert and the Bonanza Boys to so many lonely Americans.

A woman approached Buster, but he shook his head and went back to telling Louie about duck hunting. She raised an eyebrow at Lény, who, leaving my side, pulled Buster from his chair. Lény and he danced the Monkey, the Swim, the Watusi. They danced the Twist and fell down laughing after a contest to see which of them could go lower. Buster was an athlete, but Lény was a child, extraordinarily flexible and with a heart that would never wear out. When another song came on, it was all right for her friends to cut in, and from then on Buster

was the main attraction. From time to time his hoot rose
above the music. His partners laughed and laughed. He
was safe, as Marchand was not, and more fun and less
disturbing...except to their countrymen.

For when the Filipino men saw his success they pat-
ronized him; bought him drinks and talked of our losing
Vietnam and of the coming revolution in the Philippines
that would throw us out of here too. None of the conver-
sations went very far before another woman wanted to
dance with him.

I was distracted for a moment, and the next thing I
knew Lény was leading her sister, Rose, into the room. I
knew her without asking. She was eighteen but looked
older, a big, buxom girl, taller than Lény, with coarse bru-
nette skin and dramatic features heavily made up. In the
fashion of the early 70s, she wore a halter top and skin-
tight hot-pants—the amount of leg exposed was more
startling than cleavage. Her hands flew about constantly,
touching others and herself; mostly herself, as though
checking the image she projected. Her eyes with their
garish green liner had a hard, arrogant look which as-
serted her position as a woman brought early to
knowledge by the weaknesses of men. I didn't see anything about her to suggest natural leadership skills.

Lény introduced us with her arm wrapped in mine.
Rose, admiring me excessively, kissed me on the mouth
then laughed at her daring. I said the usual thing, that it
was great to meet her after hearing so much about her. I
didn't know how to act or what to think that wasn't judg-
mental. It was hard to imagine my father, though he
would certainly love Lény, welcoming Rose into his home.
Our home of kindness, reason, and decorum.

On the other hand, I felt how loving and generous
Lény was. She deserved to have the life she wanted, and
she would be just as loving and generous to me.

Of course Rose must dance with the captain. They be-gan in classic ballroom style, upright and arms extended. But when he pressed her close to him, with his other hand in the valley of her lower spine, Lény didn't like it. Rose moved as he moved, step for step: that cleft pressure told her everything. The music slowed and she draped both arms around his neck. After two dances they unwound from each other. His brutal lips formed their condescend-ing smile—he was grotesquely gallant. The tension re-laxed when she chose Louie next and Bert after him.

The hot, moist smell of the meat actually took away appetites. Twenty or thirty guests were present, but the pig remained identifiably a pig. We did drink, come what may tomorrow. We became giddy with drink and dance. People bumped into people and felt connected with them and in some cases chose them. The idea that anything could happen was in the air.

Sweaty and flushed, Buster and another dancer joined us. He and Rose shook hands, at which she exclaimed that his was all wet. Everyone laughed. Here she was, a schoolgirl after all. Another song started, and like a fool I suggested they dance. Several of the women clapped. Lény said no, not if they didn't want to, but this drew a scornful word from Rose, who reached for Buster. Some scene from the past was being replayed. Pressing her lips together, Lény looked at the floor for a moment and then at her sister with sudden distance in her eyes.

I took her in my arms. She fitted herself against me, the shape I knew so well, but her body was tense and her mind somewhere else. I could deal with that. I worked to bring her back to this moment. She let her head drop against my shoulder. With small steps we turned in a cir-cle. Her tears were warm against my neck, all about joy. I said her name. She lifted her head, alert to a life-

changing moment. Her eyes, warm and loving, affirmed
that she did trust me, had trusted me all along.

Before I could commit the rest of my life to her, she
looked off and frowned. Something had happened between Rose and Buster, I didn't know what. But it must
have been something that a worried sister would notice—
couldn't help noticing since a part of her attention never
left the other. Breaking away from me, she went to her,
spoke in her face, and dragged her from the dance floor.
Rose answered back, asserting leadership, but Lény was
furious with the authority that honest indignation gives,
and Rose, although she affected defiance, was cowed.
Lény snatched up the designer purse and jabbed it into
her sister's abdomen and pushed her out the door. She
didn't come down to the wharf in the morning. That evening was the last I saw of either of them for a long time.

Part Three
Dealing Death

At Sea Again, Eventually

People who earn their living from the sea accept its caprices. When you leave the shore you cross a line: behind you is your own life, in which you may do as you please for better or worse; ahead of you is the sea's life, where your actions have less consequence and you might as well take each day as it comes.

A different point of view makes no distinction between sea and shore. If you sin in one place, you will be punished in the other. Lawlessness, drunkenness, and lewd behavior in foreign ports have been known to cause ships to founder when they go to sea; and what is even more satisfying to this idea of justice, inattentiveness to the helm or leaving a boat fender over the side have been known to cause bankruptcy, disease, and divorce when the ship returns home. Those who borrow the sea for their purposes tend to think this way about it.

As did we in *John Shafer*. To begin with, we were late sailing—later than the boiler casualty, which had already delayed us a week. Now twenty-three of our shipmates had decided that we didn't need them as much as their hookers did. If one or two had failed to return, we would have left anyway and let the authorities in Subic deal with them. But twenty-three? On top of that, the incredulous personnelman hadn't told the XO until Sea Detail had been set, the mooring lines had been singled, and the captain was on the bridge.

He had given me the conn, perhaps feeling generous after the dance with Rose. On a slate I was drawing happy diagrams to show how I would move the ship out of this berth as smartly as Tyler had put her into it. The XO spoke to him in an undertone, holding the muster report, and the captain went below to his cabin.

The problem having fallen to him, the XO acted at once.

"Pass the word for Lieutenant DiGiovanni and Ensign Billings," he said. "Louie, my dear fellow. You are having trouble setting the boiler safety valves."

"Jerry set them last night during the pig-roast, XO."

"You are having trouble setting safeties but expect to do so by 1400 hours this afternoon. Important as this is, it's just a question of trial and error, and you don't need the shipyard's help. Ensure you info Commodore Lewis on your message.

"Buster, take ten good men who know Olongapo and bring back my crew. Include Chief Letourneau and two of his people in case you meet any reluctance. Drag them out of bed, I don't care. Spend whatever you need to spend. Also, you might try Bert, since he knows everyone. In any case, be back here by noon. By noon, do you hear me?"

"Aye-aye, XO."

A bit after noon, a motley collection of taxis, jitneys, Navy sedans, and one paddy wagon brought the defaulters back: eighteen of the twenty-three. The XO was satisfied—indeed, he was pleased—and we set Sea Detail again.

The captain, looking at the tally, said to Buster, "You should have gotten them all."

And to me, "Mr. Brock will get the ship underway."

When I couldn't hide my disappointment he added, uncharacteristically, "Sufficient unto the day, etcetera."

But that wasn't the reason. Among the eighteen was my principal subordinate, Boatswain's Mate First Class Homer Williams.

Hunting for Submarines

Triton Island was in our way. It sat so low in the water
without the curl of a reef that prudent mariners always
gave it plenty of sea room. Despite the danger, which
made us silent and tense, Marchand wouldn't change
course or reduce speed. We picked it up at the last minute
and then it was behind us and with it the worst punishment for Subic. Morale lifted, briefly. At eight the next
morning we arrived at the gunline and reported to an admiral embarked in the heavy cruiser *Newport News.*

Then came the punishment. We weren't at Mo Duc, a
hundred and twenty miles to the south, but at the Demilitarized Zone, or DMZ, and *Newport News* wasn't Charlie
Brown, who needed us. We arrived as she was firing from
her number one turret, which held three eight-inch guns.
The center gun spoke and then the left and right took
their turns. The other two turrets, the second just aft of
number one on her beautifully long bow and the third toward her stern, were centerlined. We were too far away
to see the target, whatever (or whoever) it was. The flat
uneventful reports sounded across the water as if a routine business were being carried on, like drilling for oil.
But with a crew of 1,600 (all presumably present for
duty), she could multitask. By flaghoist she gave us our
orders:

> Keep seaward of me. Screen me from sub-
> marines. Conserve fuel as practicable.

"Submarines!" XO Schmid exclaimed. "You couldn't
get a submarine in here with a shoehorn. But you know

the admiral, don't you sir?" In the captain's locker he had a stock of footballs signed by the 1963 Navy team, including Roger Staubach. Louie told me that he had sent one to every senior officer in the Seventh Fleet.

I observed that no good deed goes unpunished. Chief Beatty warned that using our powerful sonar in such shallow water would be a waste of time and also extremely annoying to the crew of *Newport News* as they tried to sleep. Chief Letourneau reported that our gun with its new barrel was in mint condition and far more accurate than anything the cruiser had. Even Tyler, whose belt buckle was inscribed with *Fidelity* and *Obedience,* commented on the misapplication of resources.

The enlisted watch were doing their share of complaining too. The bridge was a babel—unprofessional and unsafe. I called for silence just as Marchand opened his mouth to speak.

You babies, his eyes said.

"We had one good gunline period. We were there three weeks. *Newport News* has been doing this for five months, and this is her third deployment to the war. Her main battery has a broadside of three thousand pounds to our seventy. She has twelve five-inch guns to our one. Her armor can stop a round from an enemy tank. Our plating is a quarter-inch thick. How would you feel about us if you were the admiral? Anyone want to play admiral? Mr. Clarke?"

Neither anyone nor Mr. Clarke wished to play admiral.

"Let's be ready to shoot but take her at her word— Chief Beatty, ping away with our sonar so she can hear it. Who knows? She may have intel. The Germans sneaked a U-boat into Scapa Flow."

"Twice," I said.

He smiled. "I believe it was only once."

My mother taught me that contradicting someone is bad manners. She had cause: I must always be right.

"U-18 in World War I and U-47 in World War II," I said.

"You've been studying your naval history, have you?"

"Yes sir."

The smile was menacing. "In all your spare time. Thank you for clearing that up." He unclenched his fists; his hands could crush an opposing lineman's windpipe. "Let's exercise a little self-control, gentlemen, which seems to be in short supply just now."

So it did, and his warning, repeated through the ship, had a beneficial effect; if, that is, I exclude the effect on himself. For while the rest of us returned to our duties, he was increasingly out of sorts. Good news failed to please him. At the slightest suggestion of bad news he wanted to strangle the messenger.

Louie was my Virgil to Marchand's circles of hell.

"It is a fact, my dear friend, that some males of the species—and a surprising number of females—become restive in proportion to the time since their last sexual release. The horns do grow, and I don't mean the cuckold's horns, which is an unfortunate homonym. I mean the bull's horns: as they grow, the bull becomes more aggressive. Do not encroach upon his pasture."

"People are more complicated than that."

"The complication consists of other characteristics that restrain or offset the aggressive urge. You should have seen him at the ship's commissioning. He was literally pawing the ground to rut with the ship's sponsor, our namesake's widow, a respectable lady."

"Figuratively pawing," I said. "Wasn't his wife there?"

"What of it? They've been married for many years. The wedding was right after June Week if not secretly before then. She was a Baltimore belle. He was famous and ugly."

"But not all married couples behave this way."

He had nothing to say about this.

"So what now?" I asked. "Advise me, O Wise One."

Louie drew closer and glanced both ways. "First, give him plenty of sea room. Let him be your own Triton Island. Second, *do not* show your superior erudition, especially in front of the rest of us. Third, hope that Doc Dalton cures him."

"Cures him?"

"Remember Tiffany from the Texas Bar?"

"You've got to be kidding me."

He shrugged. "Why should the pathogens reject a host simply because he wears three stripes?"

"How do you know this?"

It was then that he told me about the signed footballs.

Apparently there was nothing to be done. If Louie's theory was correct, Marchand's frustration must grow every day. When not in the wardroom for meals, he confined himself to his cabin. Through the bulkhead I could hear classical music, hours of it. He was a cultivated man and proud of his taste (no doubt the Baltimore belle had something to do with that). Had we been equals—as I thought us—we might have enjoyed talking together. Under the circumstances I took Louie's advice and gave him sea room. Meanwhile the ship's clocks hardly seemed to advance, and there was much to annoy him.

What Changed

We'd been at the DMZ for more than a week, pinging away at schools of fish and sparing the enemy our lethal fire, when I couldn't avoid him any longer. Having had the forenoon watch I was late for lunch. The captain was sitting at the head of the table flanked by the XO, Tyler, and Salty Bill Wheelock, our operations officer. At the foot of the table was Buster. The senior officers were holding a post-mortem on the recent collision of a destroyer with the oiler *Mispillion* while alongside transferring fuel. I listened: *Mispillion* had been my first approach. The destroyer lost steering control, and the two ships ground against each other. No one was hurt, a few hull plates were dented, and both continued on their assigned tasks. They had been lucky.

The destroyer was in our squadron. Marchand said, "He's finished. He'll never be a commodore now."

In the pause after this I reported having been properly relieved of the deck and asked permission to join the mess.

Buster snorted, as at any formality.

The captain smiled without welcome. "Who's in CIC?"

"Mr. DiGiovanni, sir."

"What about my acey-deucy game?"

Salty Bill offered to relieve him.

"That's when we'll get the call for fire," said Marchand. "During the turnover. What about you two?" He looked down the table.

Buster said, holding up the imperious green booklet, "I need to trace systems for my junior officer journal, Captain. Mr. Clock is the wardroom expert anyway. Louie hasn't beaten him in I don't know how many tries."

Since we had never played, this was technically true.

"The wardroom expert, eh? No, finish your soup," for I had risen and threaded my napkin through the ring.

But taking my cue from the others, I thought it better to humor him and finish the meal afterwards. We moved to the sitting area and set up the board. The others left, and the stewards cleared the table. In the pantry, behind the closed door, they shifted into Tagalog.

The captain rocked back and forth in his seat, which made me think that Louie had been right about his health. He jiggled his knee. He tapped the dice cup against his massive thigh before he rolled and snapped his fingers as the dots came up. He made little provoking noises—"Got you, eh? Not now, hmm?"

An aggressive player, he deployed his skirmishers deep in my territory. He knew the odds (and was fond of reciting them for my benefit). I had never played until the Navy. But acey-deucy is mostly a game of luck, and on that day the luck was all mine. I bore on my men in a tight mass, moved them conservatively to the captain's side, and bore them off again. Whenever I needed doubles or an ace-deuce, I got them. It was very satisfying. My wall blocked him for much of the game, and when I took my last roll, he hadn't removed a single man: a skunking. "Very good, very good, all right," he said and picked up his men for another game. Which went even worse for him: a double-skunking: not only did he not remove any men, he didn't get them all onto the board.

I thought he was about to blow. There should be an emergency number to call. My father, teaching me to sail, had had to endure my early temper tantrums. I tried a pacifier in his style: "Have we inflicted enough suffering on this poor board?"

But this had no charm for the recipient.

"Are you speaking to me, mister?"

"Yes sir."

"Who the hell do you think you are?" Marchand waved his hand impatiently for the board to be set up. We played again. My first roll was an ace-deuce. "God damn it!" he exclaimed and picked up the board with both hands and threw it against the bulkhead: men and dice and dice cups flew all over. Giving me a murderous look and rising with his fists on his thighs, he stumped from the room. I was unable to move. The door opened again, and there was his voice, though not he.

"You know: you're just a goddam pseudo-intellectual, not half as smart as you think you are."

Somehow the afternoon passed. I toured my spaces, I initialed paperwork. This didn't feel like a sorrow I could share with Buster, and otherwise I had no friends except Louie, who would tell me I had got what I deserved, and Chief Beatty, whose first loyalty was always to the command. The unintended consequence of rapid advancement is the absence of peers to commiserate with.

I went back on watch. It was late, and *Newport News* was firing a mission, drilling a hole in Vietnam—North or South, we never bothered to look for the fall of shot now. She knew her business better than we could know it; our readiness to be shore bombardment heroes had lessened by the day, a cautionary tale for backup singers.

Scattered among our two ships was the Vietnamese fishing fleet, a vast extent. Sampans and junks and lesser craft were splayed out on every heading, lateen sails glowing in the light. The firing seemed not to faze them except, perhaps, in the strange way they maneuvered. From time to time one would dart across our bow so close we nearly cut her in two. I knew it had to do with luck.

I was on the engaged bridge wing watching the cruiser and the ineffable landscape she was attacking. In the distance to seaward a quadrant of waterspouts drank from the sea. High overhead were drifts of cirrus, containing at least a few motes of smoke and soot from the war. Underfoot, the sonar repeated again and again its three notes, relentless as a mourning dove.

Captain Marchand came out and stood beside me.

He gave me a sidelong glance. I had been leaning against the bulwark; I straightened to something like attention and looked through my binoculars. If he were going to cashier me from the service for disrespect to a superior officer, he wouldn't need a formal hearing. He could just do it, like the president launching a nuclear strike.

"Anything to report?" he asked.

"No sir."

"Signal from the cruiser?"

"Nothing yet, sir."

He nodded as if nothing were expected, promised, or hoped for, then he settled against the bulwark himself. The light deepened to orange then red. In Mo Duc the villagers would be switching sides now. He stared down at the water. I wondered if we would talk about *it* and who would go first. I had nothing to apologize for, other than being who I was.

A junk fine to starboard changed course and disappeared beneath our bow, leaving us with the glimpse of a homey scene: a smoky hibachi, colorful bedding being aired, a family each at his task, no one looking up.

"It would probably be good for my training," I said, "to stand in the eyes of the ship and see how close they come. But I'm afraid I wouldn't sleep afterwards."

"Do you know why they do that?"

"Yes sir."

He glanced at me again.

"No sir."

The wind had traced lines on the swell that looked like a giant seine. Or perhaps a roadmap. Or fishing fiefdoms.

"These boats," he said, "leave home possessed of a certain amount of luck. Not only fish, however, but devils swim in these waters, and before long one will latch onto each boat's transom. The devil trails his hand and picks up a comrade, who picks up another, and a chain forms, growing longer as the voyage goes on. No one can see the devils, but they're disastrous for fishing and maybe for other luck. It's a thin plank, after all, between living and eternity.

"But the fisherman has a remedy. If he crosses the bow of another boat, the chain will be cut, and the cut-off devils will slide down the side of the victim and join *her* chain. In this way it's possible to put your bad luck onto someone else. Of course you want to approach her as close as possible, to cut off the most devils.

"If only we could do that with our sins," he said after another moment. Again he looked at me, this time with a face that invited confession.

"But isn't that the promise of the New Testament, sir?"

His look turned cold—*Mr. Clarke, the pseudo-intellectual*—but apparently he no longer felt the need to put me in my place. "Yes, I suppose it is."

Although I may have avoided being cashiered from the service, I felt stupid then. Stupid and, despite all, sorry for him. The chain of devils trailing in his wake must be enormous.

Across the bow came a sharp report from *Newport News:* sharp and bitter as though lightning had split the air above her. A column of black smoke rose from her fo'c'sle.

"Something's wrong," he said. "That wasn't her gun."

He sprang inside, musings forgotten. The Navy had trained him to issue commands. "She's been hit. Head over there, Mr. Clarke—full speed. Boatswain's mate: sound the general alarm. All hands to battle stations. Away the Rescue and Assistance Team. This is no drill."

Plugging Holes

It wasn't an enemy attack, though *Newport News* had often been shot at the North Vietnamese. One of her eight-inch rounds had fused early and detonated in the middle barrel of her number two turret, and that explosion, intended for the target, had flashed through the gun house and down into the loading room: only the cruiser's rugged design had kept it from blowing up the magazines. But for the men inside, containing it made it worse. The blast hurled bodies through hatchways. Some who survived the flames died from asphyxiation. Twenty were killed and thirty-six injured. The turret itself was wrecked, and the middle barrel, nearly driven from its housing and with its breech shredded, hung like a dislocated limb at an impossibly wrong angle.

We flew over there at battle stations with our fire hoses ready—Buster, as damage control assistant, was conspicuous in his leadership—but as before we were directed to keep out of the way. By the time we came alongside the fire was out, the wounded had been taken to sick bay, and the dead were being removed from the turret.

The idea of accepting help is an added burden when you are stunned: the explosion had taken place just below the ship's bridge, in front of the captain and his watch team, with no warning in the picturesque twilight.

On board *John Shafer* everyone was sobered, but the combat veterans and a few affecting that role, like Louie, were stoic. Buster had been trained to think this way in flight school. But his face, as he looked at the rows of body bags across the water, was full of pain, and he muttered to me that it was a terrible way to end your young life. This was the first time he had seen what our own projectiles could do.

On the other hand, the accident brought opportunity. *Newport News* departed for Subic, and we were left to defend the DMZ, which meant confronting the resentful and emboldened enemy. In the moonlight a few shell splashes rose and disappeared off the bow like Moby's spirit-spout, a figment of the watch's imagination except for the chunking impacts heard on the underwater telephone. Shot at! The Combat Action Ribbon for all hands! It was tempting to reply, to engage the enemy in a duel; but after Salty Bill Wheelock reminded him of the accuracy of the Soviet-made T-64 tank (which we couldn't see in any case), the captain, mindful of our quarter-inch plating, decided that the more prudent course would be to retire out of range and await developments.

These were forthcoming. In any organization the loss of A requires B to fill in which cascades to C and so forth. The next day the light cruiser *Providence,* which had relieved us at Mo Duc, relieved us here. As important as Quang Ngai had become to the war effort, controlling the DMZ was fundamental, and the gunline commander, with more holes in the dyke than fingers, must accept the risk of assigning the smaller ship to the lesser mission. We were new and capable after all, and the Marines had

praised us and wanted us back. Our orders were to detach, to rendezvous with *Mispillion* for fuel, and then to
proceed south at best speed.

When the message came in, the XO waltzed Salty Bill
around the bridge, and even the captain allowed himself
to be pleased, though he reminded us that men had died.
Yes, *but.* Independent duty once again! Adventure and
glory! It was only a risk if you thought we might fail.

Buster's Triumph

We found *Mispillion* in the morning. The wind was calm,
and the blue-gray sea was flat with that slight bulge at
the horizon like a cup filled to the brim. I was conning.
We had overshot the rendezvous, for the oiler's industrial
silhouette poked through the mist astern of us. From the
bridge wing I ordered a small amount of rudder. The ship
turned gracefully, water hissing from her prow and the
deck heeling a few degrees, no problem for my men as
they lay out their lines. Toward the end of the turn, the
fat ship chugged across our bow. Close aboard, she was
fantastically detailed—the masts, the cranes, the king-
posts—but safe. With further adjustments in the rudder
which I could feel as if I were steering, I conned us into
her wake at five hundred yards' distance.

The captain grunted and patted my arm. Joy rose
within me and with joy clarity and power. I felt as if I
could see for hundreds of miles: the aircraft carriers
hunting the wind at Yankee Station, the sky dotted with
planes, the radar pickets, the armada of gunships bom-
barding the coast: the whole complex mechanism of the

fleet was keeping perfect time because at the center of his horizon, where each of us must live, Ensign Christopher Clarke was expertly handling his ship.

Mispillion closed up the Romeo flag, which meant *Ready for the approach.* I looked at our own halyards to see if we had responded—in a way Romeo was my own flag today, and if I made a good approach the signalmen should present it to me as a souvenir. When I turned back, Tyler was standing in front of me, with Buster. Buster would make the approach.

I looked at the captain. "You've earned sufficient distinction for one day, Mr. Clarke," he said.

Yes, but Buster. Of course I didn't like it that he was taking my place. After botching the approach on the downed aviator, his disgrace had reached its half-life, and down deep I didn't like that either. Although he continued to ridicule the surface navy and his future in it, he was taking his future more seriously. One day Marchand found him tracing systems in the torpedo room; his junior officer journal had more entries than mine.

Automatically I recited the essentials of course, speed, and stationing. Buster frowned, as if this was more than he needed, and I stopped. I showed him where to stand, by the gyro repeater, and how to speak into the brass funnel, which carried his voice through a pipe directly over the heads of the men at the helm and the engine order telegraph. The captain stood behind him ready to put in a word of advice—or, if he botched the approach altogether, to take the conn himself and get us out of trouble. I stood behind them both with the stadimeter, an optical instrument like a sextant that measured the distance to the oiler. The seas had kicked up a little; I was glad of it.

In a tentative voice Buster eased us out of *Mispillion's* wake and ordered eighteen knots. He looked forward, at the closing distance; he looked aft, at the merging wakes;

something clicked; he got the angle exactly right. The closer we came to the looming oiler—close enough to see the buckled hull plates from her collision—the taller he stood. When we could speak of it later he told me that her foreshortened side looked the same as a runway on final approach. The captain never spoke. There was nothing to say. Buster had the angle, and he slowed at the perfect time, when our bow was almost up to the oiler's stern. It has always thrilled me how far a vessel will travel on sheer momentum. With a last residuum of energy we rode a wave precisely and, as it seemed, inevitably into station. The lines went over, the rigs were hooked up, and we were taking on fuel in record time. The conning commands for the entire replenishment filled less than a page in the log. *Mispillion* hoisted the flags for *Well done!*

It was a home run on a rookie's first at-bat. Anyone could get lucky, but this seemed like more than that, like the natural ability of an athlete before whom the rest of us struggle. The other officers came by to give him a squeeze or a shove, adopting Buster's own physical style as a further compliment. The enlisted watch were now happy to obey him. That Greek chorus, my boatswain's mates at the replenishment rigs, hooted their pleasure. The XO nodded approvingly, and the captain wore a smile as if gratified by his own excellent judgment in choosing Buster.

Without taking his eye off the oiler, Buster had a friendly word for his well-wishers. His feet were braced, and the wind ruffled his hair as if he were joy-riding in a convertible. No doubt he was thinking what he had said in the sailboat: *I can do this.* The discovery promised a new start. Certainly, I told myself, that was just what I had wanted for him.

As we were about to break away, he turned to me. "Any limit to the rudder?"

Under the spell of the perfect, I replied without thinking: "None, he likes a smart breakaway, have at it."

"Let's go, let's go," the captain said when the oiler had
cast off the last line.

"Engine ahead flank," Buster said. "Right full rudder."

The forced-draft blowers wound up, and ever so slowly
we began to pull ahead. The bite of the rudder, however,
was immediate. The deck heeled and then heeled as if it
would never stop. Men on the fo'c'sle were thrown against
the lifelines. Our stern swung toward *Mispillion* until
hardly a wedge of ocean separated the two ships.

"Rudder amidships," ordered Marchand. "What the
hell are you doing?"

Buster looked at me as the deck righted and the replenishment teams, turning coat, cursed the bridge. Five
or ten seconds went by. He waited. I opened my mouth to
speak but nothing came out. Marchand was ready to
smite whoever acknowledged fault. With each second the
barrier to speech, to truth, grew impassable.

"Ensign, get off my bridge," Marchand said. "You hear
me, sir?"

Ah, but which ensign?

He was looking at Buster.

Buster lifted the binoculars from his neck and eased
them into their box. Then he turned and without another
word from any of us went through the doorway and down
the ladder.

Something of the truth became known to the wardroom; I believe Buster told Louie and Louie made sure of
it. When I went down to lunch the officers gave me the
silent treatment. As we adjourned, the XO quoted Shake-
speare: *We few, we happy few, we band of brothers.* That
afternoon he moved Buster to another stateroom, under
the mack, leaving me alone in the junior officer bunkroom

next to the captain's cabin. It was some time before the taint wore off, if it ever did. The half-life of seawater, Chief Beatty had said, was about one week; but I was now known as a back-stabber, a rate-grabber, someone who didn't care about his shipmates.

Except that I did care, I do care. In the aftermath Buster and I didn't speak. It was human nature that I too bore a grudge. If he had something say, he should have said it to me, not Louie. And it was *his* mistake—who would order a flank bell and a full rudder at the same time? I had taught him better than that when we were sailing. If you ask me is it safe to jump into the pool at the bottom of the waterfall and I say that it is, whose fault is it if you *dive* in and break your neck?

Yes, I should have spoken up. That was a moral failure, a blot on the escutcheon as my father would have said. In the years since then I have often volunteered for the blame, even when not especially guilty; in fact I see such chances coming and brace myself for them and feel better having taken the spear and then been gratified by the admiration of others for my honesty. We do learn from our mistakes, if we want to.

But: omission or commission? I was certain at the time that my motives had been innocent. Though I envied him his fine approach, I wasn't trying to ruin it. I was bemused, enervated by his astonishing skill or luck—skill. I didn't really think about what he was asking.

Or did I? Did I know, in some part of my mind, that I was giving him poison?

Fifty years later, the question still haunts me.

The First Attack

John Shafer [I wrote] answered an urgent call for fire about midnight, when a forward observation post of the 3rd Battalion, 1st Marine Regiment received indications of an impending attack east of the village of Mo Duc. A total of 47 rounds was fired, periodic illumination followed by multiple-round salvos. The initial salvo was on target. The Marines reported engaging as well with small arms. Daylight revealed unmistakable signs of preparation for a sustained assault, including areas cleared for mortar emplacement. Liaison with 3rd Battalion indicates that the manner of preparation is consistent with that of the regular troops of the North Vietnamese Army.

"Fine, fine, as far as it goes," said Captain Marchand. "But I want to tell them the O.P. was attacked and we repelled it."

"But we don't want to come across as rookies," I said. "The Marines will see this report. For all we know they want to downplay the sense of emergency—*everything's under control,* that sort of tone. This is probably just the overture. We wouldn't want them to contradict us."

"Chris is right," said the XO.

I was right, and more important, I was Marchand's creature again. The captain shook his head as he thought about it, but I knew I'd won. Like a father who has

yielded on a domestic matter, but whose supreme authority has been upheld, he pretended to be persuaded
against his better judgment when he signed the message.
"But at least change *village* to *town,"* he said. "Mo Duc is
on the chart. That makes it as good as Cambridge, doesn't
it?"

Other than a careful signature, in that round, backward-sloping script, his quick red pen hadn't touched my
draft. The XO and I grinned at each other, and I tripped
lightly down to Radio to have the message transmitted. I
felt alive.

In this, no doubt, being a sailor I had caught the con-
tagion of the ship's morale. Sailors like their routine, but
week after week of it depresses the spirit, even when the
stakes are high and there isn't a moment to spare.

We had returned to Mo Duc like Anna Karenina to the
Levin household. Charlie Brown welcomed us with a report that the area was "active," and the Viet Cong Anglo-
phone who intruded on the spotter's circuit agreed with
him. "You going to die, Snappy," he said. Once again we
fired every day—sometimes most of the day. But these
missions were preemptive, as the battalion prepared to
clear the NVA from Quang Ngai, and we seldom knew the
results. Yes, we might hear *target destroyed* or *secondary
explosion observed,* but we had no sense of what our con-
tribution meant to the impending battle, in which, of
course, we wanted to appear as heroes. We learned that
it is possible to be bored while killing people, and the re-
petitive boom and shudder of the concussions began to
get on our nerves. Ever more efficient, ever more deadly,
we observed a routine that felt like a funk.

I had been in my own funk, understandable but real
for all that. Great events were taking place around me—
we were involved in a last, desperate effort that would
probably decide the destiny of a nation—but I didn't care.

Not about the war, not about the peace to come. I was tired, lonely, dissatisfied. My father sent me a letter full of grieving. I wrote back not to him but to Lény, a false, lighthearted letter about being at sea again, toward the end of which I just mentioned that she still owed me a dance, having left me on the floor for a family argument. I thought to add that I had wanted to tell her something important to both of us, but I didn't say this. Without her actual address I sent it to the Chuck Wagon. Probably a dead letter, but at least I had tried. I wondered if I would ever complete the thought. If she were here now I would have done it and taken the consequences. I missed being in love and making love. I was disgusted by my confinement to the ship, by the same view of the blue horizon on one side and inaccessible hills on the other, as if I were a housebound man looking through a picture window.

Notwithstanding my fancy as an old salt, I didn't care about the sea, and that bothered me most of all. Being an OOD was no longer a thrill. We were eight degrees of latitude into the tropics. Even so, as October slept-walked into November, the winter monsoon was stirring, and the water was changing every day. Some days there were green depths full of light and bubbles as far down as I could see; others, the surface was dark blue or purple, oily and opaque and covered with broken vegetation from the shore. At bare steerageway the ship rolled slowly and severely in the swell. The bridge wing would swing toward the water so close it seemed I could reach my hands over the bulwark and wash my face. The sky was full of energy, if only I could tap it. I was simply weary of the effort required to keep my feet on the constantly shifting, unyielding steel deck.

No doubt I was suffering—too? primarily?—from the moral wound, which never heals quickly. Buster and I saw each other every day, we sat together at meals, from our proximate watch stations, where one enemy shell could kill us both, we passed commands and reports ... yet neither of us relented. And this went on and on like a new status quo. As with him so with the ship: I felt like Jonah.

On Monday of Thanksgiving week, at a stroke everything changed. New energy coursed through me, and I was powerful, decisive, and impervious to doubt as we are but a few times in life. And as with me so with the ship, two hundred and fifty brothers acting as one. Charlie Brown was attacked in force.

I had just come off watch when the gun began to fire. No night mission had been ordered, so this must be something else. I put my uniform back on and went across the alcove into CIC. Tyler Brock was in charge. Salty Bill Wheelock held back from relieving him, since the situation required continuity (also *no one* presumed to be as capable at war as Tyler). The captain, in CIC too, in his chair, looked tense.

Life and Death were contending in the dark not so very far from us. Here, safe within the dimmed red lighting, the war was an abstraction, a matter of faith perhaps. Over the radio Charlie Brown's voice was soft and unhurried, with that special mastery of time of the religious celebrant. He called in the fire mission. The target was plotted, and Charlie Brown's line of sight to it was converted to the ship's line of fire. Everyone wanted to see this on the chart, and I had to look over two rows of heads and shoulders. The target was partway up the face of Hill 330, between Mo Duc and the O.P. *Troops in open* was the description.

The radio talker reported, "Ready."

"Ready break fire," Charlie Brown said from the immaculate silence in which there were no sounds of battle.

The giant beat once with his sledgehammer on the forward bulkhead, and the status boards rattled in sympathy. This was the illumination round. Tyler consulted a stopwatch. Just before the bridge called down that the parachute had opened, he ordered the first salvo, a round of shrapnel timed to detonate over the enemy's heads. The giant beat again.

After a moment Charlie Brown said, "Drop five zero. Eight rounds: fire for effect."

This brought a murmur from the watch and a "Well done, Tyler" from the captain: according to Charlie Brown's spot, the first round must have landed almost on top of them, a good start. Around the table the faces I could see were resolute with the desire to kill or perhaps merely with the desire to win, for it needed a heretic's imagination to think of the target as soft humans like ourselves.

"Shot," called the radio talker with the first round, giving Charlie Brown and his Marines time to take cover. Every two seconds, while some men counted on their fingers, the *bang, bang, bang* was struck until the last round, after which the radio talker called, "Splash"— meaning it was time to look out and see where the rounds had fallen.

And so it went, until the forty-seven were fired.

Charlie Brown abandoned the liturgy. "Wonderful, outstanding! You're hanging them up on the wire. They're retreating. Dozens of them down. Great shooting."

Almost everyone was talking to his neighbor now, and the captain was the most talkative of all. Won't this read well! he must have been thinking. I was jubilant myself drafting his report, which I wrote out right there, in longhand, as it appears at the beginning of this chapter. (When I took it to Radio afterwards, I kept Mo Duc as a village).

Only Tyler was silent as he considered what might be learned. He noted on the chart the location of the Marines' perimeter: next time, a rolling salvo might drive the enemy into the prepared minefield. He decremented on his tally sheet the ship's count of ammunition (which Seaman Wolford, in the laundry, had no doubt done as well). He considered whether a more northerly firing position would have made better use of the terrain, like a hammer finding the sweet spot on an anvil. From time to time he reached for a mug of old coffee. No one spoke to him, not even Salty Bill, still waiting for their turnover. His face was expressionless, lost in the devotion to small tasks. For the true believer there is no division between moments of worship: one's whole existence is given up to the celebration of faith, if one has any faith at all.

This was the first day of the attack.

Brazen Defense

The next morning was quiet; both sides were resting. When I offered to read the news to Charlie Brown, he asked if he could get back to me. Something in his voice sounded like October turning into November. That grey grim resolve to endure the winter.

Chief Beatty and I had the afternoon watch. At bare steerageway the ship was rolling her masts out, as the old salts used to say, so I asked the captain if we could increase to seven knots to give more effect to the fin stabilizers. "Make it so, Mr. Clarke," he said cheerily. Since I had bent myself to his will, I could do no wrong.

We were still rolling enough to weary the legs, but the day was bright and the hands were happy. Tonight we would save Charlie Brown again, perhaps by killing a thousand gooks. Signalman First Class Derrick Coakley was on watch on the signal bridge, where our two .50-caliber machine guns were mounted. The chief and I made sure that as we turned around at each end of our firing racetrack, we stayed well beyond the shore. Not that we were concerned about running aground (though I always paid attention), but the last time we were here, Coakley had opened fire on three Vietnamese walking along the beach in their black pajamas and conical hats. He fired an entire belt before half a dozen of us, including the captain, could pull him off the gun. Viet Cong, he told us, sure as shit. Fortunately the range was too great even for the .50 cal. By then the targets had cleared the beach, probably without noticing. The captain went below and nothing more was said about it. Coakley had served in a fiberglass swift boat patrolling the Mekong Delta.

Homer Williams walked onto the bridge, blowing upon us like a foul breeze.

"Mr. Clarke," he said with a salute. "Chief Beatty, a pleasure. Mr. Clarke, I have in my hand a special request chit that I hope will interest you."

On quiet watches it was all right to conduct a little ship's business. This was a very quiet watch. In other parts of the world people were having their siesta.

"I would like to start an AA group," he announced.

"Why don't we take this outside," I said to both men.

"I don't mind who hears me," Williams said. "The more witnesses to my salvation, the better."

Despite this, we gathered at the XO's empty chair and spoke in low voices. "Are we talking about alcohol only?" I asked.

"Any sort of addiction, Mr. Clarke. It may be alcohol—to be sure that would be sailor-like. It may be drugs, heaven forbid, drugs on this vessel. It may be sex—as in my case," he finished in a steady voice.

It might be ambition in mine, I thought.

"Are we talking about the twelve steps?"

"Yes sir."

"Serenity, courage, and wisdom?"

"Yes sir. And honesty and acceptance. I have spoken to a number of men interested in joining such a group, Mr. Clarke. When established, we would elect a facilitator—perhaps you would consider that role?—you'd be awfully good at it. What I need now with this chit is the command's approval to start the group and to conduct the meetings in a suitable place."

Chief Beatty was expressionless. I would want to get his opinion after Williams left. This gave me an idea.

"I'll endorse the chit, certainly, and I expect Mr. Brock will too, perhaps to take effect after we leave the gunline. Whoever the facilitator is, he and the XO can work out the details. But if you ask me, if you really want support for your project, you should run it by the chiefs' mess."

"A very good idea, sir, I hadn't thought of that."

He started to leave.

I said, "By the way, bosunmate. Since we're talking about honesty and acceptance, how did you get ashore the night before we sailed? The quarterdeck still had you on the restricted men's list."

A canny gleam, well pleased with himself. "I nipped over from the fantail when no one was looking, sir. You'd be surprised how strong your legs are when you get that smell of pussy in your nostrils. The effect is profound, Mr. Clarke, profound."

I wanted to believe that he—or anyone—could reform. But the odds seemed against him. By that sly joke of fate that each roll of the dice has an equal chance, no matter how many losing numbers have come up before, Williams had contracted the clap again during his brief escape from restriction, and the doc now wanted to put him out of the Navy altogether; ostensibly for his health but I think also because he was offended. Chief Beatty had heard all about it in the mess, including Williams' gambit of the AA meeting. "You wouldn't want anything to do with that group of hard cases, sir," he told me. No, I wouldn't, and no, I didn't. Although I hadn't been threatened lately, I still suspected Williams. As I imagined the glory of helping redeemable men change their lives, I had to wonder whether his invitation to me was legitimate— whether, in fact, the .45 in my safe might be necessary— and with that thought my ardor cooled.

Having signed the chit, I felt craven asking the XO to disapprove it, but I needn't have worried. He brought it back to me in Hong Kong to say that I had been swizzled, that the captain would have to decide soon whether to send Williams away, but that given our situation First Division needed an enlisted leader and he was better than nothing.

Arc Light Strike

But I've gotten ahead of my story. The rest of the watch was uneventful, and so it was through the evening. Yet something bulked in the air. The chief and I had the mid-watch. Half an hour before then I was in the wardroom, enjoying that pre-watch snack known as midrats, when Louie phoned: "Shipmate, you'll want to see this."

"What's happening?"

"Arc Light strike."

It seemed that he had been on the phone to everyone: a crowd of officers and enlisted men overflowed the bridge wings to stand on the signal bridge and the ladder in between. It was a black and humid night. The topmast drew ellipses among the clotted stars as the swell rolled under the ship, moving on to the shore just a mile or two away. The special radio circuit patched to the bridge wing was silent. We listened and waited. Finally, a man's voice spoke a single word, then after a few seconds another, from a great distance; that was all. Neither word meant anything to me or apparently to anyone else—I can't recall them now. But people were looking landward. When nothing happened at first, they turned to their neighbors and whispered as they do in seances, as if loud talking would scare off the spirit.

A single white light flashed between two hills, casting the entire range of hills, low and dark, into relief. Then another in the same place. Then another. Then a hundred lights—or a thousand lights, both a bass and a treble clef of light, a sustained tremolo in the bass over which chord after chord was struck in the treble. The pale unshaven cheeks of my neighbors appeared in the flashes. I could see the colors of their khakis and blue dungarees.

Before the light had died out the blast came. The air hollowed and filled and slapped my face. It wasn't enough to knock me over, but it felt as if it might be or might grow to be. And then the sound: a growl rising sharply to a roll of timpani, along with knocks from weird percussion instruments. I put my hands over my ears, but it was too late: the rhythm was already inside them, being played on my own drums until the tiny bones fractured.

Around me were exclamations and awed curses as the light flickered and died and the hills vanished into the darkness.

The last to be called, I was standing closest to the bridge wing door. Just before the hills went dark again I heard a crack from the vicinity of the captain's chair. Later I found a rivet on the deck, popped out from a corner of the watertight window-frame. I had the quartermaster fill the hole with putty, but whenever it rained, drops of water would run out of the corner and soak whatever papers the captain had left in his tray.

"No one could survive that," Louie declared, and it seemed he must be right. At first light the Marines sent a Huey over the target area: its pilots reported nothing but broken sticks for several miles across; at the edges of the target area, the blasts had made stumps of the forest. The sun shone upon absolute stillness, as it will on the morning after the end of the world.

"Better field of fire," Charlie Brown remarked, which chastised us that it wasn't over. But the Viet Cong intruder was silent, perhaps silenced forever by the bombs.

That night, the third of the battle, the NVA attacked over the broken ground. It was a blunder. With their first appearance, hundreds of meters from the perimeter, they were exposed; our shooting drove them back from the O.P. and then, as Tyler had foreseen, into the Marines' minefield. Shadows crumpled and fell and were burned by our white phosphorous rounds. The attack was over in twenty minutes, by the clock, from the first stirrings to the ceasefire.

So complete was the victory and so safe the ground for now that we steamed away to refuel and rearm, officers and men working together bare-chested. A kudo came in from the admiral in *Providence* and with it a personal message for the captain that we would remain at our present station until the current battle was decided, when we would detach for our well-deserved visit to Hong Kong. *Outchop*—the end of the deployment—would come after that. We'd be home for Christmas.

Salty Bill observed that we wouldn't be going to Subic.

"You can't get theah from heah," Buster said at breakfast, but no one listened.

A Love Letter

That day, the fourth of the battle, was Thanksgiving. In the eerie calm war seemed unimaginable. Holiday routine was in effect, and those not on watch were allowed to sleep late. Before the feast our helo hopped over the horizon to collect our mail from a passing oiler. This went smoothly except that a bag was dropped in the sea. After sorting, the stewards collected the officers' mail, which was laid out on the wardroom table even as the table was being set for the festive dinner.

Only one letter had been soaked: mine, from Lény. My name and hers on the envelope were legible enough to attract the typical comments, to which I made the typical answer: *eat your heart out.* I took it back to my stateroom and opened it with the care of a spy. Although I told myself that she wouldn't have written at all if she didn't love me, my heart was pounding as I spread out the sheets on my desk. Here, perhaps, was my future. If she loved me I had an obligation. And what if—my mind leapt into this— what if she were writing to say she was pregnant?

There were four sheets of paper covered in turquoise ink with widely spaced lines. The characters were mostly printed but with some unexpected combinations in cursive as if dashed off. She connected her *u* to the next letter at the top instead of the bottom and her *v* at the bottom instead of the top. *Th* was always connected, and *t* at the end of a word always ended with a flick. I know these things now because I still have the letter.

Among the four sheets the wet patches aligned. Within these the ink had illegibly run. So too in a few other strategic spots where I needed to know the vital word. Like a codebreaker I analyzed patterns.

Dear Chris was legible, as was *Love, Lény*. This was a promising middle tone between ending the relationship and demanding too much from it. The body of the letter was largely indecipherable. Apparently she hadn't received mine. She said something about Hong Kong with a smiley face. *Long-* [smeared] *Ch* [smeared] probably meant long-legged glamorous Chinese girls, who would tempt me away from her. *Rose...* and *Bert...* probably conveyed actual news, which might affect her circumstances if not her feelings.

The most curious sentence I could make out was followed by the largest smear, which must have contained several lines of explanation: *Admiral Locke has been very kind to me.* I knew who Admiral Locke was, the commander of the naval base, the handsome virile portrait on her wall. How had he been kind to her? How had she repaid him? He was married: I had read his biography: his wife and children were named, right after a litany of personal decorations, including those for actual heroism. What could a twenty-five-year-old Filipina with a teenage sister have to do with a senior American military commander? In Subic Bay and Olongapo, what possible connection except romantic, meaning sexual?

The answer to the question might tell me everything I needed to know about Lény's character and therefore about our future. But it might be months before I knew it. As much as I loved her in that moment, or as much as I wanted her, which I might be mistaking for love, I must be careful not to commit myself.

The Importance of Football

For the holiday the traditional game between the Detroit Lions and the New York Jets was broadcast throughout the combat zone. Our technicians went aloft to rig the TV antenna, stowed away since San Diego. Each of the messes broke out its TV.

In the wardroom the stewards had prepared a feast. When I came off watch I worked my way down the buffet line until my plate was loaded. Rogelio Gozum, the leading steward, brought me a starched linen napkin folded into the shape of a turkey and set in front of me a bowl of salted nuts and a wine glass of nonalcoholic sparking cider. He seemed to enjoy Thanksgiving as much as we did. And why not? He and his countrymen—Lény's countrymen—who served in the U.S. armed forces were on a path to citizenship. Someday they'd be eating turkey and watching football in LA or Philadelphia. Or Boston. Seeing his enjoyment gave me a pang of longing for my girlfriend, who might become a citizen too.

The phone growled. The captain picked it up, listened for a moment, and spoke a word of acknowledgment. "Another mission," he explained to the table. "Charlie Brown wants us to hit the southern approaches this time."

I signaled Gozum to take my plate, but when I rose the captain waved me back to my seat. "The war can wait a couple of hours for Ensign Clarke," he said. "When was the last time you saw a football game?"

"Never during battle, I'm sure," I replied, offering a smile to dull the barb.

Deter Bain, one of the techs, fiddled with the set as other officers came in. With no warning the test pattern vanished, and there in Tiger Stadium the men were lined up for the opening kickoff. Such was the placement of the cameras that the game seemed far away (which it was) or maybe in another dimension of time (which would explain my own life). The captain and the XO made a bet, the XO switching loyalties to accept it.

Almost at the impact of the kicker's foot our gun fired; a muted concussion, which meant that the line of fire was off the bow. A long mission: the firing grew louder as the ship moved down her track and the gun trained further aft. Finally the firing was *here:* the crystal shook, and a wine glass rolled off the sideboard, crashing to the deck.

Gozum came out of the pantry with a foxtail and dustpan to sweep up the fragments. Seeing Bain, enjoying the game with us, he clucked his tongue and sent him below. The XO smiled at me.

Almost at once the signal faded. There were shadowy figures in motion, and then everything was snowed out.

"Get Bain back up here," the XO said.

"No, out of range," the captain muttered, rocking on his thighs.

The XO cranked the growler. Salty Bill was on watch in CIC. "Can you check-fire for five minutes while we come about?"

Salty Bill could. The firing stopped (at what risk to the Marines I dared not joke), and the ship heeled gently with the usual creaking of her superstructure.

The reception was excellent while we were turning, but when we had steadied on the reciprocal course it was spotty again.

"Who's conning?" the XO asked Salty Bill. "All right: patch me into the gunnery circuit. Mr. Valade: do you remember how we prosecute submarines? Yes, exactly: you have the conn, but I have *control:* repeat my orders to the helm unless immediate danger to the ship would result. *Bạn có hiểu không?* What's that? *Bạn có hiểu không?*—it means *Do you understand* in Vietnamese. *Có,* then." He stood with his eyes on the TV screen: *"Right ten degrees rudder...steady as you go.* What course? Not quite: *Come right to zero one five.* That's it! You have control again. Mr. Wheelock, you may resume firing."

He sat in a little sweat of triumph.

"At least we have our priorities right," said the captain.

Buster came into the wardroom wearing his coveralls. "Ah, the comforts of home."

"Shut up, Buster, and take a seat," the XO said.

"XO, I'm glad to see you're taking the news so calmly."

"What news?"

"The gun house is awash in hydraulic oil. It looks like the Red Sea in there. We had to stop firing."

"No we haven't. Sit down and watch."

"Do you *hear* the gun?"

The captain and the XO exchanged a look.

"Why wasn't I told?" asked Marchand.

"What happened?" asked the XO.

"Someone stepped on a fitting on the counter-recoil system," Buster explained. "The gasket's distorted and won't hold the pressure."

"Who?" asked Marchand.

"Can you take it off and reshape it?" asked the XO.

"No sir. My man Jurgelevicius is trying to weld it in place, but it won't hold a bead."

"What about a spare?" asked the captain.

"Supply says the nearest one's in Subic. Letourneau waited to give you a complete report."

"Call Tyler," the captain ordered, always his first thought whenever any professional problem arose.

Abandoning the game, we went up to the silent gun mount. Tyler was there along with the gunner's mates. Buster's account was typically overstated. The leak was serious, certainly: red fluid rolled back and forth across the diamond tread. But a patch had been applied, and pressure in the line was satisfactory. Tyler estimated that we might lose fifty gallons a day. We had two hundred onboard—the oil was common to several of the weapons systems—and we could get more from *Mispillion* before it ran out. The gunner's mates would keep cleaning it up.

"Will that oil burn if we take a hit?" I asked.

Everyone looked at me like the idiot child.

"So we're really okay," Marchand declared.

"Aye sir," said Tyler. "For now. But we'll need to have the gun fixed properly in Subic. I'll draft the report."

"Not if it shoots. Report it on the way home."

"Aye-aye, sir. The leak will get worse, Captain."

"Not on my ship, Weapons Officer."

"Charlie Brown is counting on us," I said.

"You think I don't know that, Mr. Clarke?"

"If the gun goes down—"

"If I *report* that it's down, we'll be plane-guarding *Yorktown* before the day is out, and where would that leave the Marines? What the chain of command doesn't know won't hurt them. Don't tell anyone, *including*

Charlie Brown. And not a hint of this in tonight's summary, do you hear?"

"Aye-aye, sir." That was the military ethos; and it was
easier to say *aye-aye, sir* than to argue right and wrong.
In time it becomes automatic, and then no thought is required at all.

Defilading Fire

The North Vietnamese attacked that night from the west,
the far side of the hill from us. The location of the target
presented an unusual fire control problem: if the gun
were elevated enough to clear the hill, the rounds would
carry too far. Tyler had foreseen this eventuality too and
had made notes for it on the chart. The gun was loaded
with reduced charges and "super elevated" to fifty or sixty
degrees. The rounds went up and up, as if the ship could
run under them and catch them again, and like magic
they fell on the hill's back slope.

Everyone knew this technique except Buster and me:
the barrel, pointing so high, looked like an accident waiting to happen. "Check fire," we said in unison—our first
agreement in weeks.

The door from below crashed open. Marchand glanced
at the mount without benefit of night vision, snatched up
a handset, and ordered, "Belay that: commence firing."

We did. The muzzle blast, high overhead, was anti-cli-
mactic. Above the hill the illumination round popped into
being; the candle drifted lazily downward under its parachute. Now we fired for effect. When we had finished,
Charlie Brown was a moment coming back on the radio.

"Drop five hundred," he said. Were we that far off? "Danger close," he added, meaning that the fall of shot would be near friendly troops, i.e. himself.

"Double-check your settings," Tyler warned his men. "We're inside the perimeter."

Another illumination round was followed by forty rounds for effect, more than we had ever fired in succession before. The firing went on and on like a car alarm.

"Repeat," said Charlie Brown.

"Repeat," repeated the ship's radio talker.

"Repeat," said Charlie Brown before the second forty had been completed.

"Repeat which?" asked the radio talker.

The captain shouted into the intercom, "He means *keep shooting!*"

Which is what he did mean. We fired nearly a hundred and fifty rounds—the sky over the O.P. must have rained shrapnel. The mount captain tried to make a report, but Tyler cut him off. Finally Charlie Brown came back. "End of mission," he said. "Troops dispersed. Thank you."

Captain Marchand spoke on the radio himself. "Do you need assistance?"

This was a breach of security, for any truthful answer would encourage the enemy.

"Negative. Battalion will provide. Please stand by."

"Mount Captain, go ahead now," Tyler said.

The gunner's mate reported that the prolonged firing had worsened the hydraulic oil leak. His men had had to fill the reservoir continuously. There were less than a hundred gallons in reserve.

"Mr. Brock, we really need to fix this gun."

"We're getting more oil in two days. Can we make it until then?"

"Not if we keep going like this, sir?"

Tyler came up to the bridge.

"I'm sorry about the check-fire," I said as he twisted his torso back and forth and tipped his head toward one shoulder then the other—his only sign of being under stress. "The gun just didn't look right."

"They didn't cover defilading fire at Newport, I guess."

"What's going to happen?"

"We're going to hold on. The captain doesn't want—well, you heard him."

"Tyler, that's criminal."

Strong language—a pedant would call it mutinous. He looked at me.

"The NVA will certainly try again tomorrow night," I said. "The admiral could send another ship by then. We can get it fixed in Subic and come right back."

"You must be in a hurry to go to Subic," he said.

The blasé short-timer, monitoring the Marines' radio circuit, heard Charlie Brown speak to Battalion after the attack. In the morning at breakfast he gave us the gist.

"It was close," he said. "About half the NVA got across the wire, and the Marines had to retreat into the bunker itself. Both sides were tossing hand grenades back and forth. Captain Jackson said he and his first sergeant killed six with their .45's, right at the entrance."

"What were our casualties?" asked the XO.

"Two dead and three wounded, one serious. Battalion evacuated them by Huey. Four others had wounds but refused to go."

"How many does that leave?" I asked. A voice inside of me exclaimed that two men were dead, were *dead*. They were rigidly still and had withdrawn into their small corrupting selves with the light gone from their eyes. The world was nothing to them.

"Charlie Brown expects them to follow up, maybe before dark. He asked Battalion to ask the Navy not to make any changes in gunline assignments. He said the hill would have been overrun last night except for us."

"Very gratifying," said Marchand. "I hope he puts that in writing."

"Where *is* Battalion?" asked the XO.

The short-timer grew confiding. "That's the problem. They're north of Mo Duc, blocking the route to Quang Ngai. Hard pressed as well. The O.P. has to fend for itself. I tell you, XO, those are brave men."

"They ought to get them out of there," said the XO, though ever the optimist.

Counting Pills

It was now the fifth day of the battle, Friday November 24, 1972. Elsewhere in the world the Soviet Union tested a nuclear weapon underground—we could never forget the threat of thermonuclear war. Leaders of the Republic of Ireland and the United Kingdom met about ending the sectarian strife in Northern Ireland in this, the bloodiest year of the Troubles. A former U.S. attorney general toured the Mexicali valley to learn more about the salty runoff from American farms into the Colorado River that was ruining Mexican crops. A committee of Congress met about a race riot on board the aircraft carrier *Constellation,* for which many representatives blamed the Blacks. Nixon was taking a short vacation in New York while

Kissinger and Le Duc Tho met in Paris. So far no progress had been reported while, on the ground, both sides continued to attack. In another sign of the NVA's growing confidence, General Nguyen Van Thanh, the leader of a major political-religious group in the South, was assassinated despite the supposedly high readiness of the ARVN.

I myself was running on heroic energy and power. Given the chance, I would will the NVA to retreat from Hill 330 and Charlie Brown and the Third Battalion to win in Quang Ngai. I could do it.

But now, in whatever breather we got after last night's attack, the military mundane carried on. At breakfast the XO told me that Buster and I, the two ensigns, were to count pills that morning.

"You don't mean it," I said.

"The inventory is overdue."

"We're fighting a *war*, XO."

"It might do you some good," he said, with a wink.

The last thing I wanted was to spend the morning with Buster, who would hardly look at me and whom I wanted to hate. My thoughts were aflame with rebellion, but my body did what my superior ordered: *aye-aye, sir* again.

Apart from its two beds behind a curtain, sick bay was the typical exam room in a doctor's office, only smaller, so that the padded table took up most of the space. At one end of this were a collection of milk cartons, cardboard boxes, and individual bottles, with an overflow onto the deck. Two plastic pill counters waited hopefully. A clipboard held the results of the last inventory, before I had come onboard, and Doc Daltry's best guess of what he had now.

The door banged open and Buster was there, grim of face. He looked at Doc as if no one else were in the room.

"I'll sign the report," he said. "It only takes one of us to count, and Ensign Clock is junior."

"Sir, it takes two, checking on each other. *I* can't sign the report unless two officers have done the actual counting. It's my profession, Mr. Billings."

I didn't know if Doc knew what had happened between us (but of course he did, the entire ship knew); but by some uncanny insight he had found exactly the right argument to move my friend, who was ever respectful of work and working men. *I'm just doing my job* spoke to him of human dignity. Where he came from there were fairs and barn-raisings and the 4-H.

"I'll count," he said to me, the as-yet unrecognized third presence. "You write."

But of course, as sore as we were with each other, we couldn't agree on the counting either.

"A hundred and twenty-five," he said, having segregated them with a pill knife into groups of five. These were some kind of codeine in Christmas-red capsules. Closely controlled because the addicts among our crew would love to get their hands on them. "A hundred and thirty."

"You counted that group already. *That's* a hundred and twenty-five, and *that's* a hundred and thirty."

"You don't know what you're talking about."

"I've been watching and counting too," I said. "I'm just doing my job."

"But nobody believes you"—and he looked at Daltry for confirmation of this as a general principle.

Daltry looked from me to Buster and back again. Raising his voice to the curtained-off sick quarters, he said, "Horth, we need to get you up." Behind the curtain someone mumbled. The corpsman disappeared inside, and a moment later Michael Horth emerged with his boot laces untied, and the corpsman walked him out of sick bay. "I'm trusting you," Daltry said as he left us alone, by which he meant trusting us to count accurately, not necessarily to kiss and make up. But he was an astute reader of human nature, like Chief Beatty.

Neither of us had moved. Animals look at each other as we did, and suddenly, with no sign outwardly detectable, they leap.

Buster would be the leaper. The one thing he had learned from Marchand was to clench his fists.

I wasn't afraid of him. But I was overcome by shame, remorse, a longing to be loved, and even more powerful than these, the hope of being forgiven. "I'm sorry," I said.

"Sorry for what?"

"Sorry I told you to use as much rudder as you wanted and really sorry I didn't speak up for you when he meant to throw someone off the bridge. I don't know why I didn't."

"That's easy: you're a coward."

"I was then. I'm not usually."

"And you were looking out for your career."

"I really don't care about that. What you see isn't who I am. When my hitch is over I'll go back to Boston and teach or write—history or something like it, ivory tower stuff. I don't know what has made me so ambitious. But that was a test of character, and I failed it. And I've failed it every day since then in not telling him. I'm sorry, Buster."

He nodded. His features were unmoved, but in his eyes was all the misery that I too had known these past weeks.

"I'll make it right," I said.

"This isn't who I am either. The difference is the Navy agrees with me, but it thinks you're the prize heifer."

"I've never heard of a heifer becoming an historian."

He thought about it, the witticism or my risk in bringing it out so soon. "Only the winning heifers write history. The rest of us are for the slaughterhouse. I should have gone home from Pensacola, like Marie told me to."

"*As* Marie told me to."

"*A* historian. Not *an* historian."

His eyes weren't quite dancing yet, but they were tapping their feet.

"If we can revisit the crime scene for a moment," I said, "let's not forget that you nailed that approach. No one else has done so well, not even Tyler. Certainly not me."

"She wasn't really moving. It was like landing on a runway, that same angle of approach, without the flare at the end."

"The point is, you *can* do it, you're much better with the troops than I am, and sooner or later he'll see that."

"Old Clock," he said. "One hundred and thirty-five. One hundred and forty...."

The Beach Walkers

There had been a change of air during the day; it was cooler and dryer now. Behind the hills, banks of clouds were piled high and lighted orange and pink from within, like fire in smoke. To seaward the horizon was clear and hard-edged. The breeze hadn't turned yet.

"Should be a nice sunset, Captain," Dwayne Bailey, the boatswain's mate of the watch, said.

"A beauty," the captain replied. "Pass the word."

"With the warning, Boats," I added.

But Marchand didn't like my contradicting his mood.

"For the information of all hands," Bailey announced, "a spectacular sunset may be seen off the starboard bow. All hands who wish to see the spectacular sunset are reminded to stand clear of the fo'c'sle in case of short-notice fire missions."

The burning sun dropped through the clouds and behind the hills, spreading a red and violet flush under an emerging indigo dome.

"Darken ship," Bailey passed.

The captain and I stood on the bridge wing, trying to make sense of the shore. In the fading light a large group of people, several hundred, were walking in their black pajamas and conical hats in knots of a long irregular line from right to left across our view. The ship was rolling so much I had trouble keeping my binoculars on them. Others were looking too—the gun director was pointed that way, and Derrick Coakley, the leading signalman, was looking through the big eyes.

"What does Billings see?" the captain asked, using me as an intermediary.

"It's just a long line of people," Buster reported. "Some of them are children."

"Are they carrying weapons?"

"They're civilians. Bundles, babies, household goods. No weapons. No military equipment at all."

The big eyes were more powerful than the gun director but required the user to be his own gyro. Coakley bowed and stretched and contorted himself to stay on target. "I can see them clearly, Captain," he called. "They're Viet Cong, every one of them." Coakley of the machine gun outbursts.

"Tell Billings," ordered the captain.

"Aye-aye, sir," I replied. "But aren't we expecting regular army, not the Viet Cong?"

"Tell him."

"There's no way Coakley can know that," said Buster. "It's a group of people with their lives on their backs. Probably refugees from Mo Duc, now that we've leveled the place."

"I've seen this before," Coakley maintained when I relayed Buster's response—it was ludicrous to use the phone when all of us were within thirty feet of each other. "They're moving in to support the attack."

"Piffle," Buster replied, which I didn't pass on.

"Ask Charlie Brown," the captain ordered. I relayed this to Tyler, and a moment later our radio talker posed the question.

Charlie Brown sounded calm, alert, well-rested. I shook my head at his tone of voice, so soon after two of his men had been killed and with the terrors of the night approaching. "No reported friendlies in the area," he replied. "You have weapons free for direct fire."

"That's not the same as confirmed hostile," said Buster.

"Silence on the line," Tyler commanded. "Director, CIC: synchronize Mount 51 to the director. Ten rounds with an up-spot. Commence firing."

"What at?" said Buster.

"Engage the enemy troops, Director."

"They aren't enemy troops, Brock."

In the presence of such resistance Tyler was massively calm. "The drum is loaded, and the fuses are set. Enter an up-spot of ten meters, to burst right above their heads. Begin at the head of the line. This is a classic antipersonnel solution, just what you've been trained for. The gun is yours. Commence firing," he repeated.

"How do I enter an up-spot?"

"Put the range-finder on the leading figure, and dial in ten meters on the yoke. Make sure the gun is synched to the director. You know this."

Marchand, impatient of the delay, impatient of using an intermediary—and perhaps impatient of me in that role—picked up his handset. "Director, Captain: Commence firing. You're going to lose them." This was true: the end of the line was now on the beach, and dusk was falling fast.

"Under compulsion," Buster said. "Director ready. Gun target line two six eight degrees true."

"Commence firing," Tyler ordered as though for the first time.

The mount began to hum, and the gun swung onto the beam. In the swell the ship was rolling as if it didn't know the truth, but the gun barrel, stabilized, was certain.

"Lay of the gun looks good," I said quickly.

"Shot," called the radio talker as the gun recoiled and a tongue of flame poked from the barrel. By now I was used to the muzzle blast. Like the captain I kept my binoculars trained on the target and didn't flinch when assailed. A puff of smoke appeared above the beach and almost beyond it, at the forest line. On the receiving end no one seemed to notice. The explosion may have been so far off that they didn't think it was aimed at them. Or the war may have inured them to all but immediate danger. Or after so many years of living with fear and grief they might have been letting fate decide.

"You're too long," Marchand snapped into the phone.

"No sir—too high." Buster sounded assured, like someone of eminent skill—a surgeon perhaps—who even as he performs an exquisitely delicate act has the presence of mind to evaluate it. He fired three rounds in a row; all seemed in the same place; a tree in the forest toppled.

As the end of the line crossed the beach, Coakley was jumping in frustration. Marchand shouted into the phone: "Drop two hundred. Gun Plot, Captain: drop *three* hundred."

Gun Plot, deep in the ship, normally entered the spots on their computer. As ordered they dropped three hundred. At the same time Buster, still synched in, must have entered the drop two hundred spot. Or perhaps I've got it wrong and someone made some other mistake in the excitement. In any case the aggregate was too close to the ship. Buster fired the last six rounds on a flat trajectory, and they exploded over the water—*puff, puff, puff*—each probably fusing on the detonation of its predecessor.

The last of the people disappeared.

"God: *damn* you!" exclaimed Marchand, yanking the phone from its junction box and hurling it into the sea. He started up the ladder to the gun director. It was Coakley who blocked him, speaking soft words. At this he looked back and glared for a long moment at me, who had done nothing but his bidding; then he stamped off the bridge and went below to CIC, where he berated Tyler in front of his men for the incompetence of his watch team. Tyler took it without expression. I heard about it later from Louie, but it was all over the ship in minutes. "God: *damn* you!" said Wolford in the laundry when Gozum was late bringing him the wardroom linen. "God: *damn* you!" said every displeased supervisor to every offending subordinate for days to come.

The Gun Casualty

The attack that night came from the southeast, the area toward which the people had been walking. Charlie Brown transmitted an emergency call for fire. Salty Bill, in CIC, was ready: the first illumination round left the barrel within seconds. The target coordinates were the O.P.'s position, which couldn't be true but was. Then, transmitting in the clear, Charlie Brown said, "Repeat, *Shafer.* Repeat, repeat. This is a major attack."

We fired everything in the loader drum, refilled it, and fired again. All the different fuses—anything to kill downward. The mount captain reported that the gun was running out of hydraulic oil. Salty Bill told him to do his best, sailor. I tried to call the captain; when I couldn't reach him in his cabin I had the word passed, as if we were about to collide with another ship.

The gun stopped. *Bang, bang* then silence. The cadence of shooting continued in the mind as a sense of time passing, only it was *click, click.* Salty Bill asked what the problem was, though of course he knew. On the fo'c'sle white lights revealed a scene with a crowd of men gathered at the gun mount, among the spent casings rolling around the deck. At the door to the mount, Marchand was waving his hands. Tyler Brock was at his side. Nothing could be done. The gun was hard down. The problematic fitting had blown out from the shock of firing, and no clamp or patch would hold the pressure now, even if we had the oil.

We heard twice more from Charlie Brown. "Interrogative shot?" and our radio talker had to tell him, "Wait, out." We didn't dare explain because the enemy would hear it. A few minutes later, in a hurried voice, he came on again asking Battalion for reinforcements and artillery support. After a pause, our talker told him he was on the wrong channel. He replied, "Roger" and unkeyed the transmitter. That was the last we heard from him.

I had the midwatch, which reminded me of my house the day my mother had died. At four I was relieved and went below. A light was shining under the captain's door. Without knocking I opened it and walked inside.

He was sitting in a chair with his elbows on the top of the little round table and his head in his hands, crying. His shoulders were shaking, and as I watched he sobbed and groaned.

Turning his head he looked up at me; his wet face.

I stood over him. A kinder heart would have been moved but not mine. He was responsible for getting my hero killed, a better man than himself. I just couldn't summon any sympathy for him. Now that I've retired, I have often felt it along with regret.

He had already written my after-action report, that the O.P. had gone silent while under attack. He didn't mention the gun casualty—in fact he had used the phrase "despite effective naval gunfire support." In reply the admiral, with a kudo, had detached us to go to Hong Kong. The message had come in toward the end of my watch. I had turned the ship to seaward and increased speed. If the captain wondered why, he hadn't asked, and I hadn't told him.

Now I did. When I finished with the details I added, "Nice kudo from the admiral, sir."

"You lecture *me* about honesty, Mr. Clarke?" he replied in a thick voice.

Part Four
Reunion in Hong Kong

Buster and Marie

Marie Billings, her lips pursed around three straight pins and her brow wrinkled with concentration, stood on a chair and leaned over her husband's shoulder, laying out a seam. We had come to the China Fleet Club, near the boat landing, to get a bargain in clothes. The tailor, James H. Lee, was selling civilian suits and Navy dress uniforms for less than a hundred dollars. Buster was being fitted for a suit, and Marie hadn't liked the way Mr. Lee planned to cut it. Mr. Lee stood beside her and beamed at the changes.

Buster made faces at me while Marie worked. We were all easy again. On the day after the ship moored, both of them came to the quarterdeck, for she intended to right a wrong. I, her husband's best friend, had betrayed that friendship, and partly because of this—she was sophisticated enough not to blame everything on me—he wasn't doing as well as he deserved. There it was, out in the open, and before the water taxi had crossed the harbor; out in the open, in fact, among a teeming audience of Chinese passengers. Buster protested that he and Clock had already dealt with it, but Marie replied that he was always too quick to forgive, and if she didn't stand up for him, who would? The Chinese were gratified by her tone of voice. "Well then, Chris?" she asked. I repeated what I had told him when we had counted the pills, that I was sorry and would make amends. She had us shake hands, the audience approved, and now the reconciliation was official: being a good Christian, after that she couldn't do enough for me. I felt better too.

The subject of the beach walkers and the loss of the
O.P. after our gun failed didn't come up. Nor who had
written the misleading report to the admiral.

Holding the seam together, she removed each pin from
her mouth and pushed it into place, one two three, so fast
the tailor's eyes widened. "I always allow a little more
room here," she said to him, a head below her, as she
pinched the fabric. "His whole family is big through
here."

"Massively strong," Buster said. "Handsome people."

"Big and fat," Marie said.

We left a counter full of clothes with Mr. Lee, who
promised to have them ready the next morning. Buster
and Marie had bought two suits and a sports coat, extra
trousers, and several custom-made shirts. The nicer
clothes seemed a guarantee against his returning to the
farm. It must have cost them a month's pay. Marie's
ticket here, on short notice, and their hotel room must
have cost even more. At home she had a family to feed.
Despite the expense, her mood was happy and indulgent:
relieved, perhaps, that he wouldn't be flying dangerous
jets or deploying for months at a time from home. I imagined, with longing for this kind of love, that Buster must
have grieved in her arms last night and been comforted,
that she would have put her face up to his and whispered
how much they had been blessed in life and how little this
setback would matter to them. I saw this in her adoring
eyes, which loved me now as his friend.

"And now you, Chris?" she asked.

"Clock will need a dozen new uniforms," Buster said,
which Mr. Lee wanted to believe.

"Nothing for me," I replied. "Though I'm tempted."

"Come back," said the tailor. "Ship sail Thursday."

"How would he know that?" Marie asked as we went next door for tea.

"There aren't any secrets on the waterfront," Buster assured her. "The hookers in Subic told us we were coming here, after the gunline."

"And how exactly would you know *that?*"

"Shore patrol," Buster and I said in unison.

"Boys, methinks you doth protest too much."

The arrival of the tea changed the subject. We gaped at the beautiful dishes, at the three tiers of finger sandwiches and delicate cakes, and at the ceremony of measuring, pouring, straining, and serving. In those days Hong Kong was still a British crown colony. We were English gentry.

Our window at the China Fleet Club overlooked the water, with Kowloon beyond and Red China beyond that. Surely there never was such a busy harbor—it may be the romantic lens of memory, but I don't remember it as that busy even years later, when the island had grown so crowded. Junks and sampans with distinctive red and misshapen sails cut each other's devils off and also sailed in shoals. Modern power boats with teak decks—for already the rich had settled here—were outnumbered by the smoking two-stroke stinkpots, so low in the water or pitched up so high that a moment's carelessness would swamp them. Tramp steamers came and went bearing who-knew-what cargos, vital to someone. Tankers, bulk carriers, and the early container ships operated from the burgeoning commercial docks. Barges everywhere, both moored and under tow, carried cargo, garbage, and people. The energy of it all and the excess—the alien modes of life, beginning with signs in Cantonese instead of the Roman alphabet—all this was foreign and thrilling.

And Marie was thrilled, and Buster was thrilled himself and even more so on her account. We spoke, as tourists will, of our luck or cleverness in finding this place, with this view. Behind us we could feel the mountain, on whose steep sides everything vertical must seem to lean forward like a Nordic ski-jumper. It said something for the psyche of these people that each step was either uphill or down. After Marie warned that her thighs would be so strong from climbing that her husband better watch out in bed, all of us looked costive.

"Those uniforms would have become you, Chris," she said to restore the tone. "Mr. Lee had a mannequin in the corner dressed up as a U.S. Navy commander."

"I'll be gone long before then."

"That can't be."

"Oh yes." It was pleasant to describe my encounters with Marchand, although I felt let down when I finished. My speeches didn't sound nearly as clever now. Also, I hadn't confessed to him about Buster's breakaway. But Marie was gratifyingly indignant about him: his dishonesty, his arrogance, his Rule Number Two.

"He's a sweetheart, isn't he," said Buster. "We'd better not see them. Marie is hell on wheels, Clock, at the city council meetings."

"Oh, I'll be as nice as pie. I wouldn't lower myself."

"Are we seeing them?" I asked, happy to be included.

"Dottie invited us. She left a card at the hotel."

"What's she like?"

"Very nice. Very pretty. No children to spoil that figure. She must have been a raving beauty twenty years ago. They were married in secret while he was a midshipman. Totally against the rules—if the brass had found out, they would have expelled him."

Buster agreed that of course they would have expelled their starting left tackle before the Cotton Bowl. He yawned, popped the last finger sandwich into his mouth, and stood up. When Marie protested that she hadn't fin‑ished her tea yet, he said he was going to walk to Red China and we could pick him up there in a cab.

She watched him. "I married Peter Pan."

I said, "He's a terrific officer."

She heard this as flattery and frowned. Then she al‑lowed, "He had the right personality to be an aviator. If he was going to make the Navy a career, that's what he should have been."

"He's not terribly happy where he is."

"No. I wish he were. It's a hard world."

"If he gets out, what we will he do?"

"Something at home, I guess. What will you do?"

"The same."

"Buster has always said you'll be an admiral."

"Not now I won't. The captain will make sure of it."

"But there will be other captains and other ships."

I finished my tea. "I've learned you don't get a second chance in the Navy. We're climbing Everest with no safety lines, and every so often someone falls off. Here's a story for you. In the wardroom the XO was reading one of the radio messages that announce officers' orders. He read a name they both knew and a new assignment and then said, "Get-well tour." The captain replied, "That's an oxymoron.""

"He should talk. Dottie told me that the first ship he commanded ran aground and he wouldn't be in the *Shafer* at all if it wasn't for the football team."

I hadn't heard that. My first reaction was to wonder if it might be useful to me. "But running aground isn't as serious as arguing with your captain," I said.

She smiled; smiled with affection. For a moment our radically different points of view came to rest on the same feeling. If she felt this, if she felt even the breath of it, she must have acknowledged it as a pleasant sensation no different than liking.

Buster hadn't made it to Red China, or even across the harbor. He had flagged a taxi, which took us to Aberdeen, the floating city. Just then we were the only tourists. The taxi left us, we went down a gravel road which became a boardwalk, and suddenly it was afloat and so were we and so were junks and sampans and something like houseboats all around us, connected by other boardwalks and by narrow planks: a wooden warren, a nest of humanity rising and falling with the wakes of ships in the harbor.

We were the only tourists, the only Westerners, the only people more than five and a half feet tall, and the only ones with money; even in our conservative clothes I felt like an ugly American. Of course we were noticed. A couple of dozen children and a few adults surrounded us; every one of them, even the infants, had their hands out. The old frayed pants worn by both sexes were hiked up over bony hips, however they would stay. I didn't see a shirt without holes in it.

Buster walked up and down the planks looking into their homes, never without a child and a mother beside him. Marie had something else she wanted to say.

"You have a girlfriend. What's she like?"

"What's he told you?"

"He said she's perfect for you: beautiful, smart, funny, romantic. And nice. He said you've lost your heart."

"Everyone thinks I've lost my mind."

"Because she's foreign?" Marie's easy response suggested that this had been her topic all along, presented *pro* side-first as people do in order to sound fair-minded before the devastating, intolerant *con.*

"Because it happened so fast. I have to say I agree with them. I hardly know her."

"But she's not—a hooker?"

"Not at all. She's educated and well brought up. You couldn't find a nicer young woman. Nicer in that sense. I am worried, though, what I might feel in six months if I bring her home."

"A good point."

"You don't think I should be with her?"

She looked off, under the fringe of her bangs. Her mouth was firm in that little chin with parentheses about it. No doubt generations of white God-fearing Midwestern Americans spoke through her.

"I don't think you should marry her," she said softly.

"Even if the marriage would make us both happy?"

"Your children. Yes, I know: someday we'll all be light brown and have almond eyes. But that won't help you—or our country—in this life. If you brought her home, you wouldn't be allowed to live in some states."

"Actually I would. Loving versus Virginia."

"Well, I don't know, but one of Buster's friends in Pensacola had a colored girlfriend, two nice people, and they were outcasts. He ground-looped on a check flight."

"No doubt it was cause and effect."

"Sure, laugh at me. I'm not a bad person, Chris. I'm just being practical. You'll have lots of girls to choose from back home. Who wouldn't want to marry Chris Clarke?"

A mother offered me her child to pity. The child would have been a toddler except that her left foot was missing: her leg simply ended in a knob. The woman smiled, showing about five teeth. I gave her a coin—something small.

A foolish mistake. Immediately the rest cried for their share. I gave away my change, knowing there wasn't enough for so many people—the philanthropist's dilemma. Those who received my alms didn't go away but cried for more. Buster and Marie were giving money too. The cries rose. In a minute we were out of coins and into Hong Kong dollars. Ones, fives, tens: I touched hands left and right, putting a bill into each. I was down to three twenties and a fifty, then I was down to just the fifty. I looked into the face of a man with a few long whiskers growing from his chin and said, "You'll have to share this." He grabbed the other end of the fifty and we both held it. Then he said something in Cantonese that I took to be a promise and I let it go, my last bill. Only Marie had enough money to get us home now. "No more," she declared, holding her purse beneath her chin, resolute as the Methodists in her virtue.

The virtuous feeling in me failed to survive the boardwalk. The boat people didn't let us go but continued to surround us and to clamor for more. I showed my empty pockets and my empty hands. They thought I was lying, hiding my wealth, a Chinese virtue. It was a sea of faces, yellow and brown faces, round and pinched, plaintive, rapacious, and without number; and as Lény had feared and Marie had hoped, I shuddered at the idea of Asia.

Buster's Secret

It was a nice day ending with room service, which felt like part of the adventure. After that, except for a little shopping and a memorable last night in port, I stayed on the ship. None of the long-legged Chinese beauties had Lény's sweet face. Victoria Peak, plastered with giant billboards, seemed repellently commercial. I could watch the theater of the harbor from the bridge.

In addition to duty there were *duties:* a woman named Mary Sue and her family were painting the ship, their hands wrapped in rags for paint brushes, from the main truck to the black boot topping; all in exchange for a frayed mooring line, a worn fire hose, half a dozen of our empty five-inch powder casings, and a daily haul of our trash and garbage. Williams was their nominal point of contact. Whenever I came on deck he was highly visible, "supervising" the work and pretending to hard-nose Mary Sue about the cost (but a three-fold purchase disappeared during the visit). It was then that Doc Daltry had had enough of Williams. The XO was waiting only to get the captain's attention before the Navy showed him the door.

Yet with all this I wasn't busy enough. I grieved for Charlie Brown. I grieved for my lost honor. And I grieved as a kind of down payment for my lover; for my love.

The blasé short-timer was in my duty section. Through an obliging ham operator he had set up a circuit to California as he had done for our dead Marine. One night he approached me to say that he could do the same for me back to Subic. O joy! O dilemma! Lény's farmhouse had no phone. Using the same logic as with my letter, I had the call connected to the Chuck Wagon. A Filipino answered. Yes, Bert and the Bonanza Boys were still playing there, for now. He worked the day shift, he didn't know if they had a singer. I disconnected then called back again. No, there was no "Featuring Lény" sign taped to the bass drum.

I believed—and believe today—that grief can be mitigated by self-control. Although I wanted to hide, I must stay busy. I could be a better division officer. I could study ship and warplane silhouettes in case we should ever be attacked, unlikely though that was. And I had a mystery to solve more pressing still, if for no other reason than to confirm my suspicions.

As I walked the lifelines, pretending to supervise Williams who was pretending to supervise Mary Sue, the word was passed for me. Several men stopped me to ask if I had heard it. I went up the ladder into the alcove, where one of the CIC men was buffing the deck. Navy buffers operate by *gyroscopic precession,* which means that they are designed to ram officers' spit-shined shoes. Avoiding this one, I knocked on the captain's door and entered.

He was standing by his desk, ready to go ashore, in a blue blazer, grey slacks, black loafers, and a striped tie nearly as wide as his pocket handkerchief. His freckled scalp glistened, and his body gave off conflicting sweet humid odors that must have come from a shelf of toilet products. Being in port, he would have allowed himself a full shower even though we depended on a daily water barge. With his fingers he centered and recentered his Naval Academy ring; the ring dwarfed his wedding band.

"You passed the word for me, Captain? About coming in here?" He had reason to take the hide off me for the lubberly way my men had handled the mooring shackle. But I knew better than that.

"We haven't seen each other for a day or so, Mr. Clarke. It's odd, isn't it, since we're next-door neighbors." Yet his cold, clear eyes had no regard for me as a neighbor, someone whose dog, for example, might habitually pee in your flowerbed but such a nice guy you don't say anything. "We haven't seen each other since you made a remark to me that perhaps on reflection you think was ill-natured, disrespectful."

I braced for the confrontation.

"We haven't seen each other since Charlie Brown and his men were killed, if that's what you mean, sir." This sad fact had been confirmed by message. When Hill 330 was retaken (for we were still throwing everything into the fight), the bodies of the Marines were found in their foxholes. The report from Battalion didn't mention us. It was likely that no one knew about our failure to save them. We still hadn't reported the casualty.

I added, "If my conduct was disrespectful, sir, then of course I apologize. But I doubt that revisiting the scene now, taking everything into account, would change either of our minds."

"Excuse me, Ensign, but where do you get off believing that I care what you think?"

"That's right, sir. It's of no consequence except to me."

"I'm your commanding officer. I have unlimited authority over you. If it pleased me I could make you stand here at attention until you passed out. When you flung that comment at me after the attack, I wanted to take you by your scrawny neck and choke the life out of you." He held his two fists together to show me. Involuntarily I stepped back. "And if I had I'd have gotten off. Do you think you're the only one on the ship who is sorry they were killed? What do *you* know about responsibility?"

But my real fault was that I saw him crying.

I said, "I have the same responsibility that you do, to tell the truth to my superiors."

"Ah! Very well! Just as you told *me* the truth about Buster's little shiphandling mishap."

"You're right, Captain." I was on my feet, turning about in that narrow space. "That was wrong. I've acknowledged it to Buster."

"But not to me. You were hoping I wouldn't find you out. Apparently your admirably high standards make some allowances when it's *your* ass on the line."

I had nothing to say to this.

He took me by the buttons and pulled me close. His voice was low, his breath artificially sweetened like his body: "That position was overrun before—*before!*—the gun went down. I've checked the logs. Now, what may well have contributed to the loss of that hill was our bla‐ tant failure to engage several hundred enemy troops as they were moving into position to assault it. Let's talk about that, shall we, instead of any more nonsense about timely reporting."

"You want me to inform on my friend?"

"Oh, your friend, is it. Perhaps I should ask you under oath, in a court of inquiry."

"Then I'd be required to tell the whole truth, sir."

"Stop pissing on me, Chris! What's your opinion?"

"My opinion is...." Well, what was my opinion? I was as troubled as he was. The beach walkers, if innocent by day, were guilty by night, and night was falling. As a tar‐ get they were right there. Half a dozen rounds would have eliminated them as a threat. Charlie Brown might still be alive. How could Buster have missed them?

On the other hand it would have been a slaughter.

"Some of them were certainly children," I said.

"Children have been blowing up our people since this whole damn thing started."

"All I can tell you, Captain, is what I saw."

"Did he miss them on purpose?"

Over the ship's speakers four bells were struck and the captain's departure was announced. The gig, his personal boat, was alongside. He would go ashore, and perhaps the affections of his wife would assuage him. Louie's theory of the bull's horns didn't apply to everyone—didn't apply to me, for example—but it certainly seemed to apply to James Marchand.

He buttoned his blazer and left the cabin. I followed. On the quarterdeck the usual courtiers were waiting to send him off. In his present mood I wouldn't have expected him to offer anyone a ride; and if he did, certainly not Buster; nor would Buster have wanted to be alone with him. But as I looked over the side to check on the smartness of the gig crew, there he was, Buster, behind the McNamara lace in the window of the little cabin, apparently ready to be companionable. For the sake of their wives, I supposed.

As he put his foot on the upper platform of the ladder, Marchand turned to me. "Well, Mr. Clarke?"

"I honestly don't know, sir."

I honestly didn't know, but later, as I sat in the gun director myself, I suspected what he suspected. After lunch, in possession of the duty keys, I went up to the signal bridge, climbed the short ladder, unlocked and opened the hatch, and swung into the chair where, for so many hours, Buster had observed the firing. No one was about. Two-thirds of ship's company were ashore, innocently sightseeing, I suppose. Because Hong Kong in those days had many innocent attractions but seducing its women took more than money, the straight-arrows were having their revenge on the liberty hounds. Then too we were going home next.

Buster had shown me the basic functions of the director; when I closed the main power switch, the instrument panel tested itself and the green *ready* lights came on. I tried a few movements in train and elevation. The motors had quicker reflexes than I did: I whirled through space in starts and stops as if I were learning to drive a car with a manual clutch. Eventually I was able to put myself where I wanted, and then I was able to picture what Buster had done. Synch the gun, lay the viewfinder on a target, dial in the elevation, pull the trigger. The manufacturer had made it, as we liked to say, sailor-proof: killing was guaranteed. How could Buster have missed those people? How could he have missed so badly?

I returned the director to centerline. After I had powered it down, as I sat in the seat enjoying the winter sun, an arm swung into the hatch opening, and Tyler Brock was standing on the ladder, looking down at me.

"Training?" he asked.

From now on, and especially when under pressure, I would speak the whole and exact truth. "Reconstructing the direct fire mission. How did you know I was up here?"

"Engineering saw the load spike and called up to ask if anyone was testing weapons. We only have the one generator online. You're supposed to get permission for things like this."

"Sorry. I'm sure I did know that."

"So what did you find out?"

Could I trust him? He was Marchand's creature as much as I had been, only more capable. But he was also my boss, who owed me loyalty. More than that, when you admire someone so much, confiding your secrets to him is natural, just as a bee finds his way back to the hive.

"He didn't go to school," I said. "You recall neither of us knew about defilading fire. This was his first mission actually aiming the gun himself."

"Yes, but what do you *think?*"

Yes, the same question Marchand had asked me.

"I think he did miss on purpose. Killing those people would have been easy for him."

"I agree."

"But I also think," I added, "that it doesn't matter."

"It mattered to Albert Jackson."

"He thought he'd be murdering innocent civilians. Mothers, children. How are we to do what we revolt from, what our senses tell us is absolutely wrong? It didn't help that Captain Jackson had said, in effect, that they were hostile by default. I think Buster was caught between between a rock and a hard place."

Tyler thought about it, then he said: "His duty was clear. We take an oath: *Obey the orders of the officers appointed over me.* It wasn't his call, and it wasn't yours either, by the way, to criticize the captain."

So there were no secrets on ships.

At the Polaris Room

After all this, I was surprised that the Marchands went out with us. Not that she would mind, once I knew her character a little; but by now it was clear that he hated both Buster and me. Buster had wounded his service

reputation, his vanity, and perhaps his feelings, and the
mystery of Buster's motives had only made it worse. I was
simply anathema to him, by background and sensibility.
Thanks to Louie, he knew that I had opposed the war. Now
I had accused him of dishonesty, though a liar myself. Plus
I had seen him take his hooker upstairs in Olongapo, and,
also thanks to Louie, I knew she had given him a social
disease. Here with him now was his wife. Everyone who
had been to the Texas Bar that night was a threat to him.
A little too much alcohol and—who knew?—I might start
telling tales. Why keep me around? Why not strangle me,
professionally or otherwise?

Apparently he had no fears on the latter score because
telling tales was something that men of the world didn't
do. Or perhaps he and Dottie Marchand had an understanding. Whatever his reasons, the change in his attitude
toward us was remarkable. He was witty and urbane, he
was interested in us and in Marie and their children: his
manner implied that we were valuable members of his
wardroom instead of misfits who had disgraced him and
would soon be transferred to Midway Island to join the
gooney birds.

What I still had to learn was what he too had had to
learn in his career, that his officers were assets generally,
who, subject to his orders, should be employed in the running and fighting of the ship as long as they followed those
orders. That they would make mistakes and he would call
them to account. That the Navy had assigned them to him
and their development was a part of his responsibility
along with keeping the ship off the rocks. That there was
a division between his professional relationship with them
and his social relationship that required different personae (though how a Tiffany figured in the social relationship I never *have* learned). And that he might switch between the two personae as smoothly and suddenly as a

running back reversing his field, and which one he chose to present at any time wasn't up to me either.

We called for them at the Mandarin, their luxury hotel (where Henry Kissinger stayed), and rode with them in a *White Star* ferry across the harbor to a night club in Kowloon. Buster wore one of his new suits, and Marchand looked like the snappy dresser he was. Marie looked dressed up for the first time since the prom, while Dotty looked like a woman who had once been a cover girl. I looked like a fifth wheel.

Standing on the fantail, we felt the cool land breeze.

"Oh, isn't the ship nice," said Marie. She certainly was. Her red aircraft warning lights seemed to ensure the security of Victoria Peak behind her, and her white deck lights shone like flames across the black water. Within this outline the ship was clean and freshly-painted, latent with speed and power. The rake of her bow made you imagine a more heroic image: knifing through the seas on some task vital to national security.

"How did you manage it?" Dottie asked me, in the way a political candidate sampling a blue-ribbon pie might ask about the crust. I described Mary Sue, which seemed to delight her. "Painting with their hands! And all that in three days!"

"She works fast. Time is garbage."

"You did well, Chris," said the captain, a hybrid remark between duty and socializing.

"Too bad you overpaid," said Buster.

"Opines the world's number one skinflint."

"Opines!" Buster grabbed me by the collar. "Wake up old Charlie," he said. "He's never seen a beating like I'm going to give you."

"Surely not," said Dotty with a smile. But that could have meant either reproval or relish.

"Whenever you want to try your luck," I said, after he released me, as I unobtrusively touched my collarbone.

In a high-rise we took an elevator to our nightclub, the Polaris Room, and Buster, who had arranged the evening, went around schmoozing the staff. He returned with the wine steward and a magnum of champagne. Marie teased him as the man about town.

I was at the head of the table, with her on my left and Dottie on my right. I couldn't hear what Buster and the captain were discussing. Nor was I listening to the women, for I was watching Dottie's lips. She was tall, an inch or two taller than her husband, with a voluptuous face and figure, fleshy over thin bones. She wore a dress of yellow silk that wrapped around her. The soft round lines of her hips and abdomen suggested experience; so did her husky voice. Her hair was raven black. Her skin was tanned and dusted with freckles; her face was un-lined, but there would be fine wrinkles out of sight—I would see them, for example, if I were kissing her between her naked breasts.

At some point she broke into my reverie. Her dark active eyes were fondly amused.

"And you, Chris. Married? A girlfriend?"

"Single," I said, feeling like a man who pockets his wedding ring.

"Someone in mind?" She looked up at Marie as if for confirmation.

"I'm learning as much as you are," Marie said—more dishonesty but which safeguarded my secret.

"And new to San Diego. I know some girls."

I prevaricated further: "At OCS they said a suggestion from the captain's wife was tantamount to an order."

But anyone would do what she wanted. Had the times been different she would have been a better candidate for

command than her husband. She had made herself char-
ismatic, the sort of woman who saw her good looks as a
tool to be used and who would never begin the day without thinking what she had to work with and what impression she could make and to what purpose. She was making an impression now, as certainly she knew, as she always would know. It might be selfless. It might be something else. You never knew with people's marriages. She
might be dissatisfied with her husband, so that the deployments were a relief and the homecomings repugnant,
like north to north. She might know all about his infidel-
ities. They might be part of the compact. If so, a dose of
the clap, cured, would be no problem. If so, a second hon-
eymoon in Hong Kong couldn't save them.

In contrast Buster and Marie were a delight. He was
nervous around the captain, which he covered first with
high spirits and next, uncharacteristically, with alcohol.
To help him, she was his straight-man. They teased each
other about foibles that went back to grade school.

When the band began to play, he wanted everyone to
dance. Dottie was agreeable, but Marchand only smiled—
intimacy must not be part of the compact—and I was
afraid of touching her.

Buster knelt by Marie and kissed her hands. "I love
you, dear wife."

"Hush."

"I repeat: I love you."

"So says all that champagne."

"Not true," he protested, stumbling a bit on *true.*

"I suppose you'll embarrass me in front of our friends
unless I show you how to dance?"

"Absofuckinglutely."

She slugged him.

"Exactly so," he said.

"Come on, then—if you can."

He was a good dancer, as I had seen, but nothing like
Marie. She had rhythm, she was surprisingly athletic,
and she knew the steps. She had grown up dancing, with
that love of moving her body that some children discover
is in them, and during their many years together she had
taught him how to lead. He danced as if finally he had his
partner back, which of course he did. Watching them was
a thrill. Anything done well always gives pleasure, but
watching Buster and Marie this night took me out of myself. The music slowed. They held each other in joy, comfort, friendship, and confidence. They moved half as fast
as the music. Their eyes were closed and they were thinking of home, of their children, of the life they had made.
Marie with a beautiful stretch put her arms around
Buster's neck. He drew her closer.

They were irresistible. The band members themselves
played tighter watching their effect on them. The music
and the dancing too made you long for love and sad to be
lonely. Dottie Marchand felt it. We looked at each other,
and both of us wanted what they had—Dottie and I together, I fantasized. Ever so slowly and with a wise smile,
she turned from me.

Marchand, on her other side, was leaning across the
table, transfixed. He stared at the dancers with his
tongue on his lower lip, tasting them. He was certainly
capable of recognizing love. What he felt in response was
as strong as sexual desire but more enduring. In my own
response I confused it for the thing I was feeling. Only
later did I understand what it was. Now it seems obvious.

"Jim, they're so sweet," she exclaimed.

"Yes," he replied. "Quite touching, really."

I Become a Snipe

After breakfast I was on the fo'c'sle with my division, going over how to unmoor the ship and reviewing the mistakes we'd made coming here. Whenever I explained a
step, Williams rephrased it as a command, in the voice
that drill sergeants use at boot camp. He was so worked
up that the men drew back a little. In Subic, while restricted to the ship, he had hustled a recalcitrant sailor
into the bosun's locker and knocked a tooth out of him.
(Tyler had shrugged it off as an old Navy motivational
technique.)

In my new blue uniform, tailored after the Navy mannequin in James H. Lee's shop, and having studied my
Knight's Modern Seamanship, I was feeling quite professional. Perhaps it was because there was so much activity
in the harbor, so many lives united with mine in the use of
the sea; perhaps because the deployment was almost over.
Our transit home had been posted on the mess decks.
From Hong Kong we would stop twice for fuel, at Guam
and Pearl Harbor. Assuming the weather didn't hold us
up, we would reach San Diego on December 23, seven
months away. Whatever my future was, I would know it
in about three weeks.

With one exception, important to others as well as me.
There would be no chance for a terribly romantic scene at
the Chuck Wagon as I offered Lény my hand and she put
down the microphone and left with me for the airport, full
of joy. I felt the throb of unfulfilled fantasy. If the man
had told her I'd called, she hadn't tried to reach me. She

must think we were over, and because she had been the commanding officer of our love affair, so must I.

"You had a good time in Hong Kong, Mr. Clarke," said Williams. "You observed the PCD, I trust."

"What's that?"

"Pussy cutoff date, sir. The date after which you cannot be cured of any troublesome spirochetes before reuniting with your loved ones. That date's behind us, sir."

"I'm sure you would know, Williams."

"Ha-ha-ha! Good one!" For a career sailor about to be discharged from the Navy without a pension, he certainly seemed lighthearted.

One of the yeomen brought around the watch bill. Tyler had written it. An amateur watercolorist, whenever a new watch bill was needed he wrote it on the back of a page from his sketch pad. During the deployment so far we had seen a sailor and his wife embracing on the pier in San Diego; a society of gooney birds at Midway; the six-gun *Bausell* heeled over with a bone in her teeth; and *John Shafer* at the pier in Subic, her ungainly mack— that stinting compromise between a mast and a stack— doubled in size like an erection.

Today's effort, drawn from memory but a remarkable likeness, showed Rose Rosales, hands on hips and tossing her head. Presumably dancing, but the identity of her partner was left to the imagination.

Williams whistled a catcall. I flipped the image over.

There must be some mistake. The three department heads, the short-timer, and Buster were listed as OODs— well, good for him. But I wasn't listed anywhere; not even in CIC, where I could use the experience. Nowhere. And Buster!

"Put you on the bench, did they?" said Williams.

"Carry on," I replied and walked aft, not hurrying until I was out of the sight of my men. At Tyler's stateroom I knocked and opened the door too hard, so that it crashed against the stop. A cigarette was burning in the ashtray on his desk, but he wasn't there. A few steps down the passageway, I looked into the wardroom through the porthole in the door. He was sitting at the table with Marchand, and Buster was in the XO's place. I leaned against the door with my hand on the knob. Very well: let me confront them all. I could fly home from here. Crossing the international date line, I'd be in Boston almost before I left.

"Help you, Chris?" asked a voice behind me. It was the XO, about to go into his stateroom. Carrying his flashlight and a red rag, having finished his daily inspection early, since the ship was getting underway.

"XO, is this watch bill right?"

"Which side?" he asked with a sudden smile, which faded when he saw my expression.

"Am I not wanted on the watch bill?"

"We've made some changes. You've been promoted—"

"Ah, there you are," cried Louie, coming out of the wardroom. "Walk with me to Main Control. You'll just observe today, and afterwards we'll take a tour. No, you don't go to the fo'c'sle anymore. You belong to me now."

"What the hell?"

The XO said, "If I might be allowed to finish, I was going to say you've been promoted to Auxiliaries and Electrical Officer—two divisions, twice the responsibility. And very important to your development—good engineers make good shiphandlers."

"As of when?" I asked. I really meant, *Why?*

"As of this moment," said Louie. "Come along, Ensign. Chop-chop. Those blues might be a little warm, however."

The XO nodded a benediction. This was the only notice I received of the change. No doubt, however, it would be on my fitness report, read between the lines by future selection boards. In those days, unless you'd been trained in it, engineering was for cast-offs.

"What about Buster?" I asked.

"Our new gunnery officer."

"That's a waste, with no working gun."

"Some may see it as a demotion," the XO said. "But—"

"Nothing is as important as engineering," Louie said.

"The captain wants to give him another chance on the bridge. And if, as the gods may dictate, we get called on for another fire mission, Chief Letourneau, who asked for him, could use the help."

"In the unlikely event," Louie said. "Come along, Chris."

"And what about Williams?" I asked, since it had been agreed that he was beyond redemption.

"We need someone to run First Division," the XO replied. "At least till we get home."

"Come along, Ensign. Main Control calls you."

Main Control was a booth overlooking the engine room. A normal watch there was three men, which was close quarters even so. The overhead, with its cables and pipes, was low enough that I looked for clear places to stand. The air was as confined as the space, not like my weather decks or my bridge, fresh and open with nothing nearer than the horizon. And yes, the service dress blue uniform was out of place here. I began to sweat.

At Sea Detail we were eight. I had only the vaguest idea what was going on, and if I wanted a better look I'd be in the way, a cardinal sin. Much of my first tour in the Navy, as for any new sailor, was about learning to stay out of the way. The bridge rang up its commands through the engine order telegraph; the throttleman spun a larger or a smaller wheel to open or shut the ahead or astern throttles; everyone else watched the steam pressure. The language they used might as well have been Cantonese.

Unable to make sense of it, I pictured what must be happening topside; how the ship was maneuvering in response to these engine orders. It did seem successful: back slowly away from the mooring buoy, then come ahead while gradually increasing speed.

"Who's driving?" I asked.

"Buster," said Louie. "And doing a fine job too. Let's tour your new domain. See if you know anything."

Louie believed two contradictory ideas: first, that no one in the Navy, regardless of paygrade (Marchand) or standing (Tyler), knew as much as he knew; and, next that he owed it to the great unwashed to lift them out of their ignorance. For the rest of the afternoon he used his version of the Socratic method on me. "What's this?" he would say. "All right, then: what's this? What's its primary source of power? What's its alternate source? Does it have an emergency source? How would it stand up to a fire? What if this compartment were to flood? Ah? Ah?"

As a third idea he believed how dangerous ships were. Forget groundings, collisions, battle damage: ships were constantly catching fire, letting in the sea, electrocuting sailors, suffocating them in airless tanks and voids, and crushing them under falling hatches. A ship was a battle zone all to herself. Before the deployment we had lost a man from my former division who had drowned during a swim call off Mexico; his buddy was right beside him when he sank.

"That's why the captain was so exercised when you nearly fell off the flight deck coming onboard," he said. "And when you went overboard after that pilot. A second drowning would look like carelessness, ha-ha."

"That seems a century ago," I replied.

"You've come a long way, baby."

We walked past a throbbing boiler.

"How will you know if that pipe springs a leak—a pin-hole leak?"

"You'll hear it," I offered.

"Over this cacophony?" He loved the word as descriptive of the romance of Engineering and because no one knew what it meant. "Tush, you won't hear a thing."

"Then I'll see the steam coming out."

"The first thing you'll *see,* when you walk into the leak, is your amputated arm falling to the deck. Twelve hundred pounds, my friend. Four times more pressure than a nuclear reactor."

"I'm glad I'm not in charge of the boilers."

"In many ways," he said, with no nonsense in his voice now, "you have the bigger job. Running main propulsion is mostly the same thing every day. In fact—but if you ever repeat this I'll deny I said it—these plants run themselves. Auxiliaries and Electrical take imagination. That's why I've been after the command for so long to send you down to me."

"So this was intended all along?"

"Oh, no"—under his black moustache Louie showed his teeth—"this is punishment, make no mistake. One doesn't call one's captain a liar without suffering the consequences. Even Tyler couldn't save you."

"Is the captain going to send me home, Louie?"

"As the great Danish physicist Niels Bohr once said about the future, *Who the hell knows?* The half-life of seawater is about one week, my friend. Do your best and hope he gets laid in Subic."

"We aren't going to Subic."

"Right. That's right."

"You just said so outside the wardroom."

"A simple misstatement. Or a Freudian slip, ha-ha!"

"So we've turned east?"

"We can check the gyro repeater in after steering."

We did. It said 160 degrees—south-southeast. But we needed to make some southing to clear Taiwan before turning east. Certainly we were going home. This adventure down the rabbit hole was coming to an end. All we lacked were official orders.

The last stop on our educational tour was the diesel generator room, just inside the after deckhouse by the fantail. Inside was our—my—emergency generator, the only one. If electrical power was lost from the steam-driven generators, within five seconds a valve would open automatically to admit high-pressure air to the starter. Maintaining the diesel and its associated generator and switchboard required both of my new divisions, the electricians and the enginemen.

Or, more precisely, the engine*man:* Michael Horth. He was the sailor I had seen in sick bay when Buster and I had counted pills; someone who had managed to become falling-down drunk while the ship was underway.

Apparently sober now, he was working on the diesel.

"Horth," said Louie, "meet your new division officer."

Horth held out his hand, and it was important that I shake it no matter how greasy it was. I pushed up the cuff of my sleeve first.

"How do, Mr. Billings?" he asked.

"No, Horth, this is Mr. Clarke—Ensign Clarke." As Louie said this he gave me a rag to wipe my hand.

Horth looked at me for confirmation.

"What are you working on?" I asked.

"Preventive maintenance, zurr."

"What's that involve?"

"Oh, a great host of things, Mr. Billings."

"Clarke," Louie laughed.

"Let me see the card," I said. "I'm interested."

"It's all up here, zurr." He tapped his forehead.

But certainly there must be a maintenance card. Every work center had for every piece of equipment its preventive maintenance procedures. Even my anchor swivel required two drops of oil each month.

Louie said, "Petty Officer Horth has forgotten more about diesel engineering than you and I will ever know. Listen to what he says, Chris, and you'll have no trouble from the auxiliaries gang on this deployment."

"That's true," said Horth. "This fooking endless deployment."

"Home for Christmas," I called as we left.

The diesel generator room exited to the fantail, where the ship was paving its own highway, long and straight, and waiting for no one. Hong Kong had sunk below the horizon astern of us. Marie Billings and Dottie Marchand were somewhere in the eastern skies. Night was coming on, and I had no watches: suddenly I was pleased about that. I could be an engineer. Pressure, temperature, and flow allowed for no moral ambiguities, no niceties of judgment; no temptation to lie. The command would leave me alone as long as I kept the lights on. It did feel unfair— or maybe not unfair, maybe just disappointing—that Buster had taken my place when I had finally become a capable shiphandler. He hadn't been on the bridge since his botched recovery of the downed pilot followed by his botched breakaway from *Mispillion,* and by his own admission he lost his way among moving objects. But I too had had my portion of undeserved luck. The worker who went into the vineyard at the eleventh hour was paid his penny the same as the rest.

"What's he talking about?" I asked Louie.

"One never knows with Horth."

"I mean about the deployment."

"Ah, that."

"Something's wrong. We're still headed south."

"What could be wrong, mister. The war's over, right?"

"It's not over."

"Well, then."

"My God."

By any measure I was back where I started. New to my responsibilities. Not qualified for watch. Easily lost and occasionally careless of low overheads and worn ladder rungs. Unadmired by my colleagues and possessing only one real friend. Mistaken in my patriotism and still wishing I were someplace else. But here anyway, at sea, miles at sea.

And headed back to Subic.

"What happened, Louie?"

We sat together on the bitts as the sun—in the south, nearly crossing the meridian—shone on us through the topmast. When not sharing wisdom Louie liked nothing more than sharing gossip. He tapped my knee repeatedly with two fingers to work up momentum to tell the story. The captain had held a meeting last night with the department heads. Nixon, absent an agreement in Paris, was putting the wood to Ho Chi Minh. All hands on deck, etcetera. Our deployment had been extended, we were needed in the war, and the admiral had ordered us to the gunline. When the message had come in, Marchand had had no choice but to report the gun casualty.

"Discovered during routine maintenance," Louie said, making the typical air quotes. "Somebody will blow the whistle, but at this point no one cares."

"He ought to be fired."

"You're such an innocent, my boy. Everybody does it."

Over the general announcing system the boatswain's mate piped his call: *Attention all hands.* A moment later we heard Marchand's voice. "This is the captain speaking. I want to bring you all up to date on world events." The rest of the speech was like him, articulate, impersonal, cold and remote yet couched in the two things that made them listen with respect: he knew what he was doing and he wasn't afraid of them.

While he still keyed the microphone, someone in the background of the bridge raised a cheer; one of the liberty hounds, no doubt.

A moment later the ship increased speed.

Louie stopped tapping and slapped me on the knee. "Good news for you, *Clock*: you'll get to see your true love."

Then he left me, disoriented, befuddled. My own compass was spinning. I had a true love. If she was waiting for me in Subic (although I didn't quite trust the naval portrait on her wall), she deserved her heart's desire. I had made promises to her—almost the ultimate promise.

But didn't the fact that I wanted other women—Dottie Marchand, most recently—mean that I wasn't ready to settle down yet? *All men are bachelors east of Gibraltar,* Lord Nelson said. Which implied that back home they returned to domesticity. When I did settle down, I wanted an American wife, not just someone who could sing like one. A woman who knew the presidents; who knew that Elvis in his later years had become a self-parody. The idea of *Asia* still disturbed me. I didn't want to marry into Rose Rosales.

And yet I could see Lény as my wife, in our real home. She wasn't like her sister. She wanted quiet nights and cheerful mornings, healthy pursuits, children to love and guide and through whose eyes to see the wonders of the world. She was loyal—I was sure of this—and Western enough to become American from the moment she got off the plane. That hopeful, generous spirit could be mine. I wanted it. No bell rings in the cosmos to alert us to a gift; we have to see that for ourselves.

Out of Air

When we thought we were going home, the XO had planned a dining-in, a formal meal with toasts and speeches as wardrooms had done since Moby was a minnow. Being the junior officer of the mess, I should have been responsible for the affair. Sparing me that, he planned it himself, with Rogelio Gozum, the leading steward. In Hong Kong Gozum had bought a side of beef. A friend in the White House had given him a recipe for potatoes *au gratin.* The meal would be as elegant as Thanksgiving but served in state, the mess cooks in livery acting as footmen. Pictures would be taken for the cruise book.

The junior officers wore dress blues (mine looked excellent still, despite its introduction to the engineering holes), the senior officers tuxedos with gold cummerbunds and frilly shirts. The stewards bore the roast in on a platter, the captain made a ceremonial cut, and beautifully decorated plates were slipped in front of us. Our faces in the lowered light of two candelabra looked thoughtful, bemused, perhaps a tiny degree hopeful.

The captain was determined to enliven us. Usually at meals he talked with the XO and the department heads. Tonight he cast his charm down the table and chaffed each officer in turn. It was remarkable what he remembered. The CIC officer had entered the Navy from Julliard (and after his service obligation would resume his career as a chamber musician); the captain got him to tell us why, other than from snob appeal, the violins of Stradivarius and Guarneri were so good.

With an inspired segue he asked Jerry Valade, Louie's propulsion assistant, a former enlisted man approaching middle age, about his vasectomy. Jerry made a funny story of it, just within the bounds of propriety—at the first snip the surgeon had said, "Oops." When Jerry was finished, the rest of us intoned his wardroom nickname, *Spayed Valade.* All innocent fun: he was a straight-arrow. Now we were a company together if not an actual band of brothers.

In my turn he asked me for my favorite poet; I recited some verses from *Paradise Lost.* These prompted him to quote *Macbeth:* "She should have died hereafter...." I thought of my mother. For once I wasn't tempted to correct his mistakes.

Gozum brought in a Baked Alaska, shimmering beneath a gentian wildfire. Just as he set it down in front of the captain, the lights went out, the ship went quiet, and the emergency lanterns clicked on—with the candelabra the table suggested a town in a blackout.

The diesel was designed to start in five seconds.

"Six, seven, eight," Louie counted. He and Jerry were on their feet already. It took me a moment to realize that this was now my problem too; in fact, mainly my problem. We dashed from the wardroom, leaving the others behind in their formal setting like a childhood memory. The lights stayed out. The ship was hot, dark, and quiet. "Check on the diesel," Louie told me. The two of them disappeared into main control, and I followed the emergency lighting down the short passageway to the diesel room.

I was the first to arrive there. After undogging and opening the watertight door I reached for the light switch, which of course didn't work. The emergency lanterns were as pale as a car's headlights left on too long. Someone who belonged to me was supposed to test the batteries and replace the weak ones. The diesel stood, massive, complicated, in the cabined gloom, and if it had been a crop-duster in a barn I would have felt more confident trying to start it. There ought to be a large button under a rubber seal. So there was. I was about to press it when I had second thoughts. The switchboard circuitry should have sensed the loss of load and opened the starter valve automatically: I knew that much. If I bypassed this feature by starting the diesel myself, maybe the engine wasn't ready, or maybe it would start and stop, or overdrive the generator, or explode. Better to wait for my own people, the experts.

An electrician—one of my people but I didn't know his name, and the light was too low to read it on his shirt—came in, checked the switchboard, and pushed the diesel start button. Nothing happened. He looked at me with a blank expression. This was the extent of his knowledge too.

"Where's Horth?"

"Couldn't tell you."

"Go find him."

He frowned at me in my dress blues, an alien among machinery.

"I'm your division officer. You will call me *sir.*"

"Sir." He left and didn't return, but Louie arrived with a delegation, which included Horth. Louie pushed the button: nothing. He hauled Horth in front of him to push it: nothing. Shaking his head, Horth began to trace out wires, valves, air-lines. He couldn't explain it. This was the man who had forgotten more about diesel engines than I would ever know.

"What happened?" I asked Louie, mostly out of curiosity but also in case the answer might help me, dramatically, to push the button and start the engine.

"Lost the load," he said. "Number 1A boiler ruptured a tube again—probably a bad weld in Subic—and dragged down 2A before we could isolate it. No steam, no generator, no pumps: we're dead in the water. What happened here?"

I looked at him. Did he seriously think I could tell him? Apparently he did. In an emergency speculation is data. It's how mobs discover mob-rule.

"The starter hasn't budged," I said. "Either the valve failed to open—and I imagine it isn't that, it probably fails open—or there's no air in the flask. Horth, what's the pressure on that gage?" I didn't know that there *was* a gage, but it seemed reasonable, and the darkness covered the ignorance plain on my face.

"Minus ten," he replied.

"Can't be. Look again."

"Then zero."

"There you go," I said to Louie.

"The flask is empty? Horth, you let that happen?"

"No, zurr. The gage is probably out."

"Bullshit. Why isn't there any air in the flask?"

Horth was as silent as the ship.

"You were working on the engine this afternoon."

The engineman shook his head.

"When did you do that monthly on the start system?"

"What monthly is that, zurr?"

"Monthly maintenance: you bleed down the flask, in-spect and clean the start valve, test it, and pressurize the flask when you're done. I know you signed it off, Horth."

He nodded. "I remember. 'Twas the day after Thanks-giving, when the gun broke."

"And you haven't checked it since?"

"Shouldn't it have filled automatically," I asked, "from the service line?"

"Not if the fucking cut-out valve is shut, which it is. God: *damn* you, Horth."

The only course now was to go to the bridge, where the world was bright with the afternoon sun. Buster had the watch. The ship's brain trust was gathered around Marchand in his chair. "I'll do the talking," Louie said to me. I stood beside him, looking attentive and concerned while I was really thinking how strange it was to see the ship's bow, after so many days of leaping ahead, rising and falling like driftwood. The wind and seas had worked her around to the trough, and she was rolling thirty degrees to a side. We held the grab-bars and shifted our weight back and forth.

Like many engineers, Louie's bedside manner was to set low expectations. Without air in the flask, he said, the diesel wouldn't start. Without power, there was no way to run the air compressor to charge it, no way to get fuel to 2A, the good boiler, and no way to turn the propeller.

"How?" Marchand asked, shaking his head.

"Horth, Captain."

"God: *damn* him, I'll have his crow. This is your fault too," Marchand said to me.

Louie replied calmly: "I was in the space myself this afternoon. Hindsight's always twenty-twenty, but I didn't think to look at the pressure in the flask. Of course it isn't Chris's fault." This in a longish career was Louie's finest moment.

Silence. Probably Marchand thought about choking me and finishing off the job. Finally the XO asked, "Are you saying we have to be towed, Chief Engineer?"

"Yes sir."

"Surely you can relight the boiler."

"Not without fuel, water, and air, XO."

"Why can't we jury-rig a battery-powered starter?"

"The flywheel weighs two hundred pounds."

"So you're just going say Engineering can't do it?"

"Engineering *can't* do it, XO. These ships were built to be cheap, not redundant."

"I think there's a way," said Buster, standing aside with the OOD's binoculars around his neck. He looked sure of himself. This is when I had the thought that in an emergency speculation is as welcome as data.

Everyone was waiting.

The ship rolled; Buster rolled with it like a sailor born. "The torpedo tubes are launched by high-pressure air."

"So?" said Louie.

"In the torpedo room are two high-pressure air flasks— I expect they're full of air since the torpedomen, unlike your folks, pay attention to their maintenance—and I'll bet a month's pay each one is bigger than the flask on the diesel."

"So?"

"Just reroute the air into the service line."

"Great idea," I said, seeing my chance to get a punch in. "Except the air only goes in one direction, out the torpedo tubes. How do you get it back into the service line and down to me?"

"It's designed to go that way in an emergency," he said.

"There's a check-valve. A *one-way* check valve." Again, I didn't know this.

"And a bypass," he replied. "While you were getting your beans snapped, I traced it."

Marchand looked at Tyler, who shrugged. "Find out," he said. The idea of sending for a tug, of having to report a breakdown, a failure in the most elementary practice of seamanship, which couldn't be hidden from his superiors, was worse than a dose of the clap. Plus, he had seen Buster tracing systems in the torpedo room.

We did find out. Not only was Buster right, he had taken the trouble of tagging the bypass valve *Emergency H.P. Air Supply.* In five minutes the diesel flask was charged. In ten minutes the diesel was running and my electricians had closed the main breaker. In half an hour we were making eighteen knots again.

"We'll go back up," Louie said, "and face the music."

He was resolute. Again, his finest hour.

On the bridge Marchand was telling Buster a sea story. Louie and I had nothing new to report, so we waited until he was finished. Buster was lapping up every word. Marchand, though his eyes flicked toward us once or twice, concentrated on finishing his story, reaching out for Buster at the punch-line. Buster hooted, but without his usual derision, a tone of voice I had never heard before. *Good one, sir.* something like that, something a professional yes-man would say.

Marchand swiveled toward us and jerked a thumb at his protégé. "He saved your bacon, both of you. When we get in, you should buy him a roll in the hay."

That was our dismissal.

"We could take up a collection," I said to Buster after his watch, "only it's past your PCD."

"Maybe not, if we stay in WestPac long enough."

"That's your fault. Instead of steaming on to Subic, we could have been towed back to Hong Kong."

We were sitting in his stateroom beneath the mack, which he shared with Jerry Valade. Jerry was on watch. The room was well aft of the intakes, which made it quieter than mine, but the bulkhead constantly rattled with the flow of the exhaust gasses. So much pot metal everywhere: the ship was as cheap as a Chevy Vega.

He was polishing his boots with two fingers wrapped in a rag; it reminded me of the way Mary Sue painted. Already the mirror image was emerging. In my nearly five months of knowing him, I had never seen him spit-shine his boots. In fact hardly anyone polished theirs. His dress shoes yes. But he was a company man now.

"Speaking of which did Marie make her plane all right?"

"Dottie took her. Her new best friend."

"Just as you are the captain's."

"Say what you will, he recognizes talent. And no talent."

"It works out well for me. I don't have to deal with him."

"Louie will make an engineer of you—you won't have a choice, he's like someone left the TV on—and then you'll be more employable, you English major would-be writer has-been protester pot smoker." He reached for me.

I backed away. "Eventually pot will be legalized."

"Too bad until then, you'll have to watch out for the cops. But besides engineering you've learned that other employable skill, hypocrisy. What are you and Lény going to do? When we visit you in the afterlife, will she be Mrs. Professor *Clock?*"

Will you visit? I thought. Are we still friends? Am I big enough to want to be your friend if you have slipped past me in our rivalry? If you and Marie are Captain and Mrs. Captain will it be too awkward for you to receive me in my long hair and beard with my one or two books that didn't sell and my disillusioned Filipina wife?

"I guess we'll find out," I said. "Do you think she waited?"

"Since she's loyal I'm sure she did. Unfortunately for her—and for you."

"Still not in favor of the match. Both you and Marie."

"Tell me, Clock." He tossed down the rag and polish and leapt at me from the bunk, taking me by a handful of my coveralls, pulling and pushing me. "How are you going to get out of this?"

"Did you deliberately miss those people?" I asked.

An impasse: he wouldn't answer my question, and I had no idea how to answer his.

At lunch the next day, when the ship had nearly made up time, I wondered what the captain's mood would be. I didn't have to wait for the coffee course to find out. The wardroom table was full. By seniority the XO sat on the captain's right and Tyler on his left. Then Salty Bill, then the supply officer, then Louie, third on the right, and then the rest of us with me at the foot. As the steward brought around the main dish to each officer's left shoulder so the officer could serve himself, Marchand made some trite remark about how good it was to hear the sound of the boiler intakes.

Louie said, "What a difference a day makes, skipper!"

The XO, almost undetectably, winced. The others kept their heads down. I was directly opposite Marchand the length of the table, and Louie was halfway down—an obtuse triangle of address. There was nothing obtuse about the language. Marchand never raised his voice. He began, "Another day wouldn't make any difference if I had a working engineering department." *Then* he got personal, still speaking in a monotone. He supposed it was just to be expected when the head of the department had reached his level of incompetence—what was that called, Cheng?—oh yes, the Peter Principle: when that officer had lost the confidence of his people by habitually misrepresenting the truth; and when they, following his example, misled each other. He smiled at Louie calmly. "What should I expect?"

Praise in public, admonish in private is a leadership dictum almost sacred in the Navy. But Marchand had played football, whose culture was to call out lack of effort. Perhaps coaches think that humiliation improves performance.

Louie's face was as red as a boiler wall. He stroked his moustache as if it wouldn't lie down. He continued to sit with us, making an occasional comment on desultory subjects—once with a forced laugh—and after dessert he took his coffee to go.

Part Five
How I Cut Off My Devils

Glimpses of My Lost Love

A fter such a chewing-out, Louie took no chances with our arrival in port on one (suspect) boiler. For me this meant supervising the watch in the steering gear room, where we could control the rudder directly in case the bridge had a problem. Short of battle damage, this almost never happened. Usually the watch consisted of one qualified but lesser regarded helmsman from my old First Division, ready, in principle, to engage the wheel and steer by the compass repeater overhead. Today that was Kenton Emerson, one of those who had wanted my permission to marry his hooker. If the threat to kill me and throw my body into the Shit River hadn't come from Homer Williams, it might have come from him.

Louie had also assigned me and Michael Horth, who complained that if the steering engines failed he couldn't do a fooking thing about it. Nor could I, certainly. But perhaps Louie didn't trust Emerson to steer a straight course either. The compartment, about five feet high and squeezed into the stern, barely accommodated one man. Emerson sat at the wheel while Horth and I crouched on either side of him.

In this way, with no view of the outside world, I missed the pleasure of piloting in narrow waters, and I had no idea of our approach on the pier or who might be waiting there for us. I tried to picture our surroundings from the courses ordered and our approach on the pier from the engine bells. Who was conning? I didn't know. Tyler, perhaps, who had the experience here.

A touch of a backing bell, then Bailey, the boatswain's mate of the watch, passed the word, "Moored: shift colors" and a few minutes later, "Secure the Special Sea and Anchor Detail." Emerson pushed his hands sideways from his shoulders as if we were crowding him. All of us needed air.

Stiff and sore, I recoiled from the glaring light when I emerged on the fantail. A small crowd was waiting for us: some Filipino workers milling about in their hardhats; a few U.S. officers in khakis; and a loved one, Lény Rosales in a summer frock.

I went down the brow as soon as the crane had set it in place and swam against the stream. Lény and I had our public kiss, heart to heart and lips conscious of lips but without tears—without, I thought, that surrender of our selves one to the other. "Come with me," I said, which may have meant more than just this minute: as soon as I said it I looked at her to see if she took it as joyous news. I couldn't tell, but she let me hold her hand as we went onboard. "To the wardroom," I added, where any officer's guests became by custom a guest of all the officers.

She knew the way. By the time she was settled on the couch the room was full of shipyard workers. Louie gave her a glance then took my arm and hauled me to the table as he had hauled Horth to the diesel when the lights had gone out.

Sitting in the captain's chair, he presided, with Jerry Valade, his assistant for propulsion, on his right and me on his left. Around the table were several shop foremen, all Filipinos, and an American lieutenant from the shipyard commander's office, who would superintend the work.

Louie kidded him and the foreman of the boiler shop about the failure of their tube. The lieutenant didn't like the kidding, but the foreman grinned and gave it right back.

"Operator error," he said. His name was Ramon.

"We'll plug it," said the lieutenant.

"You'll *replace* the tube and dye-penetrate the weld."

"No need to go that far."

"We'll do it," Ramon said. "Whatever he wants."

"Then, Ramon, I want both boilers hydroed again and all the other new tubes tested at both ends."

The lieutenant shook his head but without further protest. He was under orders to get us back in the war as soon as possible.

"Who's my point of contact," Ramon asked.

I made the mistake of smiling at Lény, who smiled back, a neutral smile, noncommittal.

"Mr. Clarke here will be your contact," Louie said.

"I'm not qualified," I said. "And it's propulsion."

"I'll teach you everything you'll need. Here's an excellent opportunity for professional development. I assume there's nothing on your social schedule keeping you?"

"Come on, Louie," I said in a low voice. "Jerry's right here." He was, and he was listening unhappily; but he would never challenge one of Louie's many impulsive decisions. Louie, as he often reminded us, knew boilers. "Or if you must train someone, give it to Buster. He has the engineering background." Faced with such a threat to my well-being, I jumped to the same conclusion that Marchand had done on that fateful first day.

"You must have forgotten, mister—or perhaps you're distracted. Buster no longer works for me, being the gunnery officer—over my objection, I might add. He and Chief Letourneau will fix the gun. You will remain on board to ensure that we get underway on time, the most basic and

important mission of the ship, for which *our* department—
yours and mine—has the sacred responsibility.

"Mr. Clarke will be my point of contact," he repeated
to the room. "Ramon, why don't you and he meet at the
boiler to assess the work—say, in fifteen minutes? Mr.
Clarke, that will give you time to say goodbye to your
guest and change into coveralls."

Once again there was no choice but to quell the rebellion of my entire being with *aye-aye, sir.*

Lény had no apparent reaction to the news that a nonsense duty, after three months apart, would keep me from
spending time with her. We left the wardroom. She went
up the deckhouse ladder lightly and confidently, like a
sailor, her lovely fall of hair swinging back and forth.

My stateroom door was unlocked. Inside were two new
ensigns reporting to the ship after the naval academy and
summer leave. Their names were Jon Appleby and Mark
Fuller. Their cruise boxes, brass-cornered and lacquered,
had their names in Old English script; artifacts of their
midshipmen cruises and their hopes for a long career in
positions of increasing responsibility.

"Chris Clarke," I said. "This is my fiancée, Lény Rosales."
My voice was easy and confident, as if I were used to calling
her that. Though my throat was dry and I was conscious of
my feet. It often happens that we decide what we want
when we say it. This must be what I wanted, then.

Appleby was charmed and charming. "Four point oh
news. Congratulations, sir. Best wishes, ma'am—maybe
you have a friend here I could meet?"

She laughed, not quite easily and confidently.

Other than shaking hands, Fuller had nothing to say.

They had met XO Schmid and confirmed their new
jobs. Fuller was Buster's replacement as damage control
assistant and Appleby was mine as first lieutenant.

Appleby gave a sign, and the ensigns left. In the next moment Lény was in my arms again with every sign of surrender. I wondered if we would make love now despite the orders for me to report to the fireroom—urgent love-making, brief and sweet and binding.

But she pushed us apart as we kissed.

"You called me your fiancée."

"Yes. My wife-to-be."

"For three months you've been away and I've heard nothing. Nothing!"

"But I wrote to you. I did. Your letter to me was dropped in the sea—I couldn't read it. And I tried to call you from Hong Kong. I called the Chuck Wagon. Did he tell you?"

"Who?"

"I didn't get his name. A bartender? He said he'd give you my message."

"I don't work there anymore."

"Well, that would explain it. I'm sorry, Lény. I did try. I know it's been three months. I felt them."

"Three months of silence after three weeks of prom-ises, such as any man would make after—a fling!"

"Not a fling. My feelings are the same"—which was partly false—"I've thought about you constantly"—which was mostly true.

"Three months, Chris! How could I know that you meant what you said?"

Two thoughts flowed from this: first, that if I stayed in the Navy she would have to endure other separations much longer than three months; and second, interrupting the first like a low-voltage shock, that it sounded as if she were leading up to say that she was involved with some-one else.

She took a step backward as if from the necessity of delivering unwelcome news.

"It's been three months," I said calmly, "but that's a good thing in one way. It's given us time to understand how we really feel about each other. I know that I love you. I want you to be my wife"—for I had just declared that to Appleby and Fuller. "Do you still want to marry me?"

"No," she answered quickly.

"No?"

"No. Yes. Yes, I want to, but you don't."

"Will you believe that I do when you get on the airplane? We don't know when the ship is going home, but you could fly ahead and wait for me. You can live with my father. I'm ready to make the arrangements."

"I can't leave now. There's a problem."

"With Rose?" Or with the inconvenient fact of a lover?

"With Rose."

"What is it? Do you have to be in Subic? Can I help?"

Before she could answer this, Louie opened the door without knocking and ordered me below. He would escort Lény to the quarterdeck. I would put on my coveralls and start measuring up to my responsibilities. She reached for my hand—maybe to reassure me—but they were gone before I could ask how to find her.

Water Chemistry

Fuller and Appleby, waiting outside, returned to the room. Fuller's face said he was speaking for them both.

"We'll take the lower bunks."

"Fine with me, but isn't it a question of seniority?"

"That's right. We're senior to you."

"Oh? I don't generally keep the lineal list in my pocket, but I was commissioned on May twelfth. Isn't the naval academy graduation in June?"

"It is. But our commissions are retroactive to May first." He paused significantly with something like a glower. If nothing else the academy had taught him to smite his enemies. "By law. Ahead of ROTC and OCS."

"The law!"

"The naval academy is the premier commissioning source in the service. Founded in 1845. After Vietnam, when the officer pool is reduced, Congress will abolish the other two sources. We won't need them."

"Good news! Newport in winter is just beastly."

Appleby was smiling; a smile that seemed ready to burst into laughter with the slightest encouragement.

"Let's forget all that. Seniority! Seniority among ensigns is like virginity among whores. And the inverse...or the converse...I mean, virginity among ensigns is like...you know." Even botching the joke delighted him; he was delighted with everything. His life was one happy arrival after another.

I pulled down the mattress from the upper bunk on the captain's side of the room and replaced it with my own, sheets and blanket still tucked.

"No really, Chris," Appleby protested. "I like sleeping in the upper bunk." I smiled at him. Fuller looked at him as if betrayed. The two of them wound up sleeping in the tier across from me. With, I must admit, theatrical haste to show that I at least had somewhere important to be, I pulled on my coveralls and left.

The fireroom was unbearably hot and humid. Number 1A boiler, the one that had gone down on our transit, was cool by now and had been opened so the shipyard could fix it. Number 2A, however, was still running when I got there, although the ship had shifted to shore power and it wasn't needed. The first lecture Louie gave me was how to secure a boiler safely. Jerry and his people did that with 2A while Louie and Ramon and the lieutenant and I took turns squeezing inside 1A.

A red rag had been tied around the blown tube. Ramon had agreed to test the weld at each end with penetrating dye under ultraviolet light; but before giving the order, he examined the tube throughout its length.

"Here's the rupture," he said, pointing at eye level.

A rupture in the working surface of a boiler tube has nothing to do with its installation. The culprit is either a weakness in the steel—unlikely with a new tube—or frequent exposure to contaminated feedwater.

"Where's the test and treatment log?" Ramon asked.

"You won't learn anything there," Louie said. "We're very careful."

"Just to rule out the chemistry, please."

Louie had the log brought. He handed it to Ramon with a virtuous look on his face. "Nothing out of limits."

"Yet a rupture like this is always high chloride."

"You see the pH: consistently alkaline."

"Maybe. Maybe consistently too much boiler compound. Let's test for chloride directly." A wiry man with two inches of a kinky black pigtail squeezed into a hair tie, he wiggled out from the tube bundle, hopped down to the deck, drew a sample, and ran the test.

"Eighty-five parts per million. Too much salt, Louie! And such a nice tube, though not one of mine."

Louie shifted into his confidential voice. "Eighty-five. You're right, Ramon. I'll have somebody's head for this. But there's no point in playing who-shot-John when they need us on the gunline like yesterday."

"Yes, indeed. If only your gun worked."

Louie glanced at the lieutenant and me to see how much of this had made an impression. I had heard it all, but the lieutenant's mind seemed somewhere else.

"When we report the boiler fixed, I'll make sure we give full credit to your shop—you've saved us. I would like to include a line blaming the chemistry, but the old man would never go for that. It's fitness report season, you know."

"I'll replace the tube, Louie," Ramon said. "And I'll do the hydro and dye-penetrant tests you asked for. We both know the score. Fortunately, my workload is light—all your compadres are out fighting. You didn't need to bullshit me."

"I've always been a bullshitter," Louie laughed.

"What does the rupture look like?" I asked Ramon.

"A blister."

"Oh, let me see! Novice as I am, I'll bet I can recognize a blister. This will be good for my professional development, don't you think, Louie? A gundecked rupture?"

"You didn't need to be an asshole about it," Louie said when Ramon and the lieutenant had gone to write up the work order.

"Yet I know you'll always land on your feet."

"Water chemistry's been bad since we deployed. The captain is aware of it. He refuses to tell the elephants."

"And he doesn't like being corrected. I do know that. Since we're letting down our hair, Louie, may I go now? It's nothing important, merely the rest of my life."

But my tone was a mistake. I would have done better to appeal to his vanity. Or to his sympathy, for he was capable of that too when not under pressure. He drew himself up to his full five feet six inches and sniffed. *"Au contraire,* my friend: I've put you in charge of repairing this boiler. You may go ashore when you've completed your assignment."

"That's just unreasonable."

"Or to the shop to learn from Ramon, but that's it."

"Come on, Louie. This isn't my boiler, it's Jerry's. And you're watching this anyway, boiler tech that you were. If it's more work you want from me, after I see her I prom-ise to fix the logs and records of the equipment I do own. They're a mess, as you know."

"You own what I say you own, mister. It's not a democ-racy, and we don't have a union here. You work for me, and you *will* obey orders. And don't bother going to Tyler or the XO: they'll tell you the same thing. This is good for you, *Kemo sahbee.* Ah? Ah?"

He smiled that toothy smile beneath the moustache.

No Longer the Favorite

I stayed in the fireroom until Louie left. By then Jerry and his people had shut down 2A and prepared it for the hydro test. As I was about to leave, a shipyard worker arrived with a welding machine and a new tube for 1A. Out of curiosity I watched him replace the tube. In doing so he found a blister in a nearby tube and on his own initiative replaced that as well.

The work took us past lunch. Although I did nothing but watch, my coveralls were soaked in sweat. Even the weather decks, with the impassive sun overhead and the hot wet blanket of humidity sitting on the ship, felt like a refuge. All the mistakes were piling up. I could never be an engineer; physically could never stand it.

I didn't look for Tyler or the XO, as Louie had feared I might. I looked for Buster.

He was not in the gun house, where Chief Letourneau was in earnest conversation with an American civilian about the hydraulic fitting. I waited in the door until I was noticed; despite Chief Beatty's best efforts to boost my reputation, I was not popular in the chiefs' mess. No, Letourneau said finally, Mr. Billings *had* been there—his tone suggested that all division officers should be so conscientious—but had been called to the captain's cabin.

In the alcove I listened at the other door, making out two familiar voices, one commanding, the other obliging, but not their words. Among the power panels on the bulkhead, I punched off the air conditioning. This would give me a few minutes' grace before they noticed the heat. God help me if I had punched off the compressor for CIC—I hadn't bothered to read the fine print on the label.

Fuller was in our stateroom, at his desk. Without acknowledging him I climbed into my bunk in my sweaty coveralls and lay on the woolen blanket. Through the now-silent duct the voices spoke like two tin cans and a string, but the words were clear.

Marchand was teaching Buster shiphandling, in this case how to approach the pier. Perhaps he was drawing ship silhouettes as Tyler had done for me at the Texas Bar. I was a minute understanding that this was actually a critique, that it was Buster who had made the landing coming in here, when I had crouched under the low overhead in the steering gear room.

And another minute understanding that praise was intended. Apparently Buster had conned the ship brilliantly again—there was lots of purring on both sides. He seemed happy to learn from his tutor about the effects of wind, tide, and inertia without mentioning that I had taught these same things to him in the sailboat. But Marchand spoke of other things too, I must say in fairness, things I hadn't taught him: that slower is faster; that workmanlike is safer than flashy and just as pleasing to remember; that assuming your plan will work is both dangerous and unrealistic; and that before taking the conn you should think of what might go wrong and always have an escape route.

It's a lot of responsibility, you know, the one voice said.

Yes sir, I hope to shout.

A multimillion dollar ship and two hundred lives.

Absolutely.

All the time my officers are working the ship, I am rehearsing those emergency commands.

Right: the flip side of conning.

You have a talent for this. You could go a long way. This is your life I'm talking about, mister.

I know it. Thank you, sir. Don't you think it's hot in here?

Looking for My Lost Love

In the fireroom all the problematic tubes on 1A had been replaced and the hoses hooked up to pressure-test the tube bundle. Jerry was overseeing this, as he should have been. He said that Louie was hard down, making up for the nights without sleep (and for the anxiety and guilt, I would have said). I returned to my stateroom, showered, and changed into khakis.

I left the ship and, adhering strictly to my orders, walked to the boiler shop on a last foot-pound of indigna-tion. There I met Ramon, who wanted me to sign off the job. I thought I didn't care—a job order, a confession of murder: what did it matter?—until, reading more closely, I felt a qualm about taking responsibility for such an im-portant thing before the tests had been completed.

Ramon expected me to sign, and from our short ac-quaintance I trusted him as a person. But he was a for-eigner, with his own view of the world which I couldn't know. I remembered the comments at the pig roast. Were the Filipinos really our friends? Or were they, while pock-eting our money, impatient for us to be gone—secretly rooting for the North? And did that include the woman I loved, whose country might become my country too?

After a moment I added a comment, *Pending results of testing,* and signed the order. Then he signed, without

the comment that no doubt he wanted to make: *quibbler,
weakling, coward.*

Instead of returning to the ship I walked through the
main gate, past the Marine guards, past the long list of
those arrested for violating curfew, and under the *job safety
starts here* banner, on the other side of which was Shit
River, which seemed symbolic. No Americans were throwing coins, and no Filipino urchins were diving for them. In
fact the town seemed to have emptied as if the mother lode
had run out. The importuners who came up to me didn't
seem any more interested in what they were selling than I
was. There were no smells of pot, dust, shit, tobacco, jitney
exhaust, or monkey meat on a stick. No music came out of
the night clubs, whose doors hung open with the lights out
inside.

I knew the way out of town without having to think
about it. After the last shanty the country road was im-
proved by grass and gravel, and the farms began. Lény's
farm was third on the right. I say *her farm,* but she was
only a lodger, living in the shack sanctified by our love.
The farm was poor and small: a hand-tilled crop and a
few animals hanging out near the house. This part was
all the same. Here, unless I broke my word, awaited the
rest of my life. In a moment all would be settled and on
her terms. I was aroused by the thought of this and also
afraid of it.

The door was unlocked, but no one was inside and her
belongings were gone, including the portrait. There was
no trace of her wholesome hopeful passionate self.

I went around to the other side of the house, where in
the barnyard a woman in a man's undershirt and over-
sized trousers was feeding chickens. For a surreal instant
I thought it was Lény, but it was the farmer's wife, in her
fifties, making her honest living, untouched by the sordid
town. Recognizing me, she shook her head: Lény had

moved away. Did she know where? To the base, she said, which gave me not more than a hundred places to look.

Back on the base I walked to the Chuck Wagon. A bartender was on duty, but there were no customers. Quite likely he was the man who had taken my call from Hong Kong. He hadn't known Lény then, and he didn't know her now. Nor were Bert and the Bonanza Boys playing there—the drum kit had been removed from the bandstand—he thought they had gone to the resort in Baguio. I could feel the energy draining from the place. When we withdrew from Vietnam, the ships would stop coming here. Eventually the Filipinos would get their wish, and their land would belong to them again. Olongapo would clean up its act and become the leading city of Luzon.

My presentiments were interrupted by Bert himself. He had come for the microphone, which the bartender was reluctant to let him have. They argued in Tagalog until the bartender gave in. Bert was still worked up about it when I approached him, a ghost from the past. He struggled to get control of himself, and I had to smile at this, for it reminded me of myself in the Navy. What was subordination but another kind of self-service?

Each of us remarked that it was good to see the other, then I asked about Lény.

"Hard to say. She's here somewhere, doing office work. Some new boss."

"And Rose?"

"Oh sure. Say hi to Buster."

His evasiveness didn't come naturally to him; he must be following instructions. Maybe all her friends, maybe everyone here was in on her love life. For a native woman to marry an American and leave the country might take a village.

Over a beer and a burger I tried to reason my way to
her. She was somewhere on the base. *Office work* might
include the Navy Exchange, the library, the USO, the
putt-putt, the sailing center, the bowling alley, the theater, even the chapel. But she had met the ship; how had
she known about that? After changing course to Subic
(and after Buster had solved the small problem of making
our propeller turn), we had sent our ETA by radio message. She must have seen it or heard from someone who
had (I didn't want to think that she had heard it from the
hookers' grapevine). This suggested some official place:
the shipyard, the harbor master, the base commander's
headquarters, where Admiral Locke's picture hung on
the wall by right.

Finishing my meal, I went to those places, but only
their duty offices were open, and no one, American or Filipino, seemed to know about her.

This was lunacy, as my mother used to say. Lény had
been in my arms just this morning. If she worked here,
she might be living nearby. In fact, she might be in any
of these buildings around me. If she looked out her window she would see me. If I stood here long enough there
might be another embrace, a renewed declaration of love,
a betrothal, a resolution finally.

A few hardhats moved between the shipyard and the
piers. Besides *John Shafer* two fat ships were in port: an
ammunition ship receiving her new load of death and a
tender with no clients to tend. All the sailors had been
swallowed up in the immensity of the war. As was I, alone
on the sidewalk, waiting like a fool.

On the hopeful thought that she might have returned
to the ship, I did too.

When I stepped on the quarterdeck, the watch presented Mr. DiGiovanni's compliments and would I report
to him at my earliest convenience? This traditional

phrasing, unusual in WestPac, meant *Right now, fool.*
Louie was in his stateroom with the door open, sitting at
his desk, giving me his back. Without personal address
he said over his shoulder, "Did you sign off the boiler job?"

"I did, pending the results of the tests."

"At the shipyard. With Ramon, as I instructed."

"That's where I signed it."

"And then straight back here. Awfully late."

"Will you turn around, please?"

"You will call me *sir.*"

"Will you turn around, please, sir?"

I closed the door, which completed the confinement.

His angry face. "Did you come straight back here?"

"I went to look for Lény. As you knew I would. So what?"

"The hydro failed. There's another leak. We're delayed.
Which you would know if you had obeyed orders."

"That's too bad. What's the captain going to do?"

"The point is, what am I going to do *with you?*" But he
had an answer to that, for he picked up a paper from his
desk and poked it at me. It was a disciplinary report chit
for violations of the Uniformed Code of Military Justice.
Ensign Christopher Higginson Clark, USNR, followed by
my service number (but with two digits transposed), was
accused of dereliction of duty, disobeying a lawful order,
and conduct unbecoming an officer.

"Conduct unbecoming an officer?"

"Your affair with a host national."

"That's rich, coming from you, married to a Japanese."

He leapt up. "Yes: coming from me. It all comes from
me, the rewards and the penalties. I am your lawfully appointed superior officer. Your life is mine. You do as I say."

"In a pig's eye."

"Then you can make your case at Captain's Mast. Look at Block 15."

Block 15, *Pre-trial confinement,* was checked.

"What does that mean?"

"You're under arrest. Moral arrest. You will not leave the ship. If you do—if you even try to leave the ship—I will send you to the brig in handcuffs. No, be silent. You may continue with your duties or not, as you like. I don't care: you've lost my trust. Dismissed, sir."

A Consultation

Louie would cool down. He didn't like a quarrel. He had given me the report chit so as not to go through the ship's office. Its only legal force was my sense of honor. If I left the ship right this minute and found Lény wherever she was and took her to the chapel and married her, he would be at our reception, happy for both of us. So I told myself.

I was lying in my bed with the air conditioning off. My roommates were elsewhere—probably observing the boiler work, a marquee attraction for new officers. I was dozing about various revisions of my life. The door to the captain's cabin opened and shut and two voices resumed a conversation.

It wouldn't hurt to go, don't you think? For an hour?

Why not? Can't dance and it's too wet to plow.

You know the rules are somewhat relaxed out here.

Do I! I did serve on shore patrol.

It hasn't anything to do with our lives back home.

Which is mighty convenient to think so.

They think so too, at home.

I'm not so sure. She'd about kill me.

Wardrooms have a sense of honor about these things.

She'd know in a heartbeat. She reads my thoughts.

Then don't think about it. My marriage is strong, you know. Dottie doesn't care what I do, and I feel the same about her. It works better for us. It's the modern world.

But sad, yes?

No, not sad. Monogamy is a Hallmark scam.

Surely more fun to look at it that way.

You have one life, young man. Which goes fast. It's a mistake to pass up your chances for happiness.

Or guilt.

You miss a block, you turn the page. She likes you.

This went unanswered, and *she* went unidentified. A couple of minutes passed. The door opened and shut, and footsteps climbed the ladder to the bridge. Out of the hundreds of footsteps on ladders then and the thousands since then, I will always remember his, whose every step anticipated something wonderful when he reached the top, something never there.

He was standing at the centerline compass repeater as if conning the ship but with his head down. The door clicked shut behind me. He looked up.

"Christ Almighty! Your face!"

"There's nothing particular about my face," I said.

"What happened?"

"I'm on report. Actually, I'm under arrest. Can't you see my moral handcuffs?"

I showed him the chit. Now that we were in port, the bridge had lost its wonder. The status boards had been swung up and pinned to the overhead. The stadimeter, binoculars, and code books had been locked away. Among them was the ship's wheel, locked away lest someone steal it. On the other hand the brightwork shone in the dusk like amber. XO Schmid, son and grandson of fighting admirals, had ordered all the useless brass painted over but insisted that the rest shine out of sailors' pride.

Next to the compass repeater was a table embedded with a plastic maneuvering board. On this were a grease pencil and rag, dividers, parallel rulers, and the tactical manual, as if we were underway in formation. Evidently Buster had been practicing when Marchand had called him to the cabin. Embarrassed that I had found him out, he took more time than necessary reading the chit.

"Well," he said, "what can they do: send you home?"

"Why not? And why not me?"

"Because it's all hands on deck. Because we need every man-jack in the fight until the enemy gives up. *Because the war depends on you, Clockie!*" he shouted, grabbing my arms and pinning them back, chest to chest.

"It's an abuse of power," I said after freeing myself.

"Have you ever read your Navy contract?"

"Actually, no."

"Me neither. I could take a message to Lény."

"I don't know why Louie is being such a jerk."

But this sounded like whining, and I expected Buster in his present mood to thump me again. Instead he grinned. "I can tell you that. He's under investigation for gundecking the boiler chemistry logs."

"But he said Marchand knew all about it."

"Oh, yes. And *he's* under investigation too. By the commodore. We've been running high chloride for months. The tubes in both boilers are like to have an aneurism, yet the logs are perfect. Of course it will all be white-washed, unless poor Tom Roper, the oil and water king, takes the fall."

I frowned, not at the news. Calling an enlisted man by his first name was unprofessional. Yet that was Buster's way, and the men loved him.

He started to shadowbox me. "And you thought you had problems."

"Don't," I said, and he stopped. "It all comes back to Marchand, doesn't it."

"*Captain* Marchand." But he might have been joking.

"Captain Marchand. You reap what you sow. How would you take a message to her?"

"I'm invited to a party at the Q tonight. She and Rose will be there, according to him. He says Rose is sweet on me, or I'm sweet on her, I forget which it's supposed to be. As if I would break my marriage vows—which I have never done, as you will remember—with some bosomy Lolita."

Two boxes to the shoulder, which hurt.

"What's up, Mr. Clock?"

What was up was that my fiancée, after three months of not seeing me, whom she professed to love, and on the day that I had proposed marriage and a new life to her, was taking her slutty sister to some nighttime bacchanal with her former lover. Three months: she could have slept with him or any number of men in that time. I knew how much she liked sex and how easily she consented. Then I pictured her face, her loyal loving smile. Could appearances really be that deceptive?

"You seem dangerously puissant," I said.

"Can't say I've ever heard that word before. But I certainly am dangerous."

"What happened with you and Rose at the pig roast?"

"How you carry on."

"No, I mean it, Buster."

"She got a little frisky." He grinned. "Or I did."

"Marchand is manipulating you. He's still mad about the beach walkers."

"I can see that *somebody's* mad. Or envious." Shadow-boxing. "In the next big one I'll be Admiral Nimitz."

"More like Halsey, who stumbled into two typhoons."

"Arleigh Burke, then. The quintessential destroyerman. Hey! Quintessential!"

"Do you really think you're his buddy all of a sudden?"

"What I think," he said, and now he was calm again, "is that he and his wife have an understanding, as some couples do, and even so he might be feeling what we're all feeling, that the war is lost and yet we don't know when we're going home."

"I know when I'm going home."

"Don't go home married, old son."

"Did you do it?" I asked. "Miss those people on purpose?"

"Enjoy your house arrest or whatever it is."

Doctors have a term for what happened next: *the doorknob comment;* often the real purpose of the consultation.

"I suppose I don't *have* to go," Buster said.

But if he were looking for advice, I had already begun reading the next patient's record.

A Second Opinion

In the engineering office, as an act of self-righteousness, I pulled out the maintenance records of my two divisions. I began with the emergency diesel. A third of the cards were missing, and another third didn't match the book.

Some were crossed out with a note: *Not needed don't do.*
Michael Horth! I began to make a list of discrepancies,
grew discouraged, and took the whole mess up to the
wardroom, a more agreeable setting to help me concen-
trate. Instead, of course, my attention lapsed into a reverie about my wayward fiancée.

The door opened and someone came in. I made a point
of not looking up until he walked over and stood over me.
I could identify him by aura: the XO.

"Grab your lid, Mr. Clarke. We're going to dinner."

Didn't he know? But he was second in command.

"So late, XO? It's almost eight o'clock."

"In the Navy we call that twenty hundred—eight bells,"
he said with a pleasant smile.

"Yes sir. But actually I can't. Louie wrote me up."

He recited the chit to me verbatim, including the check
in the box. "You may assume that I have the authority to
lift your arrest."

"And dismiss the charges?" But I knew he could do this.

"It depends on you. Put all that away and be on the
quarterdeck in civilian attire in five minutes."

He started to leave. I asked, "Are we going to the Q?"

"They don't serve meals there. Five minutes."

A cab was waiting at the brow, one of the many that
usually bustled through the base but the only one I saw
tonight. It took us around the bay and up a hill toward a
low rambling building at the top. This was the officers'
club at Cubi Point, the naval air station. Buster had described it from his time with the shore patrol. Then the
place had been packed with manic aviators. Their favorite bar game was *Dead Ant:* whenever the *ant-master*
would yell "Dead ant!" all of them would drop to the floor
with their arms and legs in the air; the last to die bought
drinks for the house and became the next ant-master.

Stupid fun, but when they returned to Yankee Station, some among them attacking the North would be killed, maimed, or captured, so why not? At one end of the swimming pool a primitive cockpit required you to push *the landing button* instantly when a light came on or be ejected into the water. A test of reflexes and athleticism, but also a metaphor of my own life as I groped for the button.

The club was empty tonight, of course. The headwaiter seated us beside a picture window that overlooked the harbor. *John Shafer* could just be seen at her berth, an unwieldy toy whose mack looked like a handle for lifting it from the bathtub. The two fat ships. Otherwise the view was romantic and beautiful. From this elevation it didn't seem that salty boilers or extended deployments or any other trouble amounted to much—maybe that was the XO's point in bringing me here.

The waiter, a handsome older man with long shining hair brushed back from his forehead, took our orders with his hands along his trouser seams. Buster had said that he was famous at the club, a former colonel in the Philippine army and a survivor of the Death March who could remember the orders for a table of twenty. On the jungle peninsula behind this building he must have led thousands of men. No doubt he could remember every position in the retreat, assumed, assailed, and lost. No doubt he would know what to do about me...without mercy.

When he had served the coffee, etiquette allowed the XO and me to talk about work.

"So," he asked with a smile. "Where's Chris tonight?"

"Making a mess of everything, apparently."

Schmid's face was compellingly pleasant; intelligent, interested, quick to find humor, and fair-minded both by character and experience. Beneath a receding, militarily correct crewcut his slightly protuberant, rich brown eyes shone like liquid; he used them to examine the world not to draw attention to himself—he didn't need that. His bushy eyebrows were grizzled, and his nose was large. Sometimes his shapely lips tasted the words before he spoke them.

"P-p-p-p. What part of the mess shall we tackle first? Personal or professional?"

"Personal."

No doubt this salacious item was what he wanted too, but he waited for me to begin.

"The chief personal question," I said, "is shall I marry my Filipino girlfriend?"

"That's easy: you shouldn't." He shook his head.

"Why not?"

"First, you don't know her. Second—and sorry, I'm guessing this by your age—you don't know much about women in general. Third, and wrong as it is, she will always be a drag on your career if you want one."

I could have a career, even now.

"And yet," I pointed out, "the wife of the chief of naval operations, the senior admiral in the Navy, is a Russian."

"Yes—a European. A round-eye, though I hate that term. I told you it isn't right, but that's the reality of it, and you asked for my advice. Wait until we get home then find yourself a good-looking California girl. Someone—"

"Yes?"

"—who can keep up with you intellectually. For better or worse, that narrows the pool."

"That's nice of you to say. So unlike everybody else, you don't think it's about sex."

"It might be sex. It might be love. Assume that's what it is. We humans fall in and out of love all the time. But you won't know if it's *true love* until you see how she fits into the life you want for yourself. Are you willing to take that chance sight unseen?"

"And the professional mess?" I asked.

"Quit pissing on the captain. You can't hurt him, except a little in his vanity, but he can ruin your career and your self-confidence too. Practice YARC."

"YARC?"

"You are right, Captain."

"Yes, good advice onboard the starship *Enterprise*. Or in the Nixon cabinet, apparently. Wouldn't you have reported the gun casualty?"

"I don't know, and you don't either. Who can imagine the pressure of a decision like that? When a ship is going well, there's an overwhelming temptation to project her performance as a success story, no matter what."

"No matter how salty the boilers are."

He smiled grimly. "That's to be determined. I assume you don't wish bad things for your department head. The captain's position is a bit different."

"Different how? I mean, how could it be?"

"You and I: we do our job, we get feedback constantly. The captain goes for days or weeks, and no one tells him how he's doing. He can only imagine what his superiors, miles away, must be thinking. You need a lot of faith in yourself not to hear carping voices."

"Didn't *you* advise reporting the casualty, XO?"

He tossed his napkin down. Coffee slopped over the saucer and onto the tablecloth to make a shape like the Soviet landmass. After a dinner party my mother used to grieve over coffee stains and wine stains. The advent of Axion, the enzymatic stain remover, seemed to her more representative of progress than the moon landings, and the ban on it for environmental reasons a greater tragedy than Lear. For a moment I felt bad for our heroic waiter,

having to deal with this. But human beings, besides falling in and out of love all the time, make messes.

"A very junior officer," Schmid said quietly, "no matter
how talented, doesn't get to ask a question like that. Don't
assume that you alone possess all the wisdom of the ages
and everyone else is an idiot."

"I've been told that before," I said. "It seems obvious I
don't belong here."

"That's always possible: the Navy's not for everyone.
But if so, don't you want to leave on your own terms?"

"Why was I transferred to Engineering and taken off
the watch bill? I was doing well!"

"The only reason a commanding officer needs: he'd lost
confidence in you."

"And why has he all of a sudden made a project out of
Buster?"

"The same reason: Buster has earned his confidence.
These things aren't objective."

"What's going to happen now?" I asked. "To me."

"Yes please, a refill," he said to the waiter, who had
brought a pot, a clean cup and saucer, and a new tablecloth, which he installed as expertly as a nurse changing
a patient's sheets under him. In one hand he held the
bundled linen and with the other he poured the coffee.

"To tell you the truth," the XO went on, "I don't know.
The captain and I haven't talked about you since Hong
Kong. When you told me you two had had a problem"—
but I hadn't told him that, maybe Tyler had—"I didn't
appreciate how serious it was."

"He said he wanted to choke me to death."

"I'm sure that was just the heat of the moment." He
laughed. "I guess I'm sure."

"Am I going home, XO?"

"P-p-p-p. Show a good attitude and hope for the best. He's more susceptible to flattery than you might think— he knows he's being flattered, but he thrives on it, he's been flattered since Pop Warner football. Be kind to him. We're awfully short-handed even with the new ensigns. If he forgets the whole thing and gives you another chance—probably your last chance, I might add—it will be one less headache for him."

"I think I am going home."

But he wouldn't be taking all this time with me if he thought so too.

"Why don't we leave that for the future?" he said. "Being here might relax him." Both of us knew what that meant. I must ask him about this so-called party at the Q tonight. "You, on the other hand, need to keep your eyes in the boat. Let Lény get on with her life now."

"So everyone tells me. But thank you. I do appreciate your interest."

"What was it you said to him anyway?"

"I congratulated him on the kudo from the admiral."

"Yes, I can imagine your tone of voice." Another smile flickered across his face. In that smile I saw again the three generations of Schmids, dealing with the problems of sailors, God love them, which never changed. It must be wonderful to know the rules of your life so early and so well.

The Pool Party

The XO and I returned to the ship just before evening colors. As we went onboard I looked aloft: the captain's absentee pennant was flying. I hesitated on the brow, but the XO reached back and carried me with him.

The movie had been held until he returned. It was a favorite of his, *Thunderball,* with Sean Connery as James Bond. In those days before video-on-demand, the evening movie was a treat; I cannot think of it without nostalgia. The white screen glistening like granulated sugar. The projector, hot and bright and tricky to thread, bidding us escape into other lives but threatening to melt the film unless the story advanced. The three metal reels, heavy with celluloid and promise, in their olive-green hardened cases with their double canvas security straps (how easy it is to pirate a film today!). The movies themselves, which showed life bigger than itself. Irresistible!

(Irresistible: in 1975 the cruiser *Belknap* collided with the carrier *John F. Kennedy,* killing eight and melting *Belknap's* superstructure in the fire because her captain, during a dangerous maneuver when he should have been on the bridge, couldn't bring himself to leave the movie.)

James Bond whirled and fired into a bleeding eye. I watched him with growing desire. I wished I too were swimming underwater in a bright blue sea beside a full-breasted beauty in a wetsuit. It ought to be possible to love all the beauties, savoring the best from each. This one with the nice breasts. That one with the indestructible hopes. Another who would challenge me intellectually. The XO and Marie Billings (despite her bigotry) had been right: I wasn't ready to settle down, particularly after an acquaintance of three weeks confused by sex.

And yet. I could see further than they gave me credit for. I could see this person and me in settled middle age, living in our clapboard university house; treating each other with tenderness and respect; enjoying our shared life, raising our children, mindful of our blessings and never feeling cheated that one day death would end them. She was within a year of being as well educated as I was. If not as brainy—unclear at this point—well, personality and character go a long way toward intelligence. Colleges accept applicants for many reasons besides the academic. If they see what they like, they ask only if the candidate can do the work. Lény could do the work.

The movie ended. As the beam of the projector was switched off, I went outside into the cloying darkness. Beside me was the shore steam line, rancid with its hot-canvas smell. From the shipyard came the rhythmic beat of a pile-driver.

After taps, in some guise of dedication, I made a tour of the engineering spaces. Boiler tubes were coming in and out amid the snap and flare of welding torches. Louie was at the center of it, doing his best. For a few minutes I watched from the upper catwalk without being discovered. Then I returned to my room and sat at my desk awhile. Then I went below again.

As luck would have it—better or worse luck, only time would tell—Homer Williams had the quarterdeck watch.

Giving him his due as a person of authority, I walked to the brow, turned, and saluted, saying, "I have permission to go ashore, sir." In those days enlisted men had to show liberty cards, but officers, being gentlemen, were assumed to tell the truth. No doubt at that instant the Secretary of the Navy, who had signed my commission, felt a throb of pain.

Williams, even as he returned the salute, looked at me skeptically. Notwithstanding the XO's intervention, he may have heard of my arrest; perhaps there was a note in the log about it. If he stopped me now I would be too mortified to insist. The ship would get underway tomorrow, I would never see Lény again, and my life would take a different path.

"Curfew's at midnight, Mr. Clarke."

"Thanks, bosunmate. I'm not leaving the base."

"That's right, sir. The PC are everywhere, and they're sweeping up Americans as well as Filipinos."

Which hadn't stopped him from jumping ashore himself a few months ago. But perhaps it was true that he'd reformed. Responsibility can do that. Nor was he incapable of regret. For one thing he had put on his inspection whites to stand this watch.

"I'll be careful." I stepped onto the brow then turned to him. "I'm sorry about our bad start. You'll be happier now without a division officer in your way."

Obviously, since it meant that the needs of the Navy—someone to run First Division—would outweigh his conduct, his example, even his own health. I shouldn't be surprised if he was still here when all his detractors were gone.

He saluted me again. "Mr. Appleby seems an excellent young officer, sir. Quite the seaman, like yourself."

"Right." I had forgotten that Appleby had replaced me.

Lighted by its own spotlights, the BOQ stood like a tall, self-righteous missionary among the short heathens. The swimming pool, beside the building, was also lighted, though the lights were mostly hidden from me by palm trees. To get there I had to go through the main entrance,

where a Filipino steward at the front desk asked if I was
with Admiral Locke. I said I was, no doubt causing the
Secretary of the Navy more pain. At the end of a covered
passage was a door. I pushed it open and walked onto the
slippery concrete margin, feeling that extra degree of
chlorinated heat and humidity that is a pool's own atmos-
phere and feeling too the heaviness of the hour and the
burden of my task.

Byron wrote, "There was a sound of revelry by night."
I expected revelry, the sound and sight of it. But he wrote
before the age of swimming pools, where the revelry is
wholesome by design, where the most trouble you can get
into is running instead of walking or turning yourself into
a human cannonball to rain on squealing sunbathers. If I
expected lewdness I was disappointed. Two people, a man
and a woman, were racing. Where the bottom sloped into
the deep end, my captain and Tyler Brock were playing
frisbee football with three young women; all of them up
to their necks and bouncing on their tiptoes or treading
water except for one tall beauty whom I recognized as Tiffany from the Texas Bar. The shallow end was *3'* and *4'*
by its markings, and the steps leading into it were broad
and gradual. Not just wholesome but family-friendly. At
some point, in a less dangerous time, the tour of duty in
the Philippines had been what was called "accompanied,"
and the pool had been built for families.

Two people were sitting on the steps so that the water
lapped around their hips: my friend and my fiancée.

Taking off my shoes and socks and rolling up my
pants, I sat beside my friend, who gripped me around the
shoulders to give my nipple a Texas twister. "Old Clock,"
he said. "The party crasher. Aren't you on report?"

Young as I was, old and wise as I thought myself, but
young and awkward and foolish as I look back now, I

leaned across him and offered my hand to Lény. "How do you do? I'm Chris Clarke. Pleased to meet you."

"Stop," she said softly.

Buster climbed out of the way.

"You look like someone I'm engaged to marry. Perhaps I'm mistaken."

"Who would want to marry old Clock?" he snorted from behind us.

"I must be mistaken, for my fiancée would have spent the evening with me instead of joining a bacchanal."

"Just keep talking, bacchanal-brains."

"Shut up, Buster."

"Oh, you sweetheart. You beat all."

I stepped into the water, facing her, hands on hips. "What's going on, Lény? Why are you here? What's going on with us?"

The swimmers reached our end of the pool, the woman touching first. They stood up with water streaming from their faces; laughed and shook hands, and the woman gave him a hug and a kiss in the vicinity of his ear. She was Rose, voluptuous in a midnight blue bikini with subtle dots and dashes like a message in Morse code. The man vaulted out of the pool as competitive swimmers do and put on a top, a shirt like a net, years ahead of its time. He had the physique for it, slim and muscular and deeply tanned. His black dripping hair assumed its former shape, an attractive military cut with a widow's peak. I knew him. I had seen his portrait, it was all over the base. A jock, a naval aviator, a fighter pilot, able to fling himself all over the sky and all over my life.

Seeing me, a stranger, uninvited, he came across and stretched out his hand.

"Mojo Locke."

"Yes sir. Chris Clarke."

"You're Bill Marchand's officer."

"Yes sir."

"And Buster's friend"—nodding at him. "And Lény's."

"Old Clock?" Buster said. "I've had pigs who were better friends."

"Mr. Clock is a Harvard man," Marchand said, wading into the conversation as Tyler and the women trailed him. "Raw talent. We're still finding the best fit for it."

"Clock or Clarke?" Mojo asked.

"Clarke, sir. Clock is a joke. And the captain's right, I did go to school in Cambridge, but M.I.T. not Harvard."

"*I* went to Harvard," Mojo said. "The school of government. I was a fresh-caught lieutenant commander. The happiest year of my life. Come to think of it, I had a professor there named Clarke."

"War and politics? Higginson Clarke? My father."

A slow smile broke upon Mojo's lips. He was a handsome man. At the naval academy he would have been one of those midshipmen certain to become an admiral. Louie told me later that Mojo was his academy nickname or perhaps his aviator call sign, he didn't know which. Before making flag he had commanded the carrier *Yorktown* when—another coincidence—Buster and I had ridden her to our ship. As a "fresh-caught" admiral he had been slated for Washington duty, but in the national emergency that Vietnam had become, his experience with carrier aviation was needed at Subic, and he was shanghaied here—perhaps I should say *olongapoed*—leaving his wife and children in San Diego. This year would not have been the happiest of his life. Perhaps he was making it more tolerable by taking a mistress.

My feelings were all mixed up. I was sure that my days in the Navy were numbered, and I wanted them to be. The presence of Tiffany and her friends and the way she

hung on Marchand disgusted me. I was jealous of Mojo—
he and Lény were so easy with each other: what was in
their past? what were they now?—but my more canny self
foresaw that if an officer so powerful liked me, Marchand
would find it difficult to send me home. Perhaps there
was a job here for me in Mojo's headquarters, where I
could serve out my contract and be with Lény too. To
learn how she would fit into the life I wanted for myself.
Lapsing into fantasy, I pictured a kindhearted counseling
session in which I asked him, who knew all the parties
concerned, how my father would react if I brought her
home as my wife.

Assuming that she wasn't already taken.

On the other hand Mojo's mistress might be Rose. I
thought this because, after beating him in the race and
hugging and kissing him, whose loins couldn't help being
warmed by her heat, she ignored him, as a coquette might
do—turned her back on him to slip a summer frock over
her splendid body and affected a lack of interest from
then on. Surely that meant something. If I was right, it
would be good for me and safe for Buster.

With the games concluded, the drinking got serious.
One of Tiffany's friends got so drunk, so drowning-in-the-
water drunk, that Buster and I carried her to a lounge
chair, where she began at once to snore. This reduced the
available pairings to five men and four women—something like 120 combinations and permutations. I must
work to simplify them. In ascending order of preference,
I wanted Tyler to return to the ship and prepare us for
war. I wanted Tiffany's friends to go back to Olongapo
and wait for the fleet to return. I wanted Tiffany herself
to give Marchand another dose of the clap and Dottie
Marchand to divorce him. I wanted to be Mojo's buddy.

I wanted my fiancé to be mine or at least to tell me
what the future held.

In retrospect—and the retrospective view became clear all too soon—my future might have waited. What I should have done was be a friend, a friend in need, something it has taken me years to learn. I should have separated Buster from Rose and forced him to return to the ship. I had the resources for it. I could have called Letourneau to come for him. I could have refused to leave Buster's side until his ardor had cooled. Postponing any talk about *us,* I could have persuaded Lény to make a sisterly intervention. Unfortunately I was single-minded. Here I record another failure of character.

All this time music was being piped through the pool speakers; the steward at the front desk was our DJ. Rose went inside now and put on Johnny Cash.

"Let's have a song," Marchand said, meaning that the sisters should sing.

Lény looked doubtfully at Rose, which seemed false to me, a stagey reluctance when the performer really wants to perform. They stood. A reflection off the water cast them in a shimmering light. Both their dresses were wet. Under hers Lény was a sylph, perhaps virtuous. Under hers, in that bikini, Rose was a voluptuary. If sex was all you wanted, you would choose the younger sister.

Lény began by praising a lady near and dear to their hearts, June Carter Cash. She hoped we would like it. She was performing already. Her voice sounded like English as a second language conscientiously mastered.

Putting their heads together as if before a microphone, the sisters began *We got married in a fever.* Gone was the second language: here was pure American country. Soon all of us were humming; Tiffany's sober friend sang some scat. At the words *after the fires went out* the reversal of roles between the apparent innocence of the one singer and the near violent sexuality of the other, in whom the fires would never go out, made us laugh. Lény was the husband who wanted to go to Jackson to fool around; Rose the wife who'd had enough of his philandering.

The love between the sisters was in their eyes, their smiles, and the harmonies they sang, no doubt perfected at home under the watchful eye of their uncle, the Catholic priest. When they finished everyone applauded. Then Buster scooped up a double handful of pool water and threw it at Rose.

Shocked, affronted, thrilled—instantly under control—Rose said, "You'll pay for that."

"But refreshing, right? After all that passion."

She laughed. "Be careful."

It was late. Hardly a light was to be seen in Olongapo. By now you had to be inside the base or off the streets of the town or take your chances. Mojo produced a handful of keys. Buster and I helped the drowsy hooker and her musical friend into one of the rooms. When we came down again only Rose and Lény were waiting. Rose told us where everyone had gone. Tyler back to the ship, the better for all of us. Marchand and Tiffany "over," no surprise there. And Mojo? I could feel my heart beating.

"He's turned in."

Turned into a satyr, I would bet.

"He lives here?"

"The suite on the top floor."

Lény seemed to know it.

My heart was thumping so hard it was going to seize up. She said, "I'm going back."

Buster and Rose looked at each other. She held the remaining keys.

"A nightcap?" he asked.

Rose said, "I don't drink with men who insult me."

"That was a compliment."

"I told you I'd make you pay. Besides," she added, hooking her arm through mine, "I want to have a drink with Chris, who doesn't hide a wife at home."

She smelled like her name, like the peace roses from my mother's garden on a perfect New England summer day. It was possible that both sisters wanted the same thing, a home and a family.

"I'll take you back," I said to Lény, not knowing where *back* was but relieved that it wasn't upstairs.

"As far as the gate," she replied. "Because of the curfew."

Clarity

Lény set off like a hiker who must summit and return to tree line before the afternoon storms come in. Something in this stride repelled me; self-absorbed, superior, as if she had already decided the outcome. All right: the gate would divide us: she could make her own way through life. But in the time left I would have answers.

The night had bottomed out; pitch dark and heavy. Those who died in their sleep died in this hour. The pile driver was silent; the stacks of the shipyard under lowering stars looked like something painted by Monet. On the waterfront the tracked cranes were at rest, waiting to feed. My ship, silhouetted by her deck lights, her aircraft warning lights glowing like twin rubies in a setting, might be ready to sail in just a few hours. My ship, my home, my profession, sailing with me or without me.

Lény's face was shadowed by the palm trees overhanging the putt-putt. I switched to lightward of her.

I said, "How did you know when I was arriving?"

We had slowed almost to a stop. "Arriving?"

"You were on the pier. I suppose it was to see me."

"Rose knew that."

"Rose."

"Yes. She spends time with Mojo."

"*She* does."

"Yes."

"Why?"

This she was reluctant to say. She picked up the pace. We arrived in the brilliant light of the main gate, where one Marine stood in the sentry box and the other guarded the road—a tableau of devotion to duty.

We showed our IDs. Lény had one.

The Marine saluted me.

"Sir, you shouldn't be outside the wall now."

"It's all right, Lance Corporal. I'm going to see this lady home, then I'll be right back."

"Negative, sir. If you leave, you cannot come back until six. I'd have to arrest you, sir, for breaking curfew."

"Then I'll find a place out in town."

"The PC are out in force tonight, sir. It won't be so easy to avoid them."

"She's an expert at concealment," I said.

We were at the bridge, now deserted.

"Where are we going?" I asked.

"To Rose's room. I stay there when she's on base."

I hadn't the standing to object to this.

The way was familiar: *The Flamingo, The Desert Inn, The Professional Club, Charlie's Angels,* and *Casablanca.* Absent the solicitors of vice. At *The Texas Bar* she turned in the alley and began to climb the wooden stairs.

I hung back. Even the staircase was repellent.

"Are you coming up?" she asked.

At the landing she used a key. We entered upon a hall-way of doors dimly lighted. The hallway smelled faintly of beer. She led me to the room at the end, which would be the first room coming up from the bar. As part of her duties as manager, Rose must have timed the tricks. When counting the take, she would have punished gen-erosity. That and logistics and perhaps hygiene were her job. A lot for an eighteen-year-old.

Another key opened her bedroom/office. Lény turned on the light without looking. She sat at the desk and watched me as I sank into the yielding bed.

"Now you see our life here."

"Your life too."

"I fit in to help her. Not what you're thinking."

"I wasn't thinking that. I do know you, Lény."

"I wonder."

"What I don't know is what Rose—and you—want from all this?"

She turned to the mirror and rubbed the sleep from her eyes. I remembered that other scene of her sitting be-fore a mirror with myself in the background, reaching for her, only it was she who looked like the ghost now. Her narrow shoulders sagged.

She turned toward me and sat up straight. She would do this. She said, "If Rose and I were men, we could join your navy. And we would live in the U.S. and after a cer-tain number of years be citizens. Do you know how many Filipinos go on to careers in food service or hospitality in the States? That man at the front desk of the Q has saved enough money to buy a house in Chula Vista.

"But we aren't men. I can speak four languages but for my living I sing their songs while drunken Americans pound the tables. Rose is smart. And ambitious. And tough, tough as nails. Whatever she wants she will have. She—and I—want a real life, Chris. That life isn't here."

"No, it's with me, in America." I have no idea why I said this except that it seemed called for.

She smiled, not quite an acknowledgment. "In wealthy Boston. Where you were born—by accident, yes? You could have been born in the Philippines."

"Yes! I could have been born in the Philippines. In Olongapo. Or among the boat people of Hong Kong. Or in a hamlet in Quang Ngai province in Vietnam. I know I've been privileged, Lény. Let me share that with you."

"Stop now, please. I'm trying to explain something. Trying to explain everything, really. Then you will tell me what you think. Rose." She took a breath to regroup. "Rose is a moral person. Moral by character and by upbringing. Don't be misled. She left my father in Manila because of the things he did for Marcos. I will tell you another time, it doesn't matter now. She flirts—sometimes more—with powerful men so they will arrange visas for us.

"They promise: they lie. Not Mojo. Vietnam will fall soon and in the flood of refugees he will include us—a stroke of the pen! We believe in him, So we save our money and wait. Rose and me."

"Must it always be *Rose and me?*"

She smiled a bitter smile. "Oh, you get too close."

"All right. It doesn't matter. It's you I care about."

"I'll tell you. Rose is a moral person, I said this. But the culture here: she becomes the liberty dog."

"Liberty hound?"

"Yes, hound. Good. She likes the hunt. She drinks, sometimes too much."

"So you stay with her as a duenna."

Her smile brightened.

"So you aren't using me to get to the U.S."

"Using you that way was tempting, I admit. Handsome American! But it became more. I don't need you, Chris, but I want you. You are good, good at heart. I want to make my life with you. I want what you want or what you will want. If you were Filipino it would be just the same."

"Do you love me, Lény?"

Something thumped behind the headboard. Both of us looked over. There was another thump then rhythmic thumping. God, what a job, not only to hear that all around you but to time it. A voice cried, a woman's voice. Tiffany's. Raving with an incoherence so theatrical it must be acting, the voice a part of the pleasure; raving as if her orgasm couldn't come soon enough. Nor could it. Time is money.

If Lény had shown any reaction in this moment it might have saved us. Her smile might have turned into a comic smile, complicit in the joke. But she was burdened by her heavy purpose. "I do love you, Chris, and I want you. But I need more: not just feelings but confidence. If there's no future for us—for my own family as well as yours and my family to be—love isn't enough."

Low voices next door recapitulated their experience.

"And Buster?" I asked. "If Mojo will help you and all you have to do is wait, what's Rose doing with him, then?"

"What I said. Liberty hound. She wants it with him."

"Just for sex."

"She'd marry him if he were free."

"But he isn't. He loves his wife. He's been devoted to her since they were children together."

She shrugged. "But not so much, apparently."

Her eyes were bright and hard now. In her voice was a cynicism that wanted to win above all. This was her character, as I thought.

I stood up. "Goodbye, Lény."

"Well?"

"No," I replied. "It's not possible for us. It's too much for me. This is too much. We're too different. I'm sorry."

With a nod that did catch the surprise in her face but which didn't stop me, I opened the door and left the room and took the stairs down into the darkened bar; I wanted no risk of running into Marchand. All the chairs were upturned on the tables, just like my life. I opened the front door and stepped onto the boardwalk. Just my luck, a squad car was waiting there. Two PC arrested me and carried me away from my ship to their headquarters in the hills. In a cell by myself, I listened to the shrieking of the apes, another kind of mating song or else someone was being tortured.

Part Six
The End of the Cruise

Disgrace

The sun rose, the shrieking stopped. Light escaped through the jungle, stole across the compound, and slipped through my small, deep, barred window. This was unfortunate because the place was even worse in the light. Western standards of incarceration weren't observed here. The walls were stone blocks that convicts must have quarried. The bars were rusted but tamper-proof. The toilet came in two parts: a bucket with a filthy cloth and a corner sloping to a drain. The bed was an overstuffed damask chair from one of the colonizers—the Japanese it seemed when I examined the pattern. In this I had slept for an hour or two. It was certainly out of place or would have been if prisoners hadn't pissed themselves in it. Pissed and bled, from the stains. And possibly died— there was that foul sweetness to the odor.

I had not been photographed or fingerprinted. My wallet with my military ID had been taken. Otherwise there was no record of my existence. That the PC would harm an officer of their ally was inconceivable, but the train of events going back to the draft lottery seemed to be headed toward a catastrophe. When the man had drawn my birthdate, for a time afterwards I had had dark visions of a shell being manufactured in some factory in Hanoi, the glowing metal cast into shape and lifted out with tongs, the deadly innards filled by women in white coats and hairnets, the lethal whole carried into the South on the back of a single patriotic coolie (often crawling through tunnels), to be loaded into an artillery piece and fired at

the exact spot where I stood on my ship. Long before Desert Storm I could picture the weapon's-eye-view of the
last moments of the ordnance as it bore upon the target,
my curious upturned face. Yet this would do instead.

A corridor with other cells, none of them occupied—
perhaps no one else had survived their interrogation—
led to some sort of office, where presently men began to
work. I could shout in that direction: then again, the
empty cells. I waited, for hours. No meals were served. If
your crime is serious enough to cost us a meal, we might
as well beat you to death. One of my sailors had been in
a bar when two PCs had entered and without a word had
clubbed a fellow drinker, a Filipino, senseless and hauled
him out to their car. An insurgency smoldered in the jungle, which excused Marcos his brutality; more often than
not those arrested were enemies of the president or his
shoe lady, brought to this place and disappeared.

I was sitting against the wall having these thoughts.
A policeman came up and stood at the bars.

"Transportation has come," he said.

"To take me back to the ship?"

"You will be leaving the Philippines soon, and I doubt
you will return." It wasn't clear whether he meant you in
the singular or plural. He unlocked the door and walked
me to the entrance, and a black sedan rolled up to meet
us. I was so frightened that I failed to ask for my wallet.
The car stopped. It was the captain's car. No one got out.
In the driver's seat was a sailor in dungarees. In the back
an officer or a chief, someone in khakis. I dearly hoped it
might be Chief Beatty, my enlisted sensei and friend.

It was Louie. I got in beside him and closed the door.
We wound our way down through the switchbacks with
the hazy sun overhead so the car was imprinted upon its
shadow.

"The tubes are replaced," Louie said.

"Are you telling me this because—?"

With a glance at the enlisted driver, one of mine, Louie went on: "We're hydro-testing both boilers now. If they pass, we reset safeties and leave tomorrow. Not to the gunline, worse luck. To Yankee Station, plane-guarding *Yorktown*."

"Am I going home?"

"Ah!"

"I'm sure Bartlett knows all about me. For that matter I'm sure it's all over the ship. There's no use trying to hide the scandal. Am I going home?"

Bartlett shifted the mirror to see.

"You'll have to talk to the XO. I think you've worn out your welcome. You certainly have with me."

"So we're going back to the war, on some mission we don't want and have never done before, one that depends on good shiphandling, and it would be better to be an officer short—short one of our better shiphandlers—than to carry someone who has worn out his welcome."

"Bad teammates get cut from rosters. Actually, I don't care if you complete the deployment as long as you stay out of Engineering."

"Thank you, very kind. About last night. Tyler came back early, so he'll be in fine fettle. I take it the sun rose on the captain's absentee pennant."

"That's not for you to ask. He returned for breakfast, to be informed that you were in jail. At least he knew better than to be out after curfew."

"I know exactly where he was."

"I'm sure you do."

"And Buster?"

"What about him?"

"When did he come back?"

"I don't have the Buster watch."

"And yet you always know the gossip."

"He got back just after morning colors. Apparently the worse for wear. He's been in his room ever since."

Apparently the worse for something.

At the brow Louie handed me my wallet.

These days, when in disgrace it seems better to carry on as though nothing had happened. Brazenness poses the risk of being asked if you have no shame. The spiteful sentinels of social media expect, certainly, that you should suffer from your fall and that your suffering should be public. But wiser souls understand that error is our natural state. They themselves would not wish to be judged by their mistakes; they may take a certain delight in the boldness of the disgraceful deed; and worse than brazenness they hate to see indignity. Then again, no matter who you are and what you've done, thousands of online followers will fund your defense.

But this was 1972. The duty radioman brought me the daily list of curfew violators from Mojo Locke's office. Mine was the only name on it. In the margin a round, backward-sloping red pen had written *Restricted to the ship pending my determination of his fitness for service.* I was disgraced, certainly. It might have been better for me if I were a little brazen.

But for that morning, at least, I was unable to show my face. I did shave and shower and change from my civilian clothes, which smelled of beer and cigarettes and prison. At the narrow pull-down desk I sat pretending to work, but neither Fuller nor Appleby, who were actually working, seemed to be fooled. Fuller didn't care. Appleby eyed me as though I were a celebrity criminal, disgraced but fascinating. When Fuller had left on an errand, he asked, "Do you want this?"

I thought at first he had something in his hand. "I don't think it matters," I said finally.

"And all because of a girl?"

I shook my head slowly with a smile of superior wisdom: *But what a girl!* A pity that I didn't feel it.

I ate on the mess decks, ostensibly to sample the enlisted meal, but no chit was brought to me. The chart of the Pacific showing our transit home had been left on the bulkhead; an oversight hardly good for morale. Today was December 7—allowing for the international date line, tomorrow would be Pearl Harbor day. Our track showed that we should be about halfway to Guam by now. Among the sailors who grimaced when they looked at the chart no one seemed to care about my predicament. I was alone. I had better take care of myself.

XO Schmid was in his stateroom talking to the yeoman. He waved me to the brown Naugahyde couch, which converted into his bed at night, and they continued talking even though it touched on sensitive subjects involving the crew. This was a hopeful sign.

The yeoman left. The XO swiveled to give me his full attention. At least *he* could bear to look at me.

"So here we are," he said finally.

"Here we are."

"As far as I remember, you're a pioneer, the first U.S. officer to be jailed by the PC."

"Go west, young man, go west!"

"Sometimes it's better to stay put." He ran his fingers through his hair and sighed. His naval academy ring was recharging itself from the light.

"I'm sorry, XO. I know this reflects poorly on the command." Oh yes, the command, whose behavior in any other ethical system would be the disgraceful thing.

"I suppose in time it will prove a valuable lesson."

"Am I going home, XO?"

"You asked me that last night—just last night!—when I thought we had an understanding. I'll give you the same answer now. It depends on the captain. Being embarrassed by you in front of his seniors—"

"I know." The violators' list from Locke had copied the chain of command; including our commodore, who must pick one captain out of eight to recommend for promotion.

"—hardly improves his opinion of you."

And yet he had been doing the same thing—no, worse.

"Admiral Locke has proposed to rescue you. He'll swap you for an ensign from his staff who actually wants to go to sea. The job is in port services, keeping track of ships' arrivals and departures."

"All of three a week."

"Until the fleet returns. But yes."

"I do want to go to sea," I protested. "I'm a sailor."

"It's only ashore that you act so foolishly, is that it?"

"I'm not seeing her anymore, XO. I did what you said. I ended it last night—just before they picked me up."

"Bad luck, then. Still, the problem exists."

"If he decides to fire me, I'd just as soon go home."

At this he swung a complete circle with his chair, feet up, like a kid on an amusement ride; a most undignified thing for the son and grandson of admirals, but somehow it captured the essence of the problem. In his rich brown eyes a sympathetic light was always present. He looked at me now with real pain in them.

"And you had to criticize him for the gun and Charlie Brown. Oh, Chris. Let me ask you something. Have you ever forgotten any word of criticism you've ever received? Me either. And this crude, shrewd football player is probably the most sensitive man I know. I hate to say it, but I do think you should pack your bags. He'll decide later today. I'll give him your side. Dismissed now."

Just before dinner Marchand returned and went into his cabin, moving things about. The XO came up and spoke to him. I could hear them through the air conditioning duct: the tinny words that advocated for me, the one or two words grunted in response. Then silence.

Shortly after this the XO phoned my stateroom, and I went below to see him. With his characteristic blend of authority and sympathy he informed me that the captain had decided to relieve me for cause with a recommendation that the Navy terminate my contract as a reservist, waiving the remaining time. The yeoman would bring me the paperwork. When the ship sailed tomorrow I would be left behind, to live at the Q until the base travel office arranged my flight home. The commodore had been informed and concurred. Any appeal I wished to make should be addressed to the Secretary of the Navy via the chain of command in San Diego.

Last Night in Port

Rogelio Gozum brought a tray to my stateroom, which I took up to the bridge and held on my lap as I sat in the captain's chair. Beneath me I felt the four thousand tons of responsibility. The ship was moored with her port side

against the Alava Pier; Cubi Point was off her bow. As I
sat, a dozen aircraft, one after another, took off from the
bluff toward the west. Having trained myself in recognition, I identified them as Corsairs and Intruders—replacement aircraft for those lost over the North (and, increasingly, over the South). The media predicted one supreme
final effort and then peace. Everyone in this theater would
be making that effort but me. A life lesson, the XO had
said: but it wouldn't be comfortable to think of myself forever afterwards as a shirker.

This was something I could do, and do well. I wasn't a
born leader as Buster was, but I could learn leadership—
in fact I was learning it. Be clear, be right, be reasonable,
think of how your people hear you, put their welfare
ahead of your own. If time permits, tell them why. I didn't
have to be Buster: if I conducted myself like Chief Beatty
I'd be fine.

And when I looked at the six doubled mooring lines
tying my ship to the pier, my heart quickened. Just that
image suggested how I would get her underway. Take in
all lines but number two, the aft-tending forward spring
line, and hold it. With left rudder, come ahead with a tiny
pulse of power then a few feet of glide, harnessing the
bow so the stern would swing out. Then take the line in.
Rudder amidships and back away while the stern slides
toward open water…. Routine, workmanlike, but the one
long and three short blasts of the whistle would be like
shouting for joy under a boundless sky. As Buster had
said about himself, I could do this.

I brought the tray down to Gozum with thanks, in response to which he wished me good health and happiness,
then the quarterdeck watch rang the captain ashore, and I
went out to eavesdrop again, skulking behind a flight deck
stanchion. Marchand appeared and chatted with Jerry Valade, the watch officer. Louie reported on the engineering

plant; above us the mack was hissing with steam as the safeties were tested. Marchand nodded his approval. We—I mean *they*—would leave tomorrow, first thing.

"So where is my man Buster?" he asked. "Come along, Ensign, you almost made me wait."

Wait for what? Both men were dressed for Olongapo. No one else was with them. Marchand put his hand on Buster's shoulder to go first; in the gesture was easy authority and something affectionate. Any officer would like to have his captain's hand on his shoulder in that way. The XO said we never forget criticism. Nor do we forget kindness.

I had been onboard five months, a time of nearly continuous struggle, of a few hollow successes and of many embarrassments. Of multiple lapses of character. Not to mention being a party to sanctioned murder. Other than the scant weeks when I had stood competent OOD watches, I had never known what it was like to be simply a serving officer, confident and complete. My hopes must be misplaced: I had no vocation for the Navy. And being released from my contract would allow me to get on with my life as well as square me with my politics. But here was a wound, a deep one, the first for which I was entirely responsible. Until this moment I had had no sense that my life could be damaged by my own actions. Deploring the military as I might, with more than a theoretical judgment now, I still loved ships and, in their ideal, shipboard things; I loved it that there were watches and navigation; I loved it that there was a sea.

This would be a misery for my father, always so admiring of the service officers who came through his courses. In his mild way he would want me to account for myself. If I could present my failures as resistance to evil, like the Buddhist monks setting fire to themselves in Saigon, he would take my side and be comforted. But that wasn't the truth. The truth was that I hated one man, not just his morals, though it was my duty to obey him.

And the other truth: that I hadn't called on Buster today, that I had done him further disservice as a friend. I was pretty sure what the pool party had led to last night. My own scandal was no excuse, but I tried to tell myself it was. Shame is hard to sympathize with, and any locker-room boasting by him would have disgusted me. It was also true, I could tell myself, that we were friends by the circumstance of being shipmates. I didn't love him.

But I needed a friend now, or at least someone to talk to. Oddly enough, I chose Louie.

I found him in the engineering office, typing on the departmental typewriter though he had his own yeoman for that. Fuller was there as well, examining the plastic-covered damage control plates. There were five or six of these: the master diagram showed an exploded view of the entire ship; the rest were specific to vital systems, fire main and electrical and dewatering and so forth. Perhaps he was imagining different disasters in order to be better prepared. The true professional is prepared for anything.

"You're taking work from your yeoman, Louie."

"Hey, how's it going, Chris?" Now that I was getting my just desserts, we were friends again. Some day wherever I ended up, he might visit me to talk over old times. By then his moustache, drooping and grey, would be his only reminder of having been young and resourceful.

"Super, thanks. Redoing your water chemistry log?"

He laughed. With a glance at Fuller he lowered his voice. The secretive voice, soon to be used by Deep Throat in a parking garage, was Louie's favorite.

"I'm writing my fitness report."

"You're writing *your own* fitness report?"

"Ssh." He laughed again. "It's common practice, in one sense. Reporting seniors like you to attach a list of your accomplishments so they don't have to remember them. This takes it a step further, saving him the trouble of as-signing the grades."

"Which are?"

"Can't you guess?"

"And the breakout?"—the comparison to others.

"Number one of five lieutenants. But it doesn't matter, does it." He ripped the paper from the machine as authors do when frustrated. The platen cried out. "The incomparable Tyler will be number one, of course. Salty Bill number two because of his saltiness—a virtue in sailors. I'll be lucky to hold onto number three, thanks to that other kind of salt."

"And that imaginative log."

He laced his hands behind his neck. "Did you know my class standing at the naval academy?"

"I didn't know you had gone to the naval academy." Though of course I did.

"Yeppir. Eight hundred and seventy-ninth out of 879. The class anchorman. When I graduated, my company officer, that prick, said I'd never amount to anything. Two years later, I ran into him. I'd been promoted twice and was on my way to this brand new ship while he was stuck in a dead-end job. That was quite a satisfying moment, I must say."

"Someday you and I will meet like that, maybe."

"Not likely, though. You're on your way out. I suppose it's your own fault. I was rooting for you, Chris. Truly."

"So what do you think is wrong with me, Louie?"

"You don't belong here. I won't say you're too smart for us—the Navy has a lot of smart people. But you think too much of your own opinion. Whatever decisions are made you think you could do better. And you're impatient. I hope you'll learn from this experience."

"Actually, that's helpful. Thank you. So who was the better officer, me or Buster?"

"We'll never know."

"From what you've seen."

"For ability and ambition, you. For heart, him."

"For administration it's me," said Fuller, turning away from the damage control plates. "He's left me a mess. None of the repair lockers are complete. Including the hangar. If our helo catches fire, the man in the asbestos suit is going to die."

"Write it up," said Louie. "Put it in your relieving letter. Then fix it. No one wants to hear whining. Come on, Chris. Since this is your last day on the ship, let's do something fun. I've got to stay up while we light off the plant. Let's have a movie marathon. I'll pop us an enormous bowl of popcorn, and we'll fill the coffee pot. No hard feelings."

"No hard feelings, Louie."

In that moment I meant it. Louie and I went up to the wardroom. He called down for all the movies we hadn't seen yet. There were five of these, three reels apiece in their hardened cases. Out of something like loyalty or gratitude or perhaps anticipatory nostalgia, I sat with him through the night while he ran the projector and reports kept coming to him from his people. This may well have been the first binge-watching session in history. The interest of the other officers in so much film could be plotted on a curve that peaked early then declined in a long tail. They went to bed to be well rested for meeting *Yorktown*. They were ready to be at sea again.

At sunrise the captain's absentee pennant was raised. He and Buster were still over. I packed my seabag and returned the .45 to the armory.

The XO was determined to send me off properly. At eight we were singled up, ready to leave. I stood on the quarterdeck in a fresh khaki uniform, and such officers as could be spared from Sea Detail were gathered to bid me fair winds and following seas in civilian life. Two bells were rung and the word was passed: "Ensign Christopher Higginson Clarke, U.S. Naval Reserve, departing." After the obligatory handshakes most of them disappeared. No, I was not well liked. Louie and Tyler, my department heads, stayed. "In case you try to come back," Louie said.

Then we waited. We all looked out together. Presently, with no sense of hurry, Marchand and Buster walked up the pier, chatting easily as if nothing of importance had happened last night.

Going ahead, Buster went past me without a glance. And without last words; no doubt we wouldn't see each other again. I was being dropped from all their lives— Buster and Marie and Lény and the XO and Tyler and Louie; Chief Beatty and Homer Williams and Rogelio Gozum and Michael Horth and Seaman Wolford in the laundry. Marchand, I suppose. I would just fade away without leaving a mark.

Marchand checked the clearance astern, felt the strain on the mooring lines with his foot, looked aloft to see how the wind blew, and watched the flow of the tide. He was an excellent shiphandler and wanted to be seen as such. When he stepped on the quarterdeck, the final stroke of the bell sounded. He looked pleased, content, sated. His pleasure increased as he turned to see who had come out to greet him, not excluding myself.

Showing no sign of impatience, the XO met him with my orders and a pen. The captain's smile broadened.

"I'm not sure that's necessary. Why don't you come with us today, Mr. Clock?"

Tacking to a new life, I missed stays, was taken aback.

The XO responded for me and for decency: "Captain, of course Chris needs to know where he stands."

Marchand mimed pain. "I don't want to send Mr. Clock away if he wants another chance. Do you want another chance, Mr. Clock?" And now out of that boxy haggard face that was still glowing with surfeit, as if Tiffany had patted his cheeks only a few moments ago, his eyes were cold and clear and hard with triumph. "May I count on you, sir?"

It felt like such a moment of evil I couldn't help shivering. I was being asked to endorse not only the conduct of a man I despised but a corrupt way of life in which, apparently, no one grew up. If I said yes it would be the Navy from now on. All my other ambitions, any personal desires, any family claims would be secondary to the needs of the service.

The XO understood. He took me aside. With his face a few inches from mine, and holding up the separation orders, his expressive eyes told me first of his pain and regret over *this one* outcome and next of the blessing of *this other* outcome if I could set aside my feelings, however justified. Goodness is the greatest authority of all. He was good, as many shipmates then and later have been good. "Say yes," he whispered. "You'll always know you did the right thing."

Marchand, confident of my self-interested character, waited serenely for my answer.

Ignoring him, I spoke to a theoretical and better captain who stood in his place.

"Yes sir. You can count on me."

"Capital!" he replied. "Come now, Ensign, someone needs to get this ship underway. It's possible we're a few minutes late already." Faithful to his style, he put his hand on my shoulder and guided me to the bridge.

The Rendezvous

In this recounting mostly about myself, I see that I have glossed over the changes in the morale of my shipmates, leaving it to be assumed from the circumstances. *Where you sit is where you stand,* one of my teachers at the war college liked to say. Those polls that ask whether the country is getting better or worse really tell us how the respondents themselves are doing.

Apparently most of my shipmates were doing just fine. Instead of going home, we were going back to the war, a losing war. Not only that, we had been relegated to plane guard duty, a role something like that of the cop in a squad car parked at a construction site—a long way down from investigating murder. On the other hand sailors are fatalistic. The stop in Subic had been so brief and so busy (and in truth they were so broke) that few men had gone over; consequently today they had nothing to regret or recover from. We were losing the war, but the prospect of its end suggested that when we did get home the majority of us would be civilians again. Higher morale: you could hear it in the passageways and see it on the faces on the watchstanders.

My own morale was short-lived, a spike in the curve like euphoria (or a lie in a lie detector trace). I was thrilled to get the ship underway, and I made a creditable

job of it. As in sailboats so in ships: a vessel in a fluid
medium will respond to informed control—a hypothesis
that has never failed me in forty years when so many
things in life remain mysterious. After I had cast us about
and we were headed fair, the captain dropped a word of
praise, and the XO took me aside again to say that having
knocked his man down on the football field, he would always be the first to help him up. Yes, I could do this.

Then came the crash. I remembered all the reasons why
I wasn't right for the service, and vice versa. Although I
had avoided shipwreck, I felt ashamed to have sold myself
so easily. And Buster: friends don't let friends drive drunk.
I should have locked him in his room to keep him away
from Rose; away from Marchand.

It was telling that he had locked himself there, after
the fact. At dinner Jerry Valade, his roommate, wagged
his head when asked about him. The general feeling was
that he had broken his marriage vows. I wish I could say
that we, his brothers-in-arms, felt what he was feeling,
but it wasn't so: the comments in the wardroom were in-
decent and cruel. Marchand, at the head of the table, pretended to know nothing about it, and of course no one had
the temerity to ask him. Adultery is a mortal sin for
lesser men and a feat of manhood for the all-powerful.

After dinner I went to see him. If I handled this well—
as well, for example, as Marie Billings had done with
me—we would be friends again. Friends and not rivals: I
would always cheer his success, in the service or out.

He stood in the open doorway, that squat figure of a
fighter pilot. He had shaved and was wearing a clean
starched uniform. Whatever he was feeling, he had
roused himself for the watch.

"I've got nothing to say to you, Clarke."

"I think we both have plenty to say."

"Fat chance."

"I'll start: Lény and I have broken up."

"And now I should confess that I knew that already? In that fantasyland of yours, did you think we were going to elope with the sisters?"

"I thought we could help each other."

"Fat chance."

"We both made mistakes."

"So you say. I was just having fun. As you were, if you're honest. Get out of my way now."

He pushed past me to the ladder.

But at eleven-thirty, when I came up to relieve him, he gave me a professional turnover: our position on the chart, our course and speed, the weather, the engineering plant, the readiness of our weapons, the captain's night orders, and the one contact on radar, a merchant ship heading south. There was no regard for me in his voice, but he was clear and succinct, showing a self-confidence in his mastery of the situation that might suffice for him instead. I relieved him in the same voice, one professional to another, exactly on time. He went below, followed by Appleby.

The midwatch was quiet—we still had a day's steaming before our rendezvous with *Yorktown*—which gave me an opportunity to teach Fuller the many things about our bridge and our methods that were different from his midshipman cruises; and by the time we were relieved in our turn, without insisting upon it I had shown him that I was very competent, that I knew much more than he did, and that if he listened to me I would keep him out of trouble. That sufficed for him. He was one of those rare young men more pragmatic than conceited.

Not having a job in the ship (the XO promised to speak to the captain about me), I spent the next day catching up on sleep. The wrenching events of this week, the life I had lived these past few months—indeed all sense of myself fell away in the wool. Buster came to meals but lacked his usual high spirits; no lingering over coffee, no games of acey-deucy. The gossips kept their witticisms to themselves.

An hour before the rendezvous I got up, shook Fuller, and crossed the alcove into CIC to get the briefing. Louie was there, soon to be relieved by Tyler. He stood proudly over his domain.

"Good evening, young sir. All good things await your eminence. Let us hie unto the radar plot. Here is *Yorktown,* twenty miles away. Here *Bausell,* our nemesis and the ship we are to relieve at plane guard so that she may relieve us of our lady friends. Here are we in the center of the scope, ha-ha. We have exchanged radio checks with *Yorktown,* we hear her screw-beats, we are tracking her airplanes as they launch and recover—see the circular pattern? Ah? Ah? The wind is from the west: base course, therefore, is westerly when she's flying, easterly when she's not. You will want to pay attention to her aspect, of course, as she's unlikely to pay attention to ours. Such is the picture, and I hope our much admired weapons officer is as prompt in relieving as you are."

"Thank you, old sir," I replied. "Very professional."

"You would do me a favor to tell the captain that."

With a noncommittal smile, as if the captain would care what I thought—then again Louie never failed to pull a lever—I climbed the ladder to the bridge and opened the door.

The light hurt my eyes. All the displays were turned up, and some hadn't been switched to red. None of the watchstanders cowled their cigarettes. The olive sweep of the radar scope repeated itself in the overhead. The windows were mirrors, the sea was a void, we floated on a dream, self-blinded, unguided. Below our feet were two hundred and fifty lives in a honeycomb, watertight only by eternal vigilance. There was no reality but this place, which felt like New Year's Eve.

The officer of the deck leaned against the chart table, his back to the sea, smoking a cigar and entertaining the men with a dirty joke. One of his listeners was Appleby, who was supposed to be conning.

Unable to bear the laxity, I went out to the bridge wing and cooled off in the wind, most of which was caused by our own high speed. Gradually the stars appeared, the familiar constellations and also sweeps and scatters of nameless stars as if there had been a tremendous spill. A few watery clouds rushed past. The moon, nearly full tonight, wouldn't rise for another hour, too late to help us get to station but a nice companion afterwards. A watch in the quiet moonlight, on a gracious sea, is one of the memorable experiences in life. Two officers standing that watch without much to do, speaking in undertones and working in harmony, can form lasting friendships.

I felt better, and now my night vision was as good as it was going to be. The wind brought me back to the present. I glanced ahead and felt cold. As with the naked dancer in the bar, I couldn't bear to look but couldn't look away. The horizon was crowded with lights. We were running pell-mell toward more ships than I had ever seen before—as if all the ships in *Jane's*. There didn't seem room among them for even one more. And Buster, manic, careless, aggrieved, self-aggrieved, was taking us there.

My mother said that when you feel afraid, do the next small thing. Back on the bridge, Buster expected me to relieve him, but I was busy lowering rheostats and covering indicator lights with masking tape, switching off unneeded equipment and turning intensities down. I put the rubber hood back over the radar repeater and closed the bridge wing doors. All these things were a rebuke to him, of course. The bridge grew dark and quiet. This alone, I think, made him look outside, where before us was the confusion of lights. On radar the concentration of ships was as dense as the stars.

"Clark, are you going to relieve me or not?"

As I was about to answer, the radio ordered us into plane-guard station. In theory we knew where that was— half a mile astern of *Yorktown*. Buster called the captain. Before he had washed out of flight school they had taught him that gravelly voice that says that all is under control, that there isn't even the possibility of a mishap, low fuel or shot-up ailerons or fire in the cockpit notwithstanding. My pilot in the water had that voice. The training will serve even when one's own self is bleeding out.

"Well, what about it?" he said, putting down the phone.

"Why don't we get to station first?"

"Quartermaster, make a log entry that Ensign *Clock* has refused to relieve the deck."

"It doesn't have to be that way," I murmured. "We could work together."

"Yes or no?" The question life kept asking me.

"I'd rather not," I said. "I don't like what I see."

"Yes, I'm sure we aren't up to your standards."

Kenton Emerson, at the helm, laughed at this.

Encouraged, Buster went on, "Maybe, at least, your officer would be good enough to relieve mine."

Fuller had studied the radar scope and the maneuvering board and taken bearings on the closest lights. He was standing beside me. "It's your call," I said.

"They've got *Yorktown* on the wrong course."

Buster asked mildly, "What do you know about it?"

But something in Fuller's voice prompted us to look. Suddenly we were four novices grappling with a problem beyond our experience.

Yorktown, the closest of the six carriers, was lighted up like Times Square. She had lights on her flight deck, lights on her island, lights shining through her opened hangar doors. Overhead were winking lights as planes descended in the landing pattern. Her running lights, green to starboard, red to port, would have helped reveal her aspect, but they were lost in the dazzle. Both her bow and her stern were blunt; both approximately the same distance from her island. Even on a ship with traditional lines, the broad-on-the-bow and quarter aspects can be confusing. I saw the grey curl of a wave and thought *port quarter,* but that would have meant that Fuller was wrong. Was it possible we were looking at her *starboard bow*—a collision course? Two objects arriving at an intersection at the same time, a bicycle and a cement truck?

A dark mass occulted the light: *Bausell,* the outbound destroyer, passing between *Yorktown* and us. She was heading to Subic, and Joe Montgomery must have liked his chances with Tiffany or maybe his standing with the commodore. Full of joy, she signaled; the red beam steadied on our bridge and divided itself into dots and dashes, a witty message from captain to captain, something with the words *stiff prick* in it.

"Port quarter," Buster insisted. "She's launching."

In that case she would be headed away from us; a long slog to station, but easy and safe.

A Phantom took off to our right, trailing lavender fire in the water then rising sharply into a tuft of cloud like a sleeper awakened to discover that he could fly. After a long interval, the way we count to five while awaiting the thunder, the roar of his afterburner reached us.

"She launches to the west and repositions to the east," Buster said—true when he'd taken the watch.

"The wind has shifted," Fuller said. "She's launching to the east now. I chased her for a month as a firstie. It's her bow we're looking at. Her stern is flatter than that."

"No, we're looking at her stern." Buster turned away and drew on his cigar.

"When in doubt," I reminded him, "come right."

"I'm not in doubt," he said. "Never, ever in doubt."

It is human nature in an emergency to make much of detail: *time seemed to stop,* etcetera. I'm not sure time does, except in memory. But we were certainly bogged down in detail that night. The basic truth was that none of us was qualified to command our ship, and as Marchand had warned us never to do, we were taking it away from him. We should have sought his help. The court of inquiry exonerated me because of Buster's log entry that I had refused to relieve the watch, which suggested superior judgment and self-control. It was cold comfort then, and it's been cold comfort since.

"Constant bearing, decreasing range," I said, citing that official and infallible risk of collision.

"We're ordered into a tight station astern," he said. "Her bearing wouldn't drift anyway. Just like that approach of yours on *Mispillion:* the bull and the matador."

"Five thousand yards," said Fuller from the radar. It was characteristic that, dropping out of the debate, he would make himself useful. The court of inquiry would exonerate him too.

"She's not heading away from us, Buster. We've closed to five thousand yards too fast. You need to call the captain and we need to come right."

Appleby looked at Buster for permission; he was ready to give the command. Suddenly the background chatter had stopped: Emerson was ready to spin the wheel.

Buster went to the intercom. "Combat, what course do you have *Yorktown* on?"

Louie replied: "Bridge, do you hold *Yorktown* turning?"

"That's what I'm asking you, Combat."

Steps rang on the ladder, and Louie burst onto the bridge. Unable to see, he tilted his head, rubbed his eyes, and stared through the windows. "I can't tell," he said. "We've got a problem with the plot. Is Tyler up here? Have you called the old man?"

But at this moment the captain came onto the bridge. He shuffled to his chair and sat heavily. Long nights ashore gratifying his appetites had worn him down. Afraid as I was of catastrophe, I couldn't help a stray thought that this aging ex-football player must have been a grotesque sight rutting in the embrace of the beautiful Tiffany. He sighed.

"Three thousand yards: recommend slowing to one-third," said Fuller.

"Do you have a good solution?" asked Marchand.

"We're working on that," replied Buster.

"Working on it? She's out there in front of you."

"We need to come right, Captain," I said.

"Officer of the deck, come right," ordered Marchand.

"But *Yorktown's* coming left," Buster protested.

She was out there in front of us certainly, shining across the black water.

"Come right with full rudder," Marchand said.

Too much, I started to say, recalling *Mispillion.* It was a sign of Marchand's exhaustion or self-disgust or sense of justice that he ignored this basic principle. The deck heeled to port like an amusement ride; books and codes and coffee cups crashed, people slid, and minds wondered: *How far?* From the quiet interior of the ship rose the sounds of things breaking free. None of the sleepers had been warned.

Yorktown disappeared as the world skittered past our windows.

Marchand held onto the arms of his chair, Fuller to his radar scope. Appleby, Louie, and I grabbed the heavy weather bar. In the middle of the bridge, unsupported, Buster took the roll on his sturdy legs, still smoking the cigar. We were coming around faster than our thoughts could follow. *Bausell* flew by, heading toward the horizon.

"Two thousand yards: recommend stopping."

"What's that officer's name?" asked the quartermaster, bent over his log.

"Captain!" Buster's voice had the high rasp of thwarted conviction. *"Yorktown* is coming left. She's reversing her field. We need to come *left."*

"Negative!" Louie shouted.

Who was Marchand to believe? The department head who couldn't keep the plant running and the alien being who condescended to him or the athlete he had ground down into his own image, over whom the mastery of his revenge was now complete?

"Shift your rudder," he ordered, still without raising his binoculars.

The ship rolled back, with more crashing.

I will never know what Buster saw. Another Phantom was launched; it flashed by in front of us, and at the same time we could hear it through the closed doors as if lightning had split a tree beside the house. *Yorktown* was on the same course as before, heading into the wind, launching and recovering, and now we had nearly crossed her bow. She was irresistible. We were being drawn into an infinite gravity.

Finally I was certain of her aspect; life-and-death certain. "Starboard bow," I said. When a ship sees the starboard bow of another ship that is to port of her and close aboard, the danger is extreme, and both ships must act to avoid collision. "She's coming right," I said. "See, Captain: she's stopped launching."

"One thousand yards: recommend backing down."

Backing down would admit to error. Rather than do that, Marchand must have believed he could still escape. Then again, in life as in football, almost any direction is preferable to going backwards.

Our relationship to *Yorktown* was now exactly where we had started, only much closer—close enough to see no airplanes on her catapults. She was turning right, and we had stopped turning right and were coming left, slowly, grudgingly, fighting the momentum of our earlier turn; if we held this maneuver it seemed that we *might* pass clear, that the two turning circles, hers and ours, *might* approach each other without overlapping.

Hers was much larger than ours, however. She was forever coming around. Silver light was reflected across the glassy wave-tops between us, and within the silver image were both her navigation lights, green and red. She was directly bow-on and close enough to swim to.

"Bausell, Bausell," said a young voice over the radio, speaking without call signs but confused in his own way. "My rudder is hard right."

"Hard right rudder," ordered Marchand. In the log this command was given at sixteen minutes after midnight on December 10, 1972.

"The captain has the conn," said Appleby.

"We need to stop," pleaded Fuller. "Physically stop."

"Orders to the helm?" asked Emerson.

Marchand, up from his chair like a lineman at the snap of the ball, pushed Emerson out of the way and spun the wheel as far as it would go. "My rudder is right thirty-five degrees," he said in a husky voice. He now had the command, the conn, and the helm all at once.

"We should slow," Buster said.

It was too late for that. Slightly offset, *Yorktown* and *John Shafer* were looking down each other's throats. The carrier, backing full, had still enough headway to con-tinue her turn. At some point Marchand stopped ours, taking a roughly reciprocal course. Without this we might have escaped to starboard, but just as likely we might have been cut in two. The court of inquiry spent a great deal of time on the question.

What was certain was that we were still bearing down on her at eighteen knots.

"Lost in the sea return," Fuller said in awe.

"All back full," said Marchand. "All back emergency!"

The man on the telegraph threw the handle fully astern, brought it forward once, then astern again. Over the phones he barked, "Main Control, Bridge: all back emergency. Collision, collision."

This prompted Bailey, the boatswain's mate of the watch, to sound the collision alarm. *Dee-dee-deet, dee-dee-deet, dee-dee-deet* it went, interminably. Over the general announcing system he yelled "Collision, collision: all hands brace for impact."

"Ah-h-h-h," said Marchand in disgust. He was leaning to his right, but he couldn't lean even that big willful body far enough to get us out of *Yorktown's* way.

Buster, rooted to the middle of the deck, shook his head at what life had come to. "Wake up old Charley," he said in a half-voice and tossed the cigar.

Yorktown was so close we could no longer see her island. Her whistle sounded five short blasts. In response
the quartermaster sounded ours, a rasping scream from
overhead. Marchand grabbed his scalp. The bows of the
two ships passed each other one hundred feet to port. Perhaps the pressure gradient of each hull would help to re-
pel the other. She was huge! but safe, I thought. We had
entered her gloomy realm. Effluent was streaming from
her discharge holes. A sailor watched us from a sponson.
Safe? Then the overhang of her flight deck swept above
us dark and relentless as a wing of death. The instinct is
to duck. With first a scream and then a roar, and as if in
the slow majesty of planned demolition, it smashed into
the mack behind us, cleaved everything above the point
of impact, and swept it into the sea.

Relieved of that great weight, *John Shafer* reared and
plunged. I fell. Getting to my feet, looking aft, I saw a
fireball erupt. Orange ooze shot astern of us and set the
sea alight. I turned away to see photo-flashes of the
shocked faces around me. We were still moving ahead.
The fuel spray from the carrier walked down our ship—
from the hole where the mack had been to the top of the
hangar to the fantail and the missile launcher with its
high-explosive warheads. When I looked aft, all I could
see was fire.

God help me, among the horrified thoughts and fractured impressions, I felt vindicated.

On Fire

Finally we stopped. We sat in the sea and burned. *York-town* took station on our beam, and any aircraft she had aloft were diverted to other carriers. Across the black wa-ter came alarms, ringing bells, bulled commands.

Bailey shut off our own collision alarm, and for a few seconds there was an eerie silence on the bridge while a furnace roared behind us. Before the captain could order general quarters Buster shoved the binoculars into my chest and said, "You'll take the deck now, won't you?" and was gone through the door in two strides.

I caught up to him on the ladder and called his name.

He turned. Sailors were pushing past him both ways. Even this he managed athletically.

"What?" he asked.

I raised my arms.

The world I knew, the world of order and safety and predictable effects, had shrunk to the size of a telephone booth, and I couldn't bear to think of what lay beyond it. Buster, on the other hand, looked satisfied, as if a catch had been sprung and he were now free to do the thing for which his life had prepared him. "You were right, Clock." He turned and continued below, calling over his shoulder as he disappeared, "I missed them on purpose."

In his absence I had the deck, such as it was. Louie went to main control, Fuller went to his damage control diagrams in the engineering office, and Appleby went with Buster to the helo hangar. All we could do on the bridge was monitor reports, most of them conflicting. The ship was dead in the water and without electrical power, which meant no firemain pressure. Smoke blacker than the night poured aloft to obscure our vision. Flames rose through the smoke. There were two fires. The bigger and more threatening fire reached down to the bilges under the boilers. Aft of this, in the hangar, the helo was burning with a brilliant blue light, shooting aluminum sparks into the air, and that fire had spread to the after berthing compartments, trapping sailors inside.

XO Schmid appeared regularly with updates. I kept our own picture on the bridge's copy of Fuller's diagrams and tried to fill in the blanks. It was like trying to write the history of a battle as it was being fought.

A blessed breeze carried the smoke away from us. We opened the bridge wing doors, and Marchand strode from wing to wing encouraging the troops, occasionally reporting to *Yorktown* on a portable radio. As always he needed an opponent. The fire was his opponent now. I'm sure he wasn't thinking of himself nor of consequences beyond the fire. Once he had told me about losing a football game to Notre Dame fifty-two to nothing. *A slaughter,* I said. *No, we just ran out of time,* he replied.

Suddenly the ship lurched, like a man wracked by a coughing fit. I thought it must be some internal collapse, but it was *Bausell* crashing alongside us with scattered shouts and a groan of scraping metal. Her sailors jumped across to tie the ships together. Our bridges aligned as if we were nested at the pier. Out here on the open sea, the approach was a feat of shiphandling, long to be retold. Joe Montgomery, rakish in his leather flight jacket, grinned at Marchand from his bridge wing.

"You might have told me, Joe," Marchand said.

"No time, Jim. Your midships fire is out of control. Watch this now."

He had a team standing by with fire hoses. They opened up, and convergent streams of water bore into the flames. A ball of fire rolled into the air, then all you could see were black smoke and grey steam. More sailors jumped to us from *Bausell,* and fire hoses were dragged across.

The effect was dramatic, and Marchand acknowledged that his rival had done well.

Montgomery patted his ship's old plates: "It's not as if you can hurt us, Jim."

Hopeful reports came in. The midships fire was under control. Aft and below decks, where the heat could be tolerated only behind a curtain of water, the teams were pushing the fire into a few remaining corners.

Still the bulkheads glowed. Analyzing the patterns, Fuller realized that the diesel generator room must be on fire too. Buster strapped on an oxygen mask and led men inside. With him were Homer Williams, Michael Horth, and Jon Appleby. Their response was instinctive, heroic, and fatal. Opening the door fed oxygen to the fire; while Horth set about stopping the diesel the start-air flask burst. On the bridge we heard a crump, and the two captains exchanged puzzled glances. Presently the cause was identified.

Marchand retired to his chair and sat with his forearms on his thighs; whenever someone spoke to him he flicked his hand for an answer. The XO and Montgomery took charge. Training and discipline prevailed. Now the chaos had boundaries, which could be pushed back. The full moon rose. *Yorktown,* with her fires under control, hauled off to clear for another launch—the war wouldn't wait. Crews from the two destroyers covered our fantail with foam so the diesel room could be entered. By dawn all the fires were out, the dead and wounded had been seen to, and *Bausell* had us under tow.

At Subic tugs pushed us into our berth, the berth we had left just a week before. People were waiting again, only now there were several hundred and their mood was different. They stared in disbelief. News cameras rolled. From the mack to the fantail, the superstructure of the ship, subjected to three-thousand-degree heat, had simply melted. We were a hulk with a terrible deformity on our back, thickened, hardened, twisted. And each of us crew-men, standing on deck, was a hulk as well, with guarded eyes and a misshapen sense of who we were.

Black Crepe and Folded Flags

After we arrived the XO sent me to Captain Marchand, who ordered me to fly to San Diego with the remains of my dead shipmates, eight in total. He explained: "You were his friend. You know his wife and kids."

Marchand's face had lost its elasticity. His eyes showed only a kind of dark dwelling thought. I understood that he was weighing what to say next and how to put it. I would hit him there.

"Buster's going to be blamed, and that's fair. I'm totally responsible, of course, and I was on the bridge. It was my mistake that we didn't come right and slow down in time. I'll be held accountable, no question." He meant, *You'll get your pound of flesh, Mr. Clarke.*

"But that won't be enough. The court of inquiry will also want to know why an ensign had the deck during a complicated maneuver at night—something he'd never done before. They'll ask you because I qualified you too. What was going through his mind? Why didn't he see

Yorktown's aspect correctly? What may have distracted him? What was his emotional state? Was he fit to stand the watch? Knowing you, you'll tell them just what you think, warts and all. Fine. But I would ask that you not say anything that would discredit his name. Let his wife and kids remember him as they should."

"Of course they'll remember him that way," I replied. "You met her. She would never believe that anyone—even you—could corrupt him."

"That's right, I guess." But when I got up to leave—his office was now in a trailer beside the drydock—he added, "So we end as we began: with you contradicting me."

"Yes sir."

"If you stay in the service you should lose that habit."

"Thank you."

"And one other thing you should know: your girlfriend cared about you. She asked me to take you back."

In San Diego the families were waiting on the tarmac when we rolled up to the terminal. By now, after fifty-eight thousand deaths, the military was well versed in the rites of bringing the bodies home. I stood to the side with a small uniformed group as the carry team, with precise movements, transferred the coffins from the aircraft to the private hearses and the officer in charge gave the next of kin his or her folded flag.

Now it was my duty to represent the command. I had the talking points. When pressed I fell back on truisms: first reports were often wrong, the Navy would continue to investigate until all the facts were known. I tried to speak like a human being, not an official.

The wife of Michael Horth, a tall woman with startled eyes, wearing a new dress that she had bought for the ship's return, said that Michael was afraid of fire. Yes, he was dead, she had to bury him now, but he hadn't been burned, had he? I said that it happened in an instant and he wouldn't have known anything. Yes, but not burned? I couldn't answer this. I had seen his body, which had been horribly burned, before or after he might have felt it, I didn't know.

Homer Williams too had a wife, who seemed to believe that all news, good or bad, was the result of conspiracies at high levels. There was no need to keep his secrets, first because he never wrote home—there were no stories that might have aroused her suspicions—and second because she knew him too well. He had been killed in an accident, she was entitled to benefits, that was all she needed to hear.

Jon Appleby's family were a throng, parents and siblings and nieces and nephews. Jon had written well of me; they acted as if I were the one who needed consoling. It was easy for me to reciprocate.

Marie Billings, in a pale blue dress with lantern sleeves across whose bodice she had sewn a fringe of black crepe, waited with her children, Lucinda and Tom, until I had spoken to the others. The last time she had seen me, less than three weeks ago, we were friends for life. She had danced with her husband in a place far from Missouri, and the captain and his wife had been charming. The ship would be coming home by Christmas, peace was imminent, and Buster, despite his protests to the contrary, seemed to have a future in the Navy. Now this. She didn't have to be a conspiracy theorist to want to blame someone. After the way I'd treated him once before, it was easy to blame me. Holding her children's hands she formed a line of assault.

"I have some questions," she said.

"Yes, certainly. Shall we go inside?"

"They said he was killed in the diesel room."

"Yes."

"What was he doing there?"

"Fighting the fire."

"I mean what was *he* doing there. Captain Marchand had promoted him to gunnery. He had nothing to do with damage control anymore. The officer who relieved him was sitting at a desk, safe as safe. Why was he in the diesel room?"

"He was…." I struggled to find the words. I used both hands to shape a reply. "He was Buster. Always the first."

"Yes." Her thin smile gave me hope. "Always."

"It was chaos. He saw the need. He ran to help."

"Ran to help all the way from the bridge."

"Yes."

"Well, that's my other question. He was the OOD."

"Yes."

She took a half-step toward me, forming a salient with her children, and peered up at my face. She wanted to know the truth, though she didn't trust the source.

"Was it *his* fault?"

Talking points. "The court of inquiry will go into that."

By law misconduct cannot occur in the line of duty. It wasn't out of the question that if Buster were guilty of misconduct, Marie might lose her benefits. I wondered if the administrative officer had given her that fine print. Probably not. She was sensible enough and had experience enough with the Navy to know it anyway. But that wasn't why she was asking.

"You have the answer, Chris. You were there. Tell me."

"The night was dark. It's always hard to see where a carrier is going. And *Yorktown* made mistakes too."

"It was him."

"He had the deck. Appleby had the conn. Between the two of them, yes: we ran into the carrier. It was our fault."

"You mean his fault."

"To soon to say, Marie. The captain was there too."

"His fault. That's why he ran to fight the fires."

"He would have done that anyway."

"You had that watch. Why didn't you relieve him?"

"It's good practice not to relieve during a maneuver."

"Why didn't you?"

She kicked me lightly in the foot. I understood. She would insist on knowing.

"I didn't agree with him."

"You thought he was making a mistake."

"Yes."

"The pilot who flunked formation flying."

"It was a dangerous maneuver especially at night and with ships all around. I did refuse to relieve him—that's in the log. I thought he was making a mistake. But even the captain, after he had taken over, didn't do any better. You know how sometimes you walk down a hallway and another person is coming at you, and you both keep switching to the other's side, until you bump? It was an accident, horrible. Both ships made mistakes, but there was bad luck too. Whatever the court of inquiry decides, I'm sure they'll say that much."

"And you'll be exonerated. Even praised for being right."

"I have no idea. They may well find that I should have done more. Should have insisted."

She stepped back in line. "I don't believe you."

"I'm telling you the truth. Buster was my friend."

"He was. But as we've seen, you were no friend to him. You have a lean and hungry look, Chris. You need to be a better person."

Still holding their hands, she swept the children around and walked away from me; away and out of my life. I never saw her again. Having made up her mind, she wasn't one to change it.

"You've had a long flight," said a woman's voice. "And an unpleasant task."

It was Dottie Marchand. She too had been meeting with the families, but I hadn't noticed. Her dress became her. Modest and tasteful but feminine and attractive. It carried no sign of mourning nor of the Navy.

"Easier for me than for them," I said.

"It hurts, doesn't it. Jon Appleby was new, but I've known the others through the wives' club. Edith Horth is the nicest person, and Belinda Williams is a card."

"Did you speak to Marie?"

"I didn't get to her in time. Maybe just as well."

"What's going to happen?"

"The Navy will learn it all, every mistake, down to the officer on the carrier who was chewing gum." She smiled at me as if I too were a card and now here we were, alone together. "Whatever the court decides, it's the end of the line for Jim. He'll never be promoted now. We can retire— hooray for that. Maybe the old boy network will do something for him. In a way it means freedom for me."

"Freedom?"

I wanted her to confide the secrets of their marriage as if I weren't prying.

She smiled that lovely smile that hoped we'd meet again and which didn't mean anything.

The Peace Accord

On January 27, 1973 the United States, North Vietnam, South Vietnam, and a delegation representing the Viet Cong signed a peace accord ending U.S. involvement in the war. (Real peace and the reality of our defeat didn't come until two years later, when the North completed its conquest of the South and began its reeducation.)

Beginning the next month, our POWs were released and flown to the Philippines for an emotional reception, televised around the world, followed by debriefing and medical care—in many cases lifelong care.

Meanwhile Yankee Station became again a place for sampans and junks, and the U.S. Seventh Fleet was reduced to something like a quarter of its former strength.

Accountability

John Shafer was decommissioned, made ready for sea, and towed across the Pacific to the West Coast shipyard that had built her. Her voyage back was something of an epic. For more than two months the weather was vile—in all that time the captain of the tug was unable to fix his position—and the unmanned, unballasted tow behaved abominably; kept veering off-course, turned broadside, parted the hawser. Rebuilt, she was transferred to

the East Coast and deployed regularly to the Mediterranean. As a three-star admiral commanding that fleet, I
went aboard her once. Whatever I wanted to feel, she
seemed too different to elicit memories. As I was being
led on tour, I kept looking for that awful color of green,
but there wasn't a trace of it. She's serving now in the
Mexican navy.

The small burst of good press about the towing epic
was soon swept aside by accounts of the court of inquiry,
which decided that charges should be brought against the
commanding officer for dereliction of duty and hazarding
a vessel. Many thought that the XO, being second in command, should have been charged as well. But the naval
service seemed to have a new attitude toward accounta-
bility, a stricter construction of the rules. Perhaps it was
our more exculpatory age. According to this, the XO was
not responsible for what he didn't know and didn't do.
The Naval Institute *Proceedings* aired the controversy.
We have become a society of sea lawyers, wrote a retired
captain. *Not of lawyers but of the law,* rebutted an acad-
emician, who happened to teach that subject. *Where is
the Navy of Decatur, Farragut, and Nimitz?* insisted the
first, and the Navy leadership seemed to agree with him.

But this was nothing compared to the howls of protest
when Marchand was acquitted by the court-martial. On
the advice of his civilian attorney he had elected to be
tried by a military judge instead of a jury. The hearing
was held at Pearl Harbor, thousands of miles from both
the scene of the collision and the ship's homeport. The
judge, highly respected in his community, ruled that the
captain had been called to the bridge too late to prevent
the collision. It was true that *John Shafer's* last two ma-
neuvers had been at his direction. And it was true that
either maneuver alone would probably have been effective but that in combination the two had been fatal. But

as to the first, he had been relying on the advice of his officer of the deck, qualified for the position though inexperienced; and as to the second, he had been influenced by the carrier's belated attempt to maneuver clear. Once he had taken the helm, his timely actions had undoubtedly saved lives and prevented worse damage, not excluding the potential loss of the ship. Therefore, although culpability was indicated to some extent, the fundamental and operative responsibility for the collision rested with Ambrose Thomas Billings, Ensign, U.S. Naval Reserve, deceased, and the charges proffered to the court were not proved beyond a reasonable doubt.

The decision failed to mention that neither officer had heeded Fuller's warnings to stop.

Marchand retired. Not long afterwards he and his wife, whose loyal presence at his side had made such a good impression, were divorced. She moved to Baltimore and started a business and remarried. He moved to the United Kingdom, where he took a middle manager's job with a company that operated the North Sea oil rigs. Whatever he had wanted from life—wealth, position, wisdom, worthiness—I doubt that he achieved it. In the long second half he was forever blocking the way for someone else. I lost track of him finally. Since his obituary would have made news, I assume he's still alive.

Vice Admiral Schmid (retired) tried to save his son's career; much to the surprise of both of them, he failed: with a letter of reprimand in his service record, the XO resigned from the Navy. Unlike Marchand he prospered. He became a Beltway Bandit, one of those Washington insiders who know everyone and are adept at inventing ideas for spending the taxpayers' money. His timing was excellent. After a year or two of learning the ropes, he was promoted to a high position just when people were becoming concerned about military readiness. By the end of the Reagan era he had become the chief executive of his firm. I've met him a number of times on the Navy's business, always mixed with pleasure.

Tyler Brock was recognized as one of the heroes of the disaster. He was burned fighting the fire, and his handsome face was scarred for life. From then on his career became the stuff of legends. He taught himself Farsi and Arabic. He was serving in the Persian Gulf when Iran mined it. Selected early for flag rank, he fought our nation's three wars in that region and ultimately commanded the fleet, as I later did in the Mediterranean. He was always helpful to me, seldom asking much in return. I read recently that the naval academy art museum was presenting a show of his watercolors. I will certainly see it.

Mark Fuller never got over the collision, though he was right in everything but opening the door of the diesel room. The Navy treated him for what was then called "combat fatigue" and now is better understood as PTSD. He left the service on a medical disability and lived with his parents in Colorado. I visited him once, but we had nothing much to say to each other. His thoughts and movements were slow and deliberate; his early dislike of me was frozen in time.

Louie DiGiovanni probably suffered the most; that is, the most unfairly. On the bridge he too had been right, but it didn't matter. Besides the collision his seniors remembered the salted-up boilers concealed by the logs. He was passed over twice for promotion and had to leave the Navy with a very small pension. He took a job with a shipyard but didn't keep it. His Japanese wife worked while he stayed home. He sent out resumes, carefully written to account for the gaps in his work history (I know because he sent one to me). No company hired him. Finally he became a minor official in a local shipfitters' union. At forty-seven he died of cancer.

In the accounting I will mention three others.

On the deployment Commodore Lewis was considered to have led a squadron of basket-cases. Such an opinion needn't appear in his service record: his waterfront reputation was tainted. He never did make flag, a keen disappointment after years of feeling so sure about it, years of practicing his signature to impress the bureaucracy.

On a brighter note, Mad Joe Montgomery was selected for squadron command and in that role had an outstanding deployment, even better than *Bausell's.* Because he had never served in Washington, that was as far as he went. He told me once that he didn't mind. We'd had too much to drink; standing at the bar with people around us, he insisted on showing me the tattoo on his butt: *J.M.* between two eagle's wings. "I lied to my honey that those were my initials, but of course it was Jim Marchand's bit of revenge."

Rear Admiral "Mojo" Locke, so kind to Lény and Rose (and me), was extended in command of the naval base, where his wife and children joined him after the peace was signed. He served there for more than five years, gaining a reputation as the indispensable man. Subic Bay was active during the collapse of South Vietnam and the frantic evacuation of its loyalists (compared to which the recent withdrawal from Afghanistan was a model of good planning and orderly execution). Then our national fixation shifted to oil, Southeast Asia gave off a bad odor, and Locke became a former best-seller whom nobody read any longer. He retired without getting to command a carrier battle group, his great desire, and in which he would have been superb, as I had cause to know.

A Second Act in Subic

Again I've gotten ahead of myself. Shortly after the peace accord and the return of our POWs, before Marchand's court-martial in Pearl, the court of inquiry, a fact-finding body consisting of three admirals with no connection to the case, was convened in Subic. The base theater was the scene for this, several rows of chairs having been removed to accommodate the glut of media.

I was called to testify. As I was leaving the theater afterwards, I found Admiral Locke waiting for me.

"There are no attaboys here," he said gesturing that we might walk together, "but everyone understands that you did well."

"I keep thinking I could have stopped it."

"No one had the authority over Buster but Jim. Or the XO, if he'd been up there."

"I should have called him. The first he knew of it, he was thrown out of his bed and the ship was on fire."

"Yet Navy Regs makes him the training officer."

"Not his fault," I insisted, too loudly, as Locke drew back. "I'm sorry, sir. I'm seeing a lot of dead faces."

He stopped, probably to get my attention. We were at the putt-putt. A sailor playing alone was trying to synchronize his stroke with the slowly rotating windmill. Bad timing: twice the ball hit an arm and bounced back. He put the ball on the tee, took a full swing, and bladed it over the fence; people leaping out the way as it bounced down the sidewalk.

Such behavior was beneath the admiral's notice, except to amuse him.

He said, "Of course in my community I've lost friends over the years. Bad judgment, equipment failure, enemy fire. Just like you, their faces appear to me at the oddest times. It might help you to have a new job."

"Not in the Navy."

"I was thinking you could work for me. It would help put this tragedy in perspective and also give you a chance to settle any personal questions—I don't mean to dwell on the past, but you were going to come to me in the swap anyway. You wouldn't have that painful reminder of your ship, but you'd be in touch with the fleet, which you seem to enjoy. And—I shouldn't say this—the work would be easy." He smiled, in the way that authorities do when speaking heresy. "You'd feel like you're getting your life back and in pleasant surroundings. Take away Olongapo as it is now—I suspect someone will gentrify it one day—and this place would be a paradise."

"It is already." It was. Within reason, even admirals can have an aesthetic sensibility.

"Give it some thought," he said.

I did, but I didn't need to. He had sold me by his kindness; by taking an interest in me. It was March of 1973. My contract with the Navy had two more years to run.

So I spent them at Subic, first in operations and then as his personal aide. The Lockes adopted me, and his mentoring completed my worldly education. I was recognized for my role in the emergency evacuation during the fall of Saigon, when helicopters crash-landed on any ship they could find, sometimes with refugees hanging onto the skids. Once again my head was turned. At the end of my contract I applied for augmentation into the regular Navy. That summer I transferred to the department head course in Newport and after that to my second ship. I was on my way, which has brought me here forty years later.

In the character of Mojo, of course Locke remembered the pool party. He knew that when my ship had departed for that fatal rendezvous at Yankee Station, Lény and I had been acting out a breakup despite our feelings for each other.

Now I was back and the ship was gone. Circumstances had changed. He dropped a hint. I had no trouble finding her. She had declined to sing with Bert in Baguio (his gig there lasted longer than Barry Manilow's in Las Vegas) and instead had taken a secretarial job at the shipyard. It was inevitable that we would meet. Honest and kind as she was, she responded. She knocked on my door at the Q one evening, and we sat on the couch until late at night, never touching but talking over everything. Full of the romance of it, I was tempted to love her again. If she was tempted too she didn't let me think so. Impulse cooled to common sense. Unlike many exes we agreed *not* to be friends—I couldn't bear the cliché—but that whenever we met we wouldn't make it awkward.

After that we met a lot. I never saw her with another man, but sometimes she looked so happy and good that my heart turned over with jealousy for the space in her life that a partner would fill; must someday fill.

Rose went to Manila, where Marcos had promoted her father (probably for some new act of cruelty). Then she fought with him again and returned to Subic. Ho Chi Minh was on the offensive, the fleet was beginning its build-up, the Texas Bar needed a manager: she resumed her equivocal life.

Lény was sick with worry. I couldn't help, for Locke would have no contact with someone in Rose's position— as the fleet grew, he put much of Olongapo off limits. I was afraid even to ask him about the Rosales sisters.

It was about this time that I grew up, finally. I began to see other people's problems as my own, and I began to welcome them. Having understood this in myself, I took the next step: I learned to use indirection.

When I put on my aiguillettes as her husband's aide, Mrs. Locke and I—Becca as she insisted I call her—grew close. On almost any subject, about almost any person whose actions might be judged, we could talk for hours, picking up again between interruptions. For example, I told her about protesting the war, and although she was Navy through and through she understood and sympathized. More than once she called my father, alone among his books, to praise me.

Yes, almost any subject. Her marriage was off-limits, of course. I was pretty sure that Mojo and Lény had been lovers at one time, straight-arrow that he was; and with my senses attuned to her every glance, every word said and unsaid and in what tone of voice, I was sure that she knew it. To approach her, then, about the Rosales sisters would be too hard (a legitimate reason, as I finally learned, for leaving things alone).

Nor, a true admiral's wife, did she like to be directed. In all our happy talk she had never once asked me how to solve a problem.

But I was not her best friend. Her best friend was Sheila Benedotto, wife of the CO of the air station. The Lockes and the Benedottos had come up through naval aviation together; had lived in substandard government housing, had lost squadron mates to accident and combat. Sheila was a sailor—I mean in sailboats. Like me she sometimes taught at the Sailing Center for Mr. Ruthven. I sought her there one day and proposed that we crew a boat in the two-man regatta coming up. She was pleased. We won. She had the helm when we crossed the finish line. By then I had told her all about Lény and Rose.

A few days later Sheila gave me the high sign. I took the admiral's writer into my confidence. Without a word I handed Becca a folder with its yellow tapes showing where signatures were required. A few days later and without a word as well, Becca handed it back to me.

At the shipyard Lény worked in the fabrication department, which could make anything from a steam kettle to a propeller shaft. Through the wall I could hear the snap of welding torches and the shouts of workers. She was at her desk, with a covered typewriter on one side and a dictionary stand on the other. Her inbox was empty; her outbox was full of folders, one or two bearing the red-and- white-striped borders of classified documents.

She made a fuss over my aiguillettes.

"So much power," she said with a teasing smile.

"Don't tell my boss that."

"The handsome Mojo."

"I mean my real boss, his wife. This is her work."

Saying this, I pointed to the well-known poster on the wall, of the WAVE in blues holding onto her white cap, greatly enjoying a gale:

GEE, IF I WERE A MAN, I'D JOIN THE NAVY

"What are you talking about, Chris?" She was troubled.

I put a folder on her desk. She opened it. Inside were letters addressed to herself and her sister, signed "M.J. Locke, by direction of the Secretary of the Navy." They offered enlistment in the administrative and service ratings of the Navy consistent with those of the Filipino nationality under the law. Upon signing the endorsement the addressees would be ordered to basic and specialty training, and visas would be issued them to reside in the United States, or any of its territories, on a path to citizenship dependent on full and faithful service.

"What does this mean?" But she knew what it meant.

"You're in the Navy if you want to be. You and Rose. I've taken the liberty of reserving a flight for both of you to San Diego next week. You'll be met by a recruiter, who will swear you in and send you to boot camp. Each of you may choose an "A" school afterwards, in administration or service, and so forth and so on." I rolled my hand to signify the broad and open future.

She was in my arms. We were crying, both of us. I was sobbing, her tears were mixed with laughter.

"I will never forget you," she said.

And she never has. Command Master Chief Rosales and I keep in touch, for which texting has proved such a boon. It's an odd week that I don't get something from her with a silly emoji. She served thirty years as a yeoman, quickly finding a way into the paths of enlisted states-manship. Once or twice I could have pulled strings to get her assigned to me, but we both understood that it wouldn't have been a good idea. I married, more or less happily. She never did. Rose married and left the service after her first hitch. In contrast to her own wild youth— maybe as a reaction to it—she is now the strict Catholic mother of six children.

And with this my story ends. As Buster is a charge upon my early character, Lény and Rose are in part its redemption. It goes to show, we never know what number will be drawn from the lottery drum. The best we can do is to do our best, whatever comes of it.

About the Author

Thomas Corcoran entered the Navy in 1972 and retired in 1993 as a captain, having served during the Vietnam War and Operations Desert Shield and Desert Storm. He commanded two ships and was selected for command of a destroyer squadron. He lived in Navy ports on both coasts, including Norfolk. Besides sixteen years of sea duty, he served in the Pentagon as Special Assistant to the Chief of Naval Operations and as Military Assistant to the Secretary of Defense.

A Chain of Devils is his seventh book of fiction.

www.ingramcontent.com/pod-product-compliance
Lightning Source LLC
Chambersburg PA
CBHW060405260626
47160CB00006B/2441